crested butte dreams

Ann Lain

Crested Butte Dreams

As a work of fiction, this novel makes reference to historical events, historic places, and actual locales, all of which are intended to create a realistic setting or establish historical accuracy. Other names, characters, events, or places represent the author's imagination, and any resemblance to real-life counterparts is entirely coincidental.

Published by Wheatmark™
610 East Delano Street, Suite 104
Tucson, Arizona 85705 U.S.A.
www.wheatmark.com

International Standard Book Number: 978-1-58736-867-7
Library of Congress Control Number: 2007927706

For Marissa and Tiffany

acknowledgments

Thanks to my husband, Ted, for encouraging me to write a novel in the first place. His support and unconditional love have sustained me throughout this project. My special thanks to Jean Griffith, Crystal Mazur, and Linda Fisher for reading rough drafts and offering suggestions. Richard Mazur was a big help on computer issues. I depended on the immense contributions from my two proofreaders, Myra Crawford and Mary Jane Chucko. To others who cheered me on, I appreciate each one of you.

Moreover, thanks to the ski patrollers who helped with avalanche control scenes as well as search and rescue information. At the time of my early research, Crested Butte ski patrollers Timothy Rolph and Daniel Ewert were especially helpful. For historical accuracy, I relied on Kelsey Wirth's *Reflections on a Western Town: An Oral History of Crested Butte Colorado* and Duane A. Smith's *Crested Butte: From Coal Camp to Ski Town.* Thanks also to Marcie Telander's article "Ghosts, Goddesses, and Grave Ladies" from *The Crested Butte Magazine—Silver Anniversary 1986,* for information on the legend of Little Liz.

one

etrayal will eventually find you, chase you down, thought Sarah Hansen as her husband was driving home from the 1986 Carsonville Arts dinner dance held at a Dallas hotel. Several times she had resisted the impulse to blurt out the question that had been pounding in her head. Aware of Jake's bad temper, she knew better than to bring up the subject in the car. With a fast-beating heart, Sarah waited for the moment that would come only too soon.

Once they were safely home, she went into the bedroom and emerged with a folded credit card receipt in her hand. Jake was in the kitchen, pouring himself an after-dinner drink. He had removed his jacket and tie. Taking a deep breath, she placed the innocent-looking slip of paper next to his glass.

"How long have you been seeing Rhonda Sloan?"

Now that she had actually said the words, she feared the question itself would make the possible affair a reality. Feeling the tension course through her body, she watched for Jake's reaction, wishing he would somehow come up with an explanation to make the whole nightmare go away.

"What are you talking about?" Jake slowly picked up the slip of paper, unfolded it, and took a quick glance. "What does this have to do with her?"

"Don't take me for an idiot, Jake. I saw her wearing that bracelet when she touched your shoulder and asked you to dance. Besides, your signature is on the receipt. You spent fourteen hundred dollars on that woman."

"Sarah, if you'll slow down and catch your breath, I'll explain everything."

"Stupid me," she continued without hesitation. "I've been waiting for you to give me that bracelet. I even thought maybe you planned to give it to Catrina as a special wedding gift from her father."

Jake interrupted again. "Look, Sarah, stop running off at the mouth and listen to me."

"Oh, I haven't even started about tonight. I saw the way the two of you were dancing. I felt totally humiliated. Duane and Priscilla saw it, too, and tried their best to make light of the whole scene, saying maybe the two of you had had too much to drink. I demand a straight answer, Jake. How long has this tacky affair of yours been going on?" She felt weak, and the room started spinning around.

Jake paced the room, his voice growing louder with each sentence. "Sarah, you're doing what you always do . . . jumping to conclusions and making assumptions. Look, Rhonda decorated those last million dollar houses and gave me great lighting discounts. She saved me a great deal of money. I wanted to show a little appreciation. I knew you wouldn't understand. That's why I didn't bother to tell you."

"For a bracelet like that, I imagine she gave you a lot more than discounts," Sarah said icily. She had been married to him for twenty-three years, and she knew Jake was lying to her. She felt the first sting of tears with her anger out in the open.

Jake slammed his open hand down on the countertop, startling her. "Listen to me, Sarah. That bracelet was a gift, and that's all there is to it. Don't look at me like I'm one of your high school boys in trouble." His dark eyes shot sparks of indignation.

"You know what, Jake? The real irony here is that you were stupid enough to leave the receipt in the pocket of your sports jacket. I found it when I was at the cleaners three days ago." Her voice was starting to quiver slightly. She knew that, when they got into a big argument, he would try to turn it around so that the whole sordid affair would appear to be her fault. She knew exactly where this conversation was headed, and she was furious.

"If I had been trying to hide something, I would have destroyed the evidence."

"Oh, please, Jake, you're making me tired. All those late nights when you claimed to be with clients looking at house plans, you were with her."

Jake strode toward her. "You won't stop, will you?" He reached out and seized her wrist.

"Look, what do you expect when a tall, good-looking blonde like Rhonda Sloan comes along and throws herself at a man who's starved for attention? You always have your damn papers to grade. You're always too busy to take time out for a real social life."

"Let go of me!" Sarah screamed, pulling away.

She stormed from the kitchen into the living room, blood pounding in her ears. Jake started to follow her. She whirled around to face him and said slowly, choosing her words deliberately, her voice rising in steady defiance, "You said *take time out for a social life*, not *take time out for you and me*." She drew in another sharp breath. "Again, Jake . . . how long have you been sleeping with this woman? Stop playing your games with me and give me an honest answer."

He sat down in a stuffed armchair in the living room, head bent, avoiding Sarah's glare. He ran his hands through his coal-black hair and stared at the floor. Without looking up, he mumbled, "About three months."

Sarah slumped down on the sofa opposite him. Speechless, she tried to recover from the sharp sting of his words. Now that she had an answer, she almost wished that he had continued to deny it, as he had done in the beginning. The ugly truth was out in the open. In the oppressive stillness of the room, she could hear the ticking of the grandfather clock in the foyer, like the timer device on a bomb. He had been deceiving her for three long months. How had she missed the obvious signs? These things happened to other couples, not to them. Never before had she felt so devastated. The tears ran freely down her cheeks. Her heart picked up speed.

Finally she drew in a deep breath and found her voice. "Are you in love with her?"

"Hell, no." Jake got up from his chair and walked slowly to the sofa. He sat down beside her. "Sarah, I swear I'll never be unfaithful again, never." He started to put his arm around her, but she stopped him.

"Don't . . . don't touch me." She wiped her tears away. "I can't believe this is happening to us. I mean, how could you hurt me like this?"

She stood up from the sofa to get away from him and sat down on the brick ledge of the fireplace, putting her head in her hands. Her rich chestnut hair fell forward around her delicate face.

"I'll go pack a suitcase," said Jake, rising from the sofa.

Sarah looked up at him. "Oh, no. That's totally out of the question. Catrina has her last final in the morning, and then she'll be here with us. Jake, do you realize the wedding is only three weeks away? I don't want her to know anything's wrong between us. We won't spoil the most important day of her life. At least you can do that much for me."

"Sarah, promise me you'll try to forgive me. I love you. I don't want our marriage to end. I admit it. I screwed up."

"Oh, that's for sure. Jake, I can't promise you anything right now. All I know is I cannot bear the sight of you. I feel sick to my stomach." She got up and left the room, walking quickly into the kitchen to get her car keys. She opened the back door.

Jake followed her and grabbed her arm. His six-foot frame towered above her. "Where are you going at this hour?"

She looked up at him, her hazel eyes hot with anger, her full lips a firm line. "Anywhere but here. Let go of me, Jake!"

When he released his hold on her, she ran out to the garage. As she sped away in the darkness, she wished there were somewhere to go, somewhere she could escape from the miserable knowledge of her husband's affair. Sarah pulled into a grocery store parking lot, turned off the engine, put her head on the steering wheel, and sobbed uncontrollably.

In the days that followed, divorce seemed the only solution. She wanted to punish Jake for the pain he had caused her and for the trust he had destroyed, but for the time being, Sarah and Jake's life in Carsonville continued to reflect a happy marriage. She wondered how many marriages existed where two people put up a false front and even their friends didn't know the truth until one of them filed for divorce. In the privacy of their home, Jake and Sarah dropped all pretense and went to great lengths to avoid each other.

A few days after the wedding, Sarah was relaxing by the pool, lying on a blue chaise lounge. Preparing for the chapel wedding and finishing out the school year had exhausted her. Even more stressful was the strain of hiding her grief about Jake's affair and the pressure of reaching a decision on her marriage. Her lustrous skin had paled. She had little appetite and had lost weight since she confronted Jake with the truth.

Smoothing suntan lotion on her legs and arms, she lay back and thought about her marriage. She didn't want a life without Jake; she loved her husband. Sarah knew he was right about her spending too much time on her senior English classes. She accepted a small part of the responsibility for his affair. *Maybe I need to make an effort to be the sort of exciting woman Jake is attracted to.* The image of Rhonda in her black cocktail dress flashed before her, and a sharp stab of jealousy and insecurity stung her heart.

There I was in my old white crepe pantsuit. Who am I kidding? I'm not like Rhonda, and I don't want to be. Sarah usually dressed conservatively, not wanting to draw attention to herself. For teaching, she wore the typical high school teacher's casual attire. Weekends called for jeans and tennis shoes. Although Sarah took pride in her appearance, she was reluctant to spend money on clothes and jewelry. *No,* she concluded, *Jake will have to take me as I am, as I always have been.*

More pleasant thoughts started to sift through Sarah's mind as she soaked up the warmth of the sun. She reflected on the tranquil spot Catrina and Warren had chosen for their honeymoon on Sanibel Island in Florida. Sarah was reminded of her own honeymoon: one night in a Fort Worth hotel before she and Jake had to make the long trip to Texas Tech in Lubbock for their fall classes. But those early years had been full of love as they struggled together.

She thought of the wedding. She could still see Jake and Catrina walking down the aisle of the beautiful chapel. Jake hadn't changed that much since he himself had been a groom.

Their daughter's wedding had been far more emotional than Sarah thought it would, tugging at her feelings about family and a lasting union between two people. During the entire service she had struggled to keep her composure. Jake had reached for her hand once, but she held her small beaded bag tightly with both hands. She sighed, realizing every thought that entered her mind was somehow connected to Jake.

Sarah forced Jake from her thoughts and tried to make her mind a blank. She listened to the hypnotic sound of the locusts and admired the beauty of her and Jake's backyard. The four live oak trees that they planted years ago had matured nicely. Their neighborhood was called Forestwood, but there was no sign of a native tree, and she and Jake had laughed often at that. The bright reds and pinks of the geraniums spilled out of the huge clay pots around the pool. Sarah enjoyed gardening; she wanted to make the outside of their home as attractive and inviting as the inside.

We've had such a happy life here, thought Sarah. *Will we ever know that happiness again?* It was impossible to think of anything that wasn't linked to Jake. Women forgave their wayward husbands all the time. They managed to put the past behind them and go on with their lives. Sarah didn't know if she could be one of those women.

As Jake opened the French doors to the pool, he hesitated a moment to appreciate the sight before him. The high cut of Sarah's swimsuit accented her shapely legs, and her chestnut brown chin-length bob glowed in the sunshine and gave her a youthful look. He pulled up a deck chair and sat down beside her.

"Sarah, I have some good news. I had a meeting today with J.T. Wright, an upscale home builder in Dallas. I didn't want to tell you about it until I knew more details."

"More details about what?"

"He wants me to manage a multimillion-dollar housing development at a resort in Colorado."

"Jake, what is this about?"

"How would you feel about moving to Spruce Haven, Colorado?"

She sat up straight and removed her sunglasses. "Have you lost your senses?"

"Let's get away from this rat race and start a whole new life for ourselves."

"Remember when we were in college and we used to talk about moving to the mountains someday?" There was a touch of enthusiasm in her voice. More than anything, she admitted to herself, she wanted another chance at their marriage.

"Of course I remember. Too many people make plans and then give up on them. With this opportunity, I'd have a chance to make big money. We could build a fantastic home. I could buy you nice things, like a fur coat."

"I think you've forgotten our dream. As I recall, it was to live simply in the mountains in a log cabin. I think you'd better get in out of the sun—you're not thinking too clearly."

"Listen to me, Sarah. This is what our marriage needs . . . a change in our environment, a change in our entire lifestyle."

She looked into his deep brown eyes and saw the earnestness on his intent face. "You're really serious about this, aren't you?"

"I'm trying to tell you—I want to make it up to you. The way I see it, this is an opportunity."

"I'd hate to live so far away from Catrina and Warren, but we do have to think about ourselves." She looked across the pool, lost in thought. "Moving from Carsonville might give us a fresh start." She put on her sunglasses and swung her legs to the side of the chaise lounge. Facing him again, she said, "But I don't know if it's possible for me to forget about you and Rhonda."

He looked down, silent for a few moments. "I can't undo the past, Sarah. I wish to God I could. But we can at least try to make our marriage right again. You can quit teaching. You give too damn much of yourself to that job. And I can make more money with J.T. than I can make in the construction business on my own. He knows a good banker and a couple of big money guys in Denver who want to get in on the new development at Spruce Haven." He reached out to touch her wrist. "Let's give it a chance. Please, Sarah. What do you say?"

"Tell me about the development."

"It's called Spruceland Estates. It'll have eighty home sites. The country club and golf course have already been built, and most of the roads are already in. Sarah, I can't tell you how excited I am about this."

She smiled. "I can tell you are. Isn't Spruce Haven that new resort that's not far from Crested Butte? I remember hearing about it the last time we were there."

"Right. Spruce Haven Ski Resort is about twenty-five miles northwest of Crested Butte. J.T. says in the past three years the owners of the resort have expanded it with new trails and lifts. The developers of Spruce Haven Village, which is located at the base of the ski mountain, have turned it into a town filled with restaurants and shops.

"Jake, I'm confused. Do the developers of the village have a connection with the Spruceland development?"

"No, Sarah. J.T. is the developer of Spruceland Estates. A different developer built the country club and golf course. J.T. is convinced the time is ripe to start building houses on this huge tract of land west of the village. My job will be to sell lots for home sites and oversee the construction of homes. We get to select the best lot for our future home."

Sarah looked up at him again. "There's so much to consider. We'd have to get the house ready to put on the market. When would he want us to make the move?" Hearing herself say the words made it actually seem possible that she and Jake could mend their marriage.

"He wants us to visit Spruce Haven right away and see if we like the place enough to live there. He wants us to move in by the time the mountain opens in November. I thought we could go right away and see whether or not we would want to live there. It would give the two of us a chance to be together. What do you think?"

The thought of the two of them getting away from Carsonville was appealing. The trip could be a first step toward regaining the closeness they had once shared. They hadn't been on a trip by themselves in years. Also, Sarah was touched that Jake seemed to be searching for a solution for their troubled marriage. She would make the effort to meet him halfway.

"I think I'm ready to start packing." Sarah smiled again. The lead weight on her heart had lifted. She saw the happiness and love in Jake's eyes. "I'm going inside to take a shower." She picked up her towel and headed for the French doors.

He followed her inside to the sun room and pulled her to him. "Seeing you in that swimsuit makes me ready for something else first." He lifted a strap from her shoulder and slid it down her arm.

"Jake, no, not with this suntan lotion. Let me shower first."

Ignoring her pleas, he slowly began to peel off her swimsuit as he kissed her neck. "We don't have time for that," he said.

Sarah surrendered herself like a new bride anxious to please her mate.

Jake knew she was his again. Wanting to make things right, he promised himself he would be the kind of husband that a woman like Sarah deserved. He wanted her to be a part of his future, a future that promised the material success he desired.

Even though he hadn't seen Rhonda since the dinner dance, she had continued to call him. He felt that the move to Spruce Haven would give him the distance he needed to stay away from the overpowering charms of this alluring woman. That afternoon Jake was confident that Spruceland Estates held the key to his marriage.

two

A few days later, the Hansens arrived at Gunnison County Airport, where Jake had reserved an SUV. Highway 135 led from Gunnison to Crested Butte, a route they had traveled many times on ski vacations. About ten miles outside the town of Crested Butte, Jake turned right on Evergreen Road toward Spruce Haven, which was located fifteen miles from the highway. Sarah's spirits soared at the sight of snow-covered peaks in the distance as she thought of making the mountains their home. Carsonville and its hurtful memories seemed far away.

When they reached Spruce Haven Village, they saw that it had been made to look like a quaint European town nestled in the mountains. The buildings were stucco, with accents of gray stone and dark wood. Old-fashioned black wrought iron street lamps lined the streets. The town had no traffic lights, only stop signs. A distinct American flavor, indicated by the names of the restaurants and shops, combined with the town's European air and created a cozy blend of old world and new.

Jake said, "What do you think of the town so far?" He glanced at her, his eyes gleaming with pride.

"I love the old world look, and it has the essentials—a bank, a grocery store, a medical clinic. Jake, I can't believe we're here."

He stopped to examine his map. "Let's take Timberline to Spruceland Drive. Spruceland borders the golf course. We can have lunch there at the club, or we can go ahead and check into the hotel and have lunch at the Elk Horn."

"I vote for getting settled in first," said Sarah. He turned left onto Timberline, the road that circled the base of the mountain. "Everything is so compact and neat. It's almost too perfect."

"Please, Sarah, don't start finding fault with it already."

"Oh, Jake, I'm excited. Don't misunderstand me."

Jake pulled into the underground parking garage of the recently completed three-story hotel. Thrilled to find their room so spacious, Sarah walked to the big double window to look at the view. Jake joined her, and as she stood in the circle of his arms, she felt that the two of them could mend their marriage in spite of the pain. They stood in silence, looking at the wide ski trails that tumbled down the mountain in different directions. Partially visible in the distance, one of the mountains wore a faint image of its winter crown.

After lunch at the hotel, they continued their tour, driving west on Timberline Road. Once they had left the row of condos behind, the road began to climb. Jake pulled to the side of the road and took out a map of Phase I of Spruceland Estates. "Let's pick our favorite home site. I think we should have first choice."

"Okay, but let's get out and walk awhile."

As Jake and Sarah walked along the road holding hands, a group of mountain bikers pedaled past them, and they exchanged greetings. Sarah commented on the shy wildflowers making their first appearance of the summer and the delicate green aspen leaves, stirred by a gentle breeze. "Don't you feel a sort of mystical connection to this beauty around us, a flow of energy between us and nature?"

"Sarah, sometimes you say the craziest things." He stopped and looked at his map again. "Come on—let's take a hike on this lot. I think we might like it."

Later, after a tour of Spruceland Country Club, they sat on the sun deck overlooking the emerald green golf course and watched the violets and oranges of the sunset. "Most people wait until retirement to even consider something like this," said Jake.

"I know. I was sitting here thinking how long it's been since you and I watched a sunset together. We may even take up golf." She turned to face him, her eyes gleaming with happiness. "Oh, Jake, I think you're right; the change in our lifestyle would be good for us."

The following day they met with Judd Miller, a Realtor who showed them a few office spaces and condos available for lease. Later, at his office, Judd answered their general questions about the town.

"What about your schools?" asked Sarah.

"At the present, students have to go to school in Crested Butte, but as our population grows we'll definitely take care of that situation."

"Naturally only a small percentage of our buyers would be affected by the schools, but I was curious," said Sarah.

"Also, we don't have mail delivery. Locals have to rent a box at the post office on Main Street."

"We're sold on the town, Judd, but I'd like more definite information about future plans for the ski runs," said Jake.

"The man you need to see is the mountain manager, but I've been told he's out of town this week. I'm sure Clint Turner, the ski patrol director, could answer your questions. I'll see if he's in his office; he may have already left town for vacation."

As it turned out, Clint Turner was still available. Judd volunteered to drive the Hansens to the Mountain Center, which was adjacent to the base lodge.Clint was a quiet, self-assured man who appeared to be in excellent physical shape for a man his age, which Sarah guessed to be his mid-forties.

He brought in extra chairs to accommodate his visitors in the small office. "I apologize for the cramped space. My main office during the ski season is at patrol headquarters at the top of the mountain. In the winter, I don't spend much time behind a desk." Directing their attention to maps on the wall, he said, "This time next year the new high-speed quad or four person chairlift will be in operation, which will open up the east side." He made a sweeping gesture on the map. "In two more years the back bowls on the other side of the mountain will be open, which, as you can see on this map here, are mostly above the timberline. The expert skiers love these wide-open valleys of powder."

"I understand," said Jake, "that a new mountaintop restaurant should be completed in about three years. Where will it be located?"

"Right here near the top of *Snow Chief*. The new restaurant will serve the new runs on the east side." Clint sat down at his desk. "Do you have any other questions?"

"What will the ability levels be for the new high speed quad?" asked Jake.

"It will serve primarily intermediates and advanced intermediates. Spruce Haven has a good mix of runs for the different ski levels; these plans will make it that much better. With the new bowls and runs, we're looking at a major increase in skiing terrain. We're pretty excited." He smiled, and the lines crinkled around his clear blue eyes.

"How is it working out having Crested Butte Mountain Resort so close? You must feel you're in constant competition."

Clint laughed. "I think the it works in everyone's favor. Think of the proximity of Keystone and Breckenridge, for example. Sometimes skiers think a destination that offers more variety of ski terrain is a plus factor."

Jake stood up and shook Clint's hand. "Thank you for your time. You've certainly convinced me that Spruce Haven is going to be a major resort in the near future."

"I'm glad I could be of help," said Clint.

Judd said, "And I appreciate your helping us out on such short notice."

Sarah reached out to shake Clint's hand. "I can't wait to see your mountain in November with snow if we decide to move here."

"I'll count on seeing you in November," he said, holding onto her hand and looking into her hazel eyes. She blushed and quickly turned to leave the office.

On their flight home, Jake and Sarah made a firm decision to move to Spruce Haven Village and to lease a Ridgepole condo until their new home could be built. The unit they selected was the last one on Timberline Road and was located about half a mile from the base lodge. "When we get home, I'm going to start on our house plans right away. I have some fantastic ideas," said Jake. He wanted to build a showplace, something that would make their friends envious.

"I want a lot of windows for those unbelievable views, but I don't want our house to be like any of those gigantic homes we saw. Let's not overdo it, Jake."

He loved seeing her enthusiasm, and it helped to convince him that their decision was the right one. "Trust me, Sarah. This is going to work out for us."

"I do want to trust you, Jake."

Jake knew she was trying hard to put his affair in the past. He was making the same effort.

three

When Sarah and Jake returned home from Spruce Haven, Sarah busied herself with preparations for putting their home on the market. Their good friends Duane and Priscilla, who owned a real estate company, suggested that a new coat of paint would enhance the exterior. They felt the home would sell in the next couple of months. Jake and Sarah decided to sell most of their furniture. Shopping for new pieces for the Colorado condo gave Sarah another project for the sweltering July days.

Trying to think of other details that needed her attention before the move, Sarah checked her calendar for upcoming appointments and noted she was scheduled for a mammogram the following month. With that reminder, she did her self-exam in the shower that evening and found a suspicious lump in each breast. Fully aware of the signs, she knew both lumps would have to be biopsied without delay. Her first thought was of her sister, who lived in Miami and had dealt with breast cancer a few years earlier. Lauren had been adamant about not losing her breast, choosing to have a lumpectomy followed by radiation treatment. Sarah knew that her family history of breast cancer put her in a high risk category.

She tried to ignore the fear that grew when she felt the first lump again. *I'll call the doctor's office first thing in the morning. It's probably just a benign cyst.* When Sarah climbed into bed, she wanted to wake up Jake and ask for his reassurance, but she closed her eyes and tried to sleep instead. To calm herself, Sarah thought of the crisp, fresh mountain air of their soon-to-be new home in Spruce Haven.

A week later, after her biopsies, Sarah was waiting to hear from the doctor about her pathology report. Nevertheless, the shrill ringing of the phone startled her. "Mrs. Hansen, it's Dr. Montgomery. I'm afraid I have good news and bad news to report."

Trying to sound sure of herself, Sarah said, "In that case, I'll take the bad news first and get it over with." She put her right hand up to the phone and held it firmly to steady her nerves.

"Both breasts show definite cellular change, what we call atypical hyperplasia."

Sarah spoke in a hesitant voice, "Atypical means abnormal. What does hyperplasia mean?" Her knees buckled, and she reached for a kitchen chair, pulling it toward her and sitting down.

"It means these cells have become overly large. That's more activity going on than we like to see, but it's mainly an indication for me to watch you more closely."

"And the good news?"

"Neither breast shows any positive sign of malignancy. We'll talk more when you come in to have your stitches removed."

"There's no cause for alarm, then?" The pounding of her heart subsided.

"We need to consider your medical history, but you're not to worry. I'll see you in a few days."

Later, in Dr. Montgomery's office, Sarah sat stiffly in her chair and listened intently as he explained her test results.

"What we're looking at here are risk factors, and the findings on these last two biopsies put you into a higher risk category. You already have a family history and your own history of multiple biopsies. I can monitor you closely, as I have in the past, but you have to realize these atypical cells can progress to a cancerous state and enter the lymph nodes even before a tumor can be felt, and possibly, even before a mammogram will show one." He took off his glasses and laid them on his desk. Leaning forward, he said, "What I think you should consider is a bilateral modified mastectomy. You would be a good candidate for immediate breast reconstruction."

"You mean I should take such drastic measures as a preventive move?"

"Atypical cells are the first stage of the disease. We have no way of knowing when these cells could suddenly become active and threaten your life." He put his glasses back on and continued. "I would encourage you to get another opinion. In fact, I can recommend an excellent plastic surgeon who can discuss the procedure with you and answer your questions." Dr. Montgomery scribbled down a name and telephone number and tore the sheet from the prescription pad.

"But . . . how accurate is the pathology report?"

"Dr. Simmons signed your report. He's one of the top pathologists in Dallas. Here's a copy of your report to take with you. And this is Dr. Abbot's phone number."

"I appreciate your time, Dr. Montgomery. You've given me something to think about, to say the least."

Driving home in the northbound lane of Central Expressway during the afternoon rush hour, Sarah fought to keep her mind on her driving. She rationalized that this was, after all, only one doctor's opinion. She'd get other opinions. She would not be railroaded into losing her breasts. As she was congratulating herself on remaining collected, she thought of Jake, of how he would be denied a "whole" woman. She was just getting her marriage back together, and they had such big plans for their move to Colorado. Brushing these concerns aside, she concentrated on her driving.

The following week Jake went with Sarah to meet with the plastic surgeon. Sarah liked Dr. Abbot's easy, matter-of-fact manner right away.

After he had reviewed Sarah's medical history, he said, "In view of these reports, it appears that you're in store for more of the same thing, which means more scars and more anxiety about the pathology reports now that you're on the first rung of the cancer ladder. With the next biopsy, you'll be more apprehensive than ever about the findings."

The word "cancer" lodged in her mind. "In your opinion, surgery would be in my best interest?"

He shrugged his shoulders in an almost flippant manner. "You can choose to do it now or eventually be forced into it. My opinion would be to go ahead and get it behind you . . . go on with your life."

Sarah knew some women would have been infuriated with his casual attitude, but somehow what he was saying simply made sense.

"I would do both the removal and the reconstruction at the same time."

"Isn't that a lot for her to go through at one time?" asked Jake.

Sarah saw the anxiety on his handsome face. She knew that he was dealing with what she had already experienced: the shock of hearing the cold facts from a medical authority.

"Actually, she would be better off," said Dr. Abbot. "She would have one time under the anesthesia and one hospital stay."

Dr. Abbot opened the paper gown and examined Sarah's breasts, making a sketch and notations on a yellow legal pad. Jake looked at the floor, the ceiling, anywhere but at his wife's breasts. When the doctor finished the examination, he gently pulled the paper gown closed and made more notations. He showed Jake and Sarah the sketch he had drawn.

"The incision will come across the middle of the breast, beginning here, a little under the arm, and going across, toward the middle of the breasts. You can see that such an incision will permit you to wear low-cut gowns and swimsuits without showing scars," said Dr. Abbot.

"Why can't the incision be underneath the breasts?" asked Sarah.

"Because we can do a more thorough job of removing all the breast tissue this way. In your case, I would recommend removing the areola and the nipple on each breast, excising the tissue, and using them as grafts."

You make it sound simple, but it isn't. I know there can be complications."

"It's not an easy surgery. The breasts you end up with are not going to look the same. The implants will be placed beneath the chest wall muscles. The breasts will have a more rounded appearance; that's called the breast mound. Your breasts will no longer have any sensitivity. You'll have to deal with the scars, which fade more quickly for some women than for others."

"What about the risks of the implants?" asked Sarah.

"Only in the rarest of circumstances would implants present a risk to the patient. You are at much greater risk of losing your life to breast cancer. Implants make it easier for most women to give up their breasts. I think you'd be pleased with the results."

Jake was grateful when the consultation ended.

On the way home they stopped at Houston's on Belt Line and ordered lunch. The place was crowded and noisy with business people taking their lunch breaks.

"It's hard to figure," said Jake, "if the guy really thinks you need this operation or if he needs another trip to Hawaii."

Sarah knew that when Jake tried to be humorous about a serious subject, he was really concerned. "I know. He was a bit pushy, but I liked him. He was confident without being arrogant. Dr. Montgomery thinks he's the best, and I wouldn't know where to start to find another plastic surgeon."

"I think you need more information about whether or not you need the surgery, not just how it's done. Why don't you try to see one of those breast cancer surgeons that you found out about through the cancer society?"

"Would you come with me?"

"Yeah. I want to hear what an expert has to say."

She could see the fear in his eyes, a fear that matched that of her own heart.

Several weeks later, Sarah and Jake met with Dr. Frazell, the surgeon they hoped would give them a better perspective on Sarah's situation. He was direct, speaking in short, clipped sentences from the moment he entered the conference room. She sensed he was going to answer her questions before she asked them.

"If you're going to have it done, have it done right and be thorough about it. Don't leave five percent of the tissue behind. You'd just be defeating your purpose. That's why I would be opposed to a subcutaneous mastectomy. I'm in agreement with the procedure that Dr. Abbot has described for you, but you need to be a hundred percent certain you're willing to give up your breasts to avoid developing cancerous cells. A hundred percent certain," he repeated. "And you need to know that with the reconstruction you still end up with fake breasts and fake nipples. That's the bottom line. Or you can choose not to have the surgery, and have your doctor monitor you closely with mammograms."

"I've been told it could be too late by the time a mammogram detected cancerous cells," said Sarah.

"Yes, that's true. It's a risk. Mammograms miss a small percentage of cancers."

"And which option would you recommend, in view of my total medical history?"

His answer struck her speechless for a moment. "I cannot give you the answer. That's a decision that you must make." He paused, looking at Jake. "I must tell you that some men can deal with mastectomy and reconstruction, and others cannot. I've seen marriages destroyed in certain cases. If you have a strong marriage, going through this ordeal can make it even stronger. You see, there are variables here. It isn't my decision, as I said before. If you had come to me with a malignant tumor, our discussion would be entirely different."

"I guess we expected too much of you," said Sarah. She looked at Jake and then at Dr. Frazell. "We wanted you to give us your medical advice."

"Atypical cells in this early stage don't present us with a clear choice. And that's why it has to be the patient's decision."

"Can't you at least give us her percentage of risk for these little monsters becoming active?" asked Jake. Sarah could hear the frustration in his voice.

"Percentages in a case like your wife's are pretty rough, but with her atypical cells I'd say fifteen percent, and with her medical history I'd add another twenty-five percent. We could say your wife has about a forty percent risk," concluded the doctor. Sarah could feel herself accepting what needed to be done. The idea of allowing cancer to sneak up on her was intolerable. She wondered what Jake was thinking. "And if I have the surgery," asked Sarah, "would you say I would be a hundred percent free of the disease?"

"Nothing in medicine is a hundred percent, but yes, you would reduce the odds greatly." He smiled at Sarah for the first time, putting her more at ease.

On the way home Jake concentrated on his driving as he merged with the rush hour traffic. Sarah remained quiet.

"I thought he would give us an indication of how he felt," Sarah said at last.

"I know. I couldn't read him either. I thought we paid him a hundred bucks to get his opinion."

When they reached Carsonville, she glanced at the hideous water tower beside the freeway that blasted through the middle of town. There wasn't a whole lot that Sarah would miss about Carsonville, with the exception of friends. She wished this horrendous decision making would end.

"Jake, he said I'd have to make the decision, but I'm going to need your help. So far you haven't told me how you really feel about all this. I mean, you say you want what's best for me, but you haven't actually discussed any of it."

In a hesitant voice he said, "I see the doctor's point, in a way. It's your body, and it has to be your decision."

She hugged herself tightly and closed her eyes again. What an absolute nightmare this whole thing had become. She hadn't told family members about it because she didn't want their reactions and well-meaning advice to cloud her decision. But she needed her husband's opinion because he was more directly involved than anyone else.

"Do you think you're one of those men who can't deal with the surgery? After all, I couldn't even get you to look at the pictures in the book I bought."

"I love you, and whatever you decide, I'll still love you."

"Do you think our marriage is strong enough to stand the strain if I have the surgery?"

"I don't know of any marriage that doesn't have its ups and downs. I think the trip to Las Vegas this weekend with J.T. and his wife couldn't have come at a better time. You need to forget about doctors and opinions and all those books you've been reading. Give yourself a break, Sarah."

"Maybe you're right."

"We need to get in good with J.T., because he's the reason we're getting this chance to move to Spruce Haven. He's been wanting to meet you. Besides, you've never seen Vegas."

They pulled into their driveway. Before Sarah got out of the car, she said, "I'll do my best not to think about any of this for the next two days." She was considering giving up her breasts if she thought Jake could deal with the surgery.

When Sarah entered the lobby of the MGM Grand, a sea of red carpet spread before her, along with row after row of slot machines and gaming tables. Her first impression of Las Vegas was one of suffocation. For the next two days she learned what it was like to exist in a world that never stopped, in this adult fantasyland of spinning wheels and blinking neon lights. Sarah loved the outdoors, and this was not her idea of a vacation.

J.T. had made reservations for the big stage production at the hotel on Friday night. They took their seats at a table near the stage. "Phoebe and I have seen this show three times before," said J.T. "Believe me, these are the best seats in the house. From here, we won't miss a tit . . . ah, I mean, we won't miss a thing." J.T. had a bigness about him that matched his offensive manner. He appeared uncomfortable in his too-tight clothes, his sports coat straining across his shoulders.

Wearing a reptile-print silk caftan, Phoebe giggled and exclaimed, "This show always gets J.T.'s pulse up to its maximum level."

She sparkled with jewelry, but her diamond drop almost disappeared in the valley of her wrinkled cleavage. Her lacquered silver hair had the look of a six-day-old beauty parlor style, complete with swirls.

The spectacular staging and special effects thrilled the audience. As Sarah was about to relax and enjoy the production, the showgirls appeared onstage in little more than feathers and elaborate headdresses.

Later, when Sarah and Jake returned to their room to get a few hours of sleep, she was unable to hide her anger and frustration.

"I didn't expect to have to sit through an evening watching bouncing boobs. What happened to the idea of going to see Wayne Newton or taking in some other celebrity who's in town?" She kicked off her high-heeled sandals.

"Sarah, I'm sorry. J.T. and Phoebe are in charge of the plans. We are their guests. We haven't paid one penny for this trip."

"Oh, it's all right. I guess I'm on edge after seeing Frazell, and I'm really tired."

"Too tired to mess around?"

Sarah sat on his lap. "What do you think?" She ran her fingers through his dark hair and kissed him fully on the lips.

Jake swept her up and rolled her onto the bed. He kissed her neck, tugging at the gold buttons of her top.

"Jake, I've never asked you this and don't get mad."

"What, Sarah? Not a serious conversation now!"

She pushed at his chest slightly. "I have to clear the air once and for all."

Jake rolled over on his back and groaned. "I don't believe you."

"Maybe it's this hotel room, this town, but I can't seem to forget about your affair. I have to know one thing."

Jake slid off the bed in a quick panther-like movement. "We're trying to have a good time and you want to drag up the past." He buttoned his shirt and reached for his wallet on the dresser.

"Jake, please, just listen to me. I have a reasonably nice-looking body, and you were attracted to another woman. What if I have the breast surgery? I can't help but wonder if that attraction for another woman would be even greater."

Jake swung his arms in a motion of hopeless desperation. "I thought you were going to put that surgery stuff aside for this weekend." He snatched the hotel key from the table. "I'm going down to the casino."

She lay there in the dimly lit room without moving for a long time. *Jake's affair with Rhonda definitely complicates my thinking about the surgery. I'm going to have to dump these insecurities if I have the operation. Jake has a right to be upset with me. This stupid trip came at a bad time.*

When their plane touched down at Dallas/Fort Worth Airport, Sarah was glad to be home. The trip had served as a reminder of how much emphasis society puts on a woman's body. She continued her struggle about having the surgery and tried to convince herself Jake would be able to accept her new body image. *As long as Jake can still think of me as desirable, that's all that matters,* she reasoned.

Sarah watched the next two weekends in July pass in a blur of backyard pool parties. It was a boring repetition of previous summers, but Jake was happiest when he was either going to a party or giving one. She had never needed the constant social life that Jake required, but she tried to please him by entertaining during most weekends in the summer. At one of their backyard cookouts, Sarah talked about her contemplated surgery to her friend Priscilla.

"That's exactly why I don't have regular checkups," said Priscilla, taking off her sunglasses to look directly at Sarah. "Doctors are always looking for something wrong, like garage mechanics."

"But wouldn't you want to find out what was wrong with your car before it broke down on you, maybe in the middle of a remote location where you couldn't get help?"

"As a matter of fact I wouldn't, but that's the difference between you and me. I'd have to be told that the operation was absolutely necessary."

Sarah changed the subject, realizing that she didn't want to explain her risks to Priscilla. She later thought how different their conversation would have been if she had said that she had cancer. Then her friend would have shown the concern and support that Sarah needed. She had found yet another angle to her predicament if she had the surgery: people like Priscilla would see it as needless and even foolish. Sarah reminded herself that she had never cared what other people thought of her actions.

In the days that followed, she continued to sift through the pros and cons about breast treatment until she made her final decision. She called the plastic surgeon's office to schedule her surgery for sometime in September. Because of another patient's cancellation, Sarah could go into the hospital earlier, on the last Friday in August. She took a deep breath and scheduled for that day.

Once that was done, Sarah was immediately relieved to have made the decision, to have taken control. She gathered up her books on breast cancer and stacked them on the bottom shelf of the bookcase. She would tell Jake when he got home, and she would call the family the next day.

When Jake came home in a bad mood about a contract he'd lost on a house, she put off telling him until that evening. She went upstairs to take a shower while he was watching TV. Seeing her reflection in the mirror, she knew that her next ordeal would involve the physical loss of her breasts. She wrapped herself in a white terry cloth robe.

She entered the bedroom, surprised to see that Jake had already come upstairs. He sat on the edge of the bed and reached out to her. She took a few steps and stood before him as he undid the sash on the robe and ran his hand down her thigh. Overcome by a pang of sadness, Sarah knew this was to be one of the last times that she and her husband would share such intimacies while she still had her breasts. After their lovemaking, she told him about her scheduled surgery. He was shocked that she hadn't discussed it with him first.

"Jake, I'm sorry, but you kept telling me to make up my own mind. If you're having second thoughts, I'll cancel the appointment."

"No, it's just that I hate for you to go through this."

She rolled over next to his warm body and said, "Hold me."

He could feel her tears on his shoulder. "Honey, don't cry; please don't cry."

Jake dreaded what lay ahead for her. He tried to imagine Sarah with her breasts reconstructed, but it was pointless. *She has to do this for her own peace of mind*, he told himself. *Maybe she's right. Maybe she is saving her life from cancer, and I sure don't want to lose her.* He held her closer, knowing how she had struggled to make her decision. He could tell by her steady breathing that she had finally gone to sleep, but sleep for Jake was hours away.

The date for Sarah's surgery arrived. They had decided there was no point in Jake's staying at the hospital after he had helped to check her in. Sarah knew she was in for a series of routine tests and X-rays. She kissed him good-bye, and the door closed behind him.

She stood in her hospital room, realizing the time had come, the time she had dreaded the most, when she was alone to face the demon of her fear. *By this time tomorrow I will have returned from recovery. It'll be behind me.*

As she began unpacking her small bag, she reminded herself again that her surgery wasn't anything compared to the loss of a limb. Unlike so many women having a mastectomy, she wasn't facing that horrible dread of cancer spreading to other parts of her body. Dr. Abbot didn't expect her pathology reports to bring bad news.

Sarah walked to the window and looked out at a freeway in the distance. She could see the top half of the Ferris wheel at the state fairgrounds, its giant skeleton looming on the horizon, its motionless ribs spread out, a reminder of bright October cotton candy days to come. She wrapped her arms around herself and considered the Ferris wheel she had ridden for the past few months, going in dizzy circles as she made decisions that led her to this hospital room and this window on a blazing hot August afternoon.

The wheel had stopped. She was alone, sitting in the top seat, buckled in, waiting for the ride to the ground below.

A week later, on the morning Sarah was to leave the hospital, Dr. Abbot removed the tape that had been so bothersome. She expected a sudden rush of relief once the skin was able to expand, but instead she felt as if the tape were still cutting into her soft skin.

"Dr. Abbot, I can't tell any difference. It still hurts."

He cocked his head to one side and said, "It'll take a while for your skin to soften up."

Sarah knew better than to expect sympathy. She reasoned that doctors had to keep that professional distance from their patients to help them deal with reality. She reminded herself how fortunate she was that her pathology reports hadn't revealed new concerns. He cautioned her about doing her daily arm exercises and demonstrated them again. He handed her an appointment card and said, "I'll see you in two weeks."

Sarah called Jake to come get her and began to pack her things. Leaving the sanctuary of her hospital room made her feel uneasy. She would be returning to familiar surroundings, but she wasn't the same. She closed her bag, leaned against the wall, and looked out toward the fairgrounds. Unconsciously she began to spider walk her index and middle fingers up the wall, her arm held straight. When her fingers reached shoulder height, the tight constriction under her arm seemed to dig into her flesh. She knew that she would have to work hard to reach straight up above her head. She inched her fingers up a tiny bit more, proud that she could do it, determined to overcome this temporary soreness. Her eyes rested on the huge Ferris wheel in the distance, and she recalled the afternoon she had first arrived at the hospital. Sarah smiled and said to herself, *I'm ready to get back on the ride. I won't be left behind. I'll get on with my life and not ever look back and wonder if I made the right decision. I know I can deal with the outcome of the surgery. I hope Jake can.*

That night at home, Sarah was changing her dressings when she heard Jake in the bedroom. She called to him, "Jake, I really think you ought to go ahead and take a look. That way, you won't have to wonder."

When he came into the bathroom, she turned around and watched his face as his eyes traveled to her chest. She saw his dark brows come together, and he looked up at her. "I'm sure it'll look a lot better when you're healed."

"Oh, I realize that, but don't you think they're pretty remarkable?"

"I think you're pretty remarkable," said Jake, and he left the bathroom. Sarah was let down by his reaction. She thought, *I've had days to look at them, and he'll get used to the new me in time.*

*A*s the doctor had predicted, within three weeks Sarah had resumed most of her normal activities. She knew that it was difficult to get rid of the tightness under the arms, so she worked extra hard on stretching her arms above her head every day. A slight tightness was a small price to pay for putting the worry of breast cancer behind her.

Their Realtor friends sold the Hansens' house the first week in November. As Sarah packed their belongings, she clung to the memory of the special time that she and Jake had shared in Spruce Haven. She marked off the days on her calendar until their departure date: Thursday, November 21.

*O*n that day, Jake saw Rhonda for a farewell visit that began in an upscale restaurant with champagne and appetizers and ended in a motel room, where his promise of loyalty to Sarah vanished into the characteristic stale air.

After their frantic moments of passion, Jake quickly left the bed and headed for the shower in an effort to remove traces of Rhonda's strong perfume. Too much early afternoon champagne and satisfying sex had left her in a relaxed state. She lay curled up in bed like a lazy cat.

Jake's booming voice startled her back to reality, and she leapt from the bed in one smooth motion and began to dress. "Rhonda, I never intended for us to end up here. I've been making a strong effort in my marriage, especially now that we have a chance to get away from here and have a fresh start." He slipped into his shoes and looked around for his briefcase. Mentally, he was already rehearsing an explanation for Sarah about running late.

"Jake, you don't play this loyal husband part well, so save your breath." She finished buttoning her silk blouse and reached for her belt. "Your moving away from here is not going to erase our good times together. You won't be able to forget me. She ran a brush through her shoulder-length honey-blonde hair and applied fresh lipstick.

"You're the one who's fooling yourself if you think this isn't over." He looked at his watch and grabbed his jacket and briefcase.

"In another twenty minutes, I'm Colorado bound." He opened the door for her and said, "Rhonda, go work on your own marriage."

As she was leaving, she put one finger under his chin and looked up at him with her blue-green eyes. "We'll see how long it takes for you to get bored up there in the mountains, isolated from the real action."

Her hips swayed as she walked away from him in her tight leather skirt and high-heeled pumps. Jake's eyes followed her for a moment, and then he made a quick exit.

On his way to get Sarah, he tried to make himself feel better by remembering he had been faithful to her for six months by resisting Rhonda's repeated calls to tell him she wanted to see him again. None of this reasoning seemed to help, however. Jake dreaded facing his wife and keeping up the pretense again.

On that crisp fall day, as the moving van pulled away from the curb, Sarah felt sad. The emotion of endings was powerful. Waiting for Jake to return from checking on one of the houses he had just completed, she wandered through the lifeless rooms, stripped bare of furniture . She thought of happy times their home had given them the past sixteen years, and memories flooded her mind. Standing in the foyer, Sarah looked up the stairs and recalled how lovely Catrina had been in her pale yellow prom dress. *Now she's a married woman with her own life.* Sarah looked forward to the skiing trips and summer vacations they would have together at Spruce Haven and Crested Butte.

When she saw Jake pull up out front, she closed the front door, locked it, and dropped the key in the mailbox for the new owners. As they drove away from their home that autumn afternoon, Sarah put away her sadness and concentrated on their future in Spruce Haven.

four

Wearing a velour jogging outfit, Sarah made herself comfortable on the beige leather sectional sofa and watched Jake stack the logs in the fireplace of their new condo. Their new furniture and other belongings had arrived safely that afternoon. She thought how striking Jake looked in the soft glow of the fire, his hair combed back neatly from his temples. She knew he was taking great pains to get a roaring blaze started. They had spent the previous night in Pueblo and had agreed to make their first night in Spruce Haven a special occasion. Jake had already opened a bottle of champagne.

In her relaxed mood, Sarah looked around the room, pleased at the other furniture choices they had made. A large wrought iron and glass coffee table was the focal point for the living room. For the dining room, Sarah had selected a dark distressed pine table and six chairs.

Sarah closed her eyes and leaned her head against a large sofa pillow, thinking about the task of unpacking boxes stacked in every room, trying to convince herself there was no rush to unpack everything. She and Jake had already put linens on their bed and towels in the bathroom, and she would take her time getting the kitchen and closets organized. *Besides, tonight we're sharing the start of our new life*, she thought. *It's been such a long time since Jake and I have been this excited about anything . . . I want tonight to be really special.*

As Jake poured the champagne, he said, "Let's make a toast to our new place. Then you can change, and we can go to the club to see what's happening on a Saturday night in Spruce Haven.

We need to start introducing ourselves to people right away." He handed her a glass of champagne.

Startled, she felt the disappointment rise in her throat as she put the glass on the table. "We just arrived this afternoon, Mr. Friendly. I thought one of the reasons we moved here was to learn to appreciate each other more." She took a breath and sighed, turning to look out the window filled with darkness before her.

Anger flashed from Jake's dark eyes. "I thought you said you were going to relax and have fun with our new adventure."

"Go on by yourself. I'm exhausted from the trip and dealing with the movers this afternoon. Besides, I want to go to bed early, so I can get up at a decent hour and go skiing."

"Go skiing? With all this unpacking to do?"

"I've always wanted to ski on the first day a mountain opens. Don't you realize Spruce Haven has opened four days early because of this fantastic snow?"

"What I realize is that you have years to ski this damn mountain. Sarah, we've moved here; we're not here for a week's vacation."

"That's true, but we're also going to be here for years to make new friends," she insisted, glaring at him.

Grabbing his red parka from the coat closet, he said, "Don't wait up for me."

Opening the massive oak doors of the club's arched rock entrance, Jake lost no time finding his way to the bar. Since all the seats were taken, he found an empty cocktail table nearby and ordered a scotch. He began to feel guilty about disappointing Sarah. After being with Rhonda on Thursday, he knew that his nerves were on edge and he had taken it out on his wife. Although he looked forward to his new job, he also felt apprehensive. As project manager, he knew he would enjoy overseeing the construction of new homes, but as sales manager, he would not be as familiar with the promotion and advertising part. With the opportunity before him, he hoped he could meet the demanding responsibilities he faced. He ordered a second drink.

After Jake left, Sarah sat on the sofa staring into the fire, listening to the popping noises made by the aspen wood. With each pop she jumped, startled by the sharp contrast to the silence around her. She picked up the glasses, took them into the kitchen, and poured out the champagne.

Sarah was too agitated after their argument to go to bed, so she started rummaging through boxes, retrieving certain possessions that had meant so much to her over the years. Everything around her was too new; she longed to see something familiar, something that said *home.* She located her favorite woodcarving, a graceful antique white swan, and placed it on the dark wood mantel. The pewter candlesticks and ivory colored candles were the next items she discovered. They promptly found their places on the new dining room table. Soon she had filled the shelves on either side of the gray rock fireplace with books and framed family photographs. Carefully unwrapping the mantel clock that had belonged to her grandmother, Sarah placed it in the center of the mantel. Once she had adjusted the pendulum, the comforting sound of the clock's ticking reassured her that she could make their new surroundings feel cozy. The clock struck twelve, a grim reminder that Jake had not returned.

"Excuse me—mind if I join you? This place is really crowded on Saturday nights." A young, redheaded woman stood in front of Jake.

"Of course not. Have a seat."

"I'm Veronica Townsend."

"Jake Hansen. Nice to meet you."

"Are you a new member? I don't recall ever having seen you here before."

"Yes, I am. My wife and I are from Texas. I'm with Spruceland Estates."

"How interesting. I've heard about Spruceland. I just moved here about a month ago myself, from Phoenix. I'm an instructor with the ski school."

He couldn't help but see her ample cleavage, revealed by an unzipped black jumpsuit. He finished his drink and stood up. "Nice to have met you. I really need to be going."

"Good luck with your project. I'm sure I'll see you around."

Driving home, Jake reflected on how certain women were obvious in their pursuit of men. Veronica Townsend, with her aggressive nature, reminded him of Rhonda. Veronica was a woman Jake intended to avoid in the future. He was sorry he had left Sarah alone on their first night in Spruce Haven. He wondered if she had waited up for him.

Sarah climbed the stairs to the master bedroom and dressed for bed. She considered changing into one of her new provocative gowns, but she loved the soft fleecy warmth of flannel. *In Jake's mood tonight, he could care less what I wear to bed*, she thought.

With the lights off, she looked out the bedroom window across the road at the condominiums silhouetted against the clear winter sky and thought about how Jake's construction would soon add to the growing number of new homes. She hated to think of bulldozers destroying the stately blue spruce and the ponderosa pines. Sarah shivered. Their new home would be in the midst of that wilderness. She considered how isolated their condo was since it was the last unit that backed up to the hill. Her underarms felt tight after traveling; she stretched her arms to the ceiling. Pulling back the rich rust and gold comforter, she got into bed, dozing until she heard Jake's key in the door. She pretended to be asleep when he got into bed.

The following morning Sarah found a note on the kitchen counter that read:

> *I'm sorry things didn't get off to a better start. Meet me at Timberhouse around 1:00 for lunch and we'll ski this afternoon. I'm on my way to see about the office space. Love, Jake.*

After reading the note, she began to feel that the entire argument had been her fault. She reasoned that Jake had been in a mood to celebrate, which to him meant going out. They could have their special time that evening. Deciding to surprise him by appearing for lunch in a flattering new ski outfit, she decided to visit the ski shop in Spruce Haven village, which was less than a mile from their

Ridgepole complex. Timberline Road led to the base lodge, a large three-story cedar structure with a clock tower that could be seen from any point in the village.

Sarah watched lift 3 whisking skiers up the mountain. Turning left onto Main Street, she looked at the row of shops and galleries with their pitched roofs intended to hold the snow, as if in a fairy tale setting. Spruce Haven was a pedestrian village with an underground parking garage on the east side of the resort. A smooth shuttle system moved skiers from the outlying condos to the base of the mountain.

At the end of Main Street, Sarah could see Evergreen Road, where she would do her marketing at the only supermarket in town. A light snow was falling as she pushed open the oval glass door of the Powder Hound Ski Shop.

With their extensive collections of ski clothes and equipment, resort ski shops attracted Sarah. In this one, clothing racks bulged with a bright assortment of parkas, and wool sweaters in vibrant colors lay stacked on shelves. In the next room, sleek new skis lined the wall.

She was determined to try on a pair of stretch pants, but when she saw how they revealed the imperfection of her figure, she had her doubts about buying them. *Why can't I look like those tall, skinny women I see wearing these pants in the lift lines?* she thought. She laughed to herself, realizing that she was stuck with her five-foot-four height. She walked out of the dressing room to look in a larger mirror.

"I really like those on you," said Kathy Castleberry, who owned the shop. Sarah knew the mirror told the truth, but she needed a boost to her ego and gratefully accepted the compliment.

"They're really a little tight," admitted Sarah, "but I'm going to get them as an incentive to lose a few pounds." Turning from her reflection in the mirror, she said, "I'm Sarah Hansen." She was eager to introduce herself to Kathy, a petite woman with short blonde hair and a pleasant smile.

"And I'm Kathy Castleberry. How long are you staying in Spruce Haven?"

"For a number of years, I hope. We just moved here from Texas. My husband is the sales and project manager for Spruceland Estates."

"Really? My husband works with me here in our shop. He took the day off to ski before the Thanksgiving crowds arrive in full force. We were swamped during the holidays last season. Of course, two years ago we didn't have much snow, so I'm not complaining about the crowds."

"I guess a ski shop is a seasonal business. What do you do in the off season?"

"Oh, we love the summers here, so it's nice to have the free time. We thought about starting a line of golf and tennis clothes, but we'd have to work too hard," Kathy laughed.

Sarah bought the black stretch pants and a flattering lavender parka with a black fur-lined hood that would keep her warm on cold days. As she paid for her purchases, Kathy asked Sarah for her phone number. "My husband and I have heard rumors about Spruceland Estates, and we'd like to know more about it. Why don't I give you a call before long and the four of us could get together at the club for drinks one evening?"

Sarah left the shop, proud that she could tell Jake she had already found a prospective client. Returning to the condo, she changed into the new outfit. Adding a touch of rose-colored blush to her high cheekbones, she admitted she was beginning to feel more like her old self than she had since her breast surgery. A renewed energy seemed to flow through her veins.

She promised herself she would make a real effort to meet Jake halfway and to make a special effort to be more social. With these optimistic thoughts, she gathered her skis and other equipment and set forth for what she believed would be a good day.

Stepping into the crystalline mountain air on that Sunday morning, Sarah thought about how lucky she was. Since she and Jake had already received their season passes in the mail, she could simply walk to the rear of their complex, where a cleared path in the snow led to the last half of *Lonesome Trail*, a short beginner run. She had studied the trail guide to select the runs she would try first.

When the trail of packed powder came into view, Sarah felt an inner peace she hadn't known for a long time. She wished that Jake were with her to experience the adventure of the first run of the season. As a privileged guest in this serene world of white, she watched a rabbit scamper away. Seeing the fresh, delicate tracks of small animals in the snow, she decided that they had made a beautiful life for themselves, just as she and Jake were about to do. The anxieties she had lived with for the past months seemed to vanish into the crisp morning air. When she clicked into her bindings, the sharp sound of metal snapping into place echoed around her, shattering the silence. Taking hold of the poles, she shoved off.

The cold morning air brushed away her concerns from the night before. Although Sarah hadn't skied since last spring, the turns came easily, and her rhythm felt natural and smooth. She was pleased to see that the tightness under her arms didn't bother her as she skied. The thought of being able to ski had given her a strong incentive to work extra hard on her arm exercises and her general body conditioning.

At the bottom, Sarah joined a group of enthusiastic skiers standing in line for the chairlift. During the ride, an attractive young woman with long red hair struck up a conversation with her. Sarah always dreaded rides with strangers who felt compelled to ask the same trite questions.

"Where are you from?" asked the woman.

Sarah looked straight ahead. "I live here. My husband and I moved here yesterday from Texas."

"I'm one of the new ski instructors here, but ski school doesn't open until Wednesday. Last night at the club, I met a man who had just moved here from Texas and plans to build homes."

"Really?" Sarah was conscious of the steely edge in her voice, but she didn't care. "That must have been my husband."

The woman didn't make any further effort to talk to Sarah, who felt a familiar knot in her stomach, not unlike the feeling she had when she saw the bracelet on Rhonda's wrist. Instead of being angry with Jake for meeting a beautiful redhead on his first night in Spruce Haven, Sarah reminded herself that she should have gone with Jake to please him. When their chair reached the upper terminal, she could see lift 2, which would take her to the top.

As Sarah skied down the ramp of lift 2, she saw photographers taking group pictures with snowcapped peaks and ridges in the background. Turning away from the postcard view, she let her skis run straight until she picked up speed to initiate a turn. She had already planned to take *Hillcrest* all the way to the base lodge in time to meet Jake.

About halfway down, she stopped, puzzled by a fork in the trail. A trail sign before her with a black diamond for advanced read *Hillcrest*, and to her left another trail sign with a blue square for intermediates read *Windsong*. A patroller skied along beside her. "Can't decide which way to go? There's a big difference."

Sarah turned to face the man. "I believe we met last June. I'm Sarah Hansen. My husband Jake is in charge of Spruceland Estates."

He moved his sunglasses up into his tousled sandy hair and smiled. "Oh, yes, I remember. Welcome to Spruce Haven."

"Thanks. It's hard to believe we've really moved here." She looked at his name tag to refresh her memory.

Again, he gave her a broad smile, showing deep laugh lines on his rugged face. "I'm Clint Turner."

"I'm usually better at remembering names. And I'm usually better about bringing along a trail map. I was so eager to get started this morning that I forgot it. Until I got to this point, I thought *Hillcrest* was blue all the way down."

"It is, except for this one short black." Using his ski pole as a pointer, he said, "You need to take Windsong. It's a blue run that feeds into *Hillcrest* by lift 5 and runs down to Timberhouse." He reached into his rust-red patroller's parka and pulled out a trail map.

She took it from him and said, "Thanks. I'm supposed to meet Jake at one o'clock, and it's almost that time."

"As they say in Texas, I hope y'all like it here." Clint smiled and pulled his sunglasses down over his blazing blue eyes.

"I'm sure we will. With all this snow, it's as breathtaking as I had imagined." She pushed off with her poles and skied in the direction of *Windsong*. She could hear his skis slicing through the snow close behind her. When she reached the bottom of the run, she stopped to rest and saw Clint disappear into the lift line crowd. She rested for a few minutes and then took *Hillcrest* down to the base lodge.

Clint Turner, ski patrol director of Spruce Haven, opened the door to patrol headquarters at the top of lift 2 and entered a spacious room with a large trail sweep board, where his forty patrollers signed up for various assignments. He poured himself a cup of coffee and went into the dispatcher's office to listen to radio communications, hearing the dispatcher say, "We've got a 1050 on lower *Baby Doe's*. Over."

"Patrol headquarters, this is Randy. I'm about to get off lift 7. On my way to lower *Baby Doe's*. Over."

Clint watched lift 2 dumping skiers at a steady rate. He had chosen this profession because it combined his love for the mountains with the personal satisfaction of helping injured skiers and controlling the menace of avalanches. He saw groups congregated at the top, checking maps and adjusting boots and goggles. Two of his patrollers were returning an orange toboggan to its proper station. The constant radio banter rolled into the room with the rhythm of waves on a beach, sometimes with the softness of a gentle rippling of water and other times with the crashing sound of a big roller.

His mind no longer registered the messages coming in over the radio. He was thinking of Sarah's bright smile, the same smile that he remembered from last summer, when he first met her in his office. She had a vitality about her that he found appealing, but he reminded himself that she also had a husband.

At one o'clock Sarah arrived at Timberhouse Lodge, made of rough-cut Douglas fir and Alaskan cedar. Timberhouse offered a ski rental shop, coin-operated ski lockers, photo emporium, day-care for children, and a deluxe cafeteria. The lower level of the lodge was accessible from the rear of the building, where the clinic and ski patrollers' locker room were located. As she looked for

Jake, she decided not to bring up the previous night, even though she wanted to say something sarcastic about the redhead who had met him at the club.

"Hey, Sarah, " yelled Jake, amid the noisy confusion of hungry skiers clumping through the lodge looking for empty seats as they carried trays of hamburgers and steaming cups of hot chocolate. Nudging her way through the crowd, Sarah claimed the seat Jake was saving for her. She waited for him to comment on her bright new parka, but he didn't say anything.

"Jake, I have had the best morning. I can't wait for us to try different runs."

"Whoa, Sarah, slow down. I want you to meet a couple of friends who own a ski repair shop. Meet Willy and Cliff. Their place is on Evergreen Road next door to the office space that I leased this morning. It will be be a convenient location for the sales and construction office. Guys, this is my wife, Sarah."

The two young men acknowledged Sarah with the usual courtesies. She realized for the first time since she had sat down that Jake wasn't wearing his ski clothes; he had on jeans and the red wool sweater she had given him last Christmas. Her enthusiasm for their afternoon together faded. She wasn't surprised that he had wasted no time in meeting some locals. People seemed naturally attracted to his open friendliness, his greatest asset or, at times, his greatest downfall, Sarah thought. She tried to hide her disappointment and appear cheerful.

"Is it the office space we found in June?"

"Yes, it was only a matter of signing the papers."

"Now that you are official residents of our fair town," said Willy, "no one can call you a gaper."

"A what?" asked Sarah.

"Gaper," answered Willy. "It's a term used to refer to tourists, especially Texans, no offense, who go around with their mouths open, gaping, like at posted menus, trail signs, that sort of thing."

"Yeah, I used to work at one of the warming houses," said Willy. "A guy would come up to the counter, gape at the signs, and say 'How much is a large Coke?'"

"And you gotta figure these guys are smart people," said Cliff.

"They're doctors, businessmen, lawyers. But something strange happens to their brains when they get up to this altitude. They'll be on the hill, gaping and asking dumb questions like 'How do you get to the bottom?'"

"The locals sometimes call tourists turkeys," said Willy. "I have a friend who's a cook here at Timberhouse. He's always hearing people say things to him like `Must be a rough life, flipping burgers and skiing all day.' My friend flips about a thousand burgers a day and skis one day a week. The average turkey thinks everybody's job around here is simple."

"I'm glad you guys have clued us in on the inside terminology," said Jake.

Seeing that their luncheon and ski date were both hopeless, Sarah decided to make a quick exit. "Nice to have met you," she said as she stood up from the table, nodding in the direction of Cliff and Willy and adjusting her ski cap. "Jake, I'll see you at the condo later. We have a great deal of unpacking to do." As an afterthought, she added, "Oh, and I'll need the truck later this afternoon in order to shop for groceries." She hoped Jake caught her icy tone as she put on her sunglasses and left him with his new friends.

Sarah was upset with him for not returning to the condo until hours later, but after she got home from the grocery store, her anger was gone. Hoping to set the right tone for a relaxing evening at home, she prepared Jake's favorite meal, pork tenderloin with fresh green beans. During dinner their awkward silence was almost unbearable. She waited for Jake to apologize for not keeping his promise.

"Dinner was great, but let's agree to eat at the club three or four times a week."

Anxious to have a pleasant evening, Sarah said, "That sounds like a good idea." She didn't want to start nagging him about his lack of consideration that afternoon. She could tell he was trying to atone for the way he had behaved toward her since they arrived in Spruce Haven, and she didn't want to spoil his efforts.

"I realize you're upset about today, and I don't blame you. I'll make it up to you tomorrow by going skiing with you, but first I'll make it up to you tonight," said Jake in a husky voice that caught Sarah by surprise. "Why don't we take a bottle of wine with us to the hot tub . . . and no swimsuits allowed." He reached across the table for her hand. "I'll help you clear the table."

Sarah wanted to keep Jake in his present mood. She hadn't seen him that amorous in a long time. "The dishes can wait until later."

When she eased her body into the swirling warm water, Jake slipped his arm around her waist, kissing her softly on the neck, and Sarah closed her eyes. She felt a twinge of insecurity, wondering if Jake was bothered by her surgery. She took his hand from her waist and moved it slowly to her chest. "See how much softer they've become."

"Yeah, feels like the real thing to me. Can you feel me touching you there?"

"Oh, Jake, remember it'll never be like it was before."

Jake had a sinking feeling when she said that. He missed her breasts, and there was no getting around it. He wished he could talk to her about it and make her understand that he didn't love her any less. The ringing of the phone interrupted his thoughts.

"What timing," he said. Reaching for a towel, he lifted himself out of the tub. "I'll get it; it could be important." For a fleeting second he feared Rhonda could be calling him.

"Duane, what's happening?" After a short conversation, he hung up the phone with a dazed look on his face.

Standing near him with a towel wrapped around her, Sarah said, "I gather from what I could hear that Priscilla and Duane are coming up in a few days." The couple had brought them a gift the night before Jake and Sarah left for Spruce Haven. Sarah was surprised by the call and even more surprised at the impending visit.

"Can you believe those two?" said Jake. "They called Information for our number. They'll be here Thursday, Thanksgiving Day."

"I assume they're flying."

"Right. Duane said they'd be here around five o'clock Thursday afternoon, and he already made arrangements to rent a car."

"Jake, this is too much. I expected to see them during the

Christmas holidays or some time in the spring, but certainly not this soon. We just left Carsonville. Besides, we can't possibly be unpacked by Thursday."

"Hey, Sarah, relax. I'll help you unpack, and we'll go to the club for a late Thanksgiving feast. You won't have to do a thing. I can't wait to show them this place."

She knew she was being unreasonable and selfish, but she hadn't expected to contend with visitors so soon. At the same time, she remembered that she had decided to work harder on compromising with Jake. "You're right. I know they're curious to see Spruce Haven, and we'll have a good time showing them around."

"Now that we have that settled, let's go to the bedroom and continue where we left off in the hot tub," said Jake, pulling Sarah to him. "You can put on one of those sexy new outfits that turn me on."

Their lovemaking had the effect of lulling Sarah into a sense of warmth and security. She felt protected, wrapped in his arms, listening to the wind outside murmuring sweet assurances.

The next morning Sarah found herself skiing down an intermediate run she had already learned to love. Unlike Sarah, Jake had always been athletic. He skied much faster than Sarah did. He seemed to swoop down the mountain like an eagle diving for his prey, making effortless turns and disappearing from sight. When he paused to catch his breath, she skied below him, sliding to a quick stop.

"Why did we wait this long to move up here, Sarah? This beautiful, rugged country is unbelievable."

Before them spread a wide expanse of blue mountain ranges with snow covered peaks in the distance as far as they could see.

Trying to put guilty feelings aside, Jake realized how much he had taken Sarah for granted. He lowered his head and kissed her cold cheek. "I'm proud of you."

"What made you say that?"

"For being you, skiing three months after your surgery. You're a gutsy woman."

"I think knowing we were coming here is what gave me such

motivation to work on my exercises. Oh, Jake, our dreams are coming true. Look behind you at our fresh tracks in the snow, our new beginning."

They stood there, drinking in the natural beauty and the hushed stillness. They felt the mountain belonged to them.

"These are going to be the best years of our lives together. You wait and see," said Jake.

five

Late Thursday afternoon, Priscilla and Duane arrived, bearing two bottles of wine. "Hey, come in, you two. Did you have any trouble following my directions?" asked Jake as he helped Duane with the suitcases.

"No problem, Jake," said Duane, who was always jovial. "In fact, we saw your Suburban parked in front before we even saw the number on the building. Here—we brought you something for letting us barge in on you like this."

Removing the bottles of wine from his tote bag, he handed them to Sarah, smiling broadly, showing the spaces between his teeth.

"Thanks. I'm so glad to see you both," said Sarah, reaching for the wine. An unexpected warmth spread through her.

"Oh, Sarah, I feel as if we're really imposing coming this soon, but we decided to take off Friday and have a getaway from our hectic office. We called you the other night on an impulse," Priscilla said breathlessly. She gave Sarah a quick hug and walked around the room, swinging her arms in a flutter of birdlike movements as she continued her stream of chatter. Her quick brown eyes darted from place to place, giving the living room and dining room a quick inspection.

"Impulsive trips are always the most fun," said Jake.

"Jake, honey," said Sarah, "Help them with their coats and show Duane where to put their skis in the garage."

"Right. Let's put your parkas here on this coat rack. Duane, let me give you a hand with those ski bags. Wait until you see this heated garage." Jake led Duane toward the back door.

"For goodness sakes, Sarah, give me the guided tour," said Priscilla.

"You'll have to excuse the boxes. We shoved a number of them into the corners."

*T*hat evening a crowd of people who had spent the day skiing, putting off their holiday celebration until that night, filled Spruceland Country Club. A glowing fire in the huge rock fireplace dominated the center of the main room. Since the fireplace was open to two dining rooms, most of the diners were able to enjoy its coziness. Oriental rugs in rust and blue graced the polished wood floors, and brass lanterns lined the dark walls to give a soft glow. A small stage and dance floor were on one side of the room, along with a massive reproduction antique bar, set off by an ornately trimmed mirror. Several couples on the dance floor swayed slowly to the band's music.

The Hansens and their friends managed to find four chairs around one of the small tables near the bar. The cocktail waitress recognized Jake right away, asking if he wanted the usual, and then took the others' drink orders.

Duane said, "Jake, looks like you've already made yourself known around here." Duane's statement pained Sarah as she reflected on Jake's visit to the club without her on Saturday night.

Ignoring Duane's comment, Jake said, "Actually, Sarah and I have decided to come here a couple of times a week for dinner."

Priscilla sighed and said, "I really envy you two. With our real estate business, Duane and I are lucky if we get to have a microwave dinner together twice a week." She reached over to pat Duane's arm.

Sarah said, "Take a look around you and tell me what makes this bar scene different from one in Dallas."

"Everyone's wearing after-ski boots. Is that it?" teased Priscilla.

"Go ahead, Sarah, give us your startling theory," said Jake.

"Oh, forget it. You'll all laugh at me."

"Come on, Sarah. Tell us what's on your mind," said Duane.

"With these radiant faces and sounds of laughter, it seems as if the people here are really enjoying themselves, not just going through the motions." She finished her statement, realizing that no one really understood what she was trying to express.

"Sarah, I'm going to clue you in on something that may shock you, but keep in mind that this is a resort environment. Naturally, people are going to appear more relaxed than in an urban setting," said Duane. "These people haven't been fighting traffic jams on North Central all afternoon. And their radiant faces are called sunburned faces."

"I'm aware of that, but I don't think your resort idea is the real reason for this genuine merriment," said Sarah. "To me, it's as if the people in this room share a spirit of camaraderie because they each have a unique connection to the mountain. Think about comparing this group to a bunch of sailors who are gathered in a cozy tavern after a trip on the high seas."

Jake turned to Sarah and asked, "And how many times have you been in a cozy tavern full of sailors?"

They laughed, including Sarah. She knew it was pointless to continue her line of reasoning.

"Have Warren and Catrina found a house in Fort Worth?" asked Priscilla.

"No, they've decided to stay in their apartment for a while longer until Warren gets established with the investment firm. Of course, Catrina is in college this semester, and she still has her part-time job at the dance studio," said Sarah.

"Your parents must have hated to see you move way up here," said Duane.

"I don't think they'll ever get used to the idea," said Jake. "We've tried to assure them that if anything happens, we can be on a plane to DFW in no time and rent a car for the short drive to Fort Worth or Waco."

The waiter came to tell them their table was ready and led them to their seats near the fireplace. Once they had ordered, Sarah told Priscilla about her decorating plans for the new house, while Jake and Duane discussed development prospects in Spruce Haven.

At the close of the evening the four of them agreed it had been a wonderful Thanksgiving celebration. Sarah felt that the evening had contributed to a closer bond between her and Jake. The four of them had discussed old times together, bringing her marriage into sharper focus.

*E*arly the next morning, Jake and Duane left early to get in a few runs ahead of their wives, agreeing to meet them at Sprucetop for lunch.

As the two women lingered at Sarah's new pine dining table, Priscilla was in her usual talkative mood. "Oh, Sarah, I meant to tell you that our friends are shocked about Rhonda and Kevin Sloan getting a divorce. We just found out about it a few days ago. You remember Rhonda, the interior designer who owns that studio on Mulberry Street?"

Afraid that Priscilla would see her trembling hands, Sarah put them in her lap and tried to hide her reaction. She didn't dare pick up her cup of coffee. "Of course, I remember her. Do you know why they're getting a divorce?" asked Sarah, trying to remain calm.

Proud to be a bearer of news from home, even if it happened to be bad news, Priscilla said, "Yes, but let me explain how Duane was one of the first to get the news. You see, Kevin and Duane play racquetball every Tuesday at that new club in town. It seems Kevin was really upset Tuesday, and he finally told Duane that he was leaving Rhonda. Anyway, last Thursday Kevin had called Rhonda to have lunch with him, but she told him she was meeting a client and couldn't make it. Kevin had a business appointment in Dallas for later, so he decided to call the man and arrange to meet him for lunch. As he was driving into Dallas, he spotted Rhonda's blue Mercedes several cars ahead of his." Priscilla's brown eyes narrowed as she looked straight into Sarah's face. Lowering her voice as if someone might be listening, she continued, "He saw her exit onto the service road and turn into this motel. Well, he followed her." Priscilla stopped to take another gulp of coffee. "Yuck, this stuff is cold. Stay put; I'm gonna grab a quick refill. You want another cup?"

"No, not for me," said Sarah, who felt a sudden desire to leave the room. Last Thursday at noon . . . a motel . . . she didn't want to hear any more, but she knew there was no exit for her. *Please, dear God, not Jake; it must have been someone else, not Jake.* She remembered waiting for him at home last Thursday and the excuses he had made for running late. Her heart hammered, but she managed to appear unshaken.

Returning with a steaming cup of coffee, Priscilla resumed her seat, continuing her story. "Let's see. Where did I leave off?"

Sarah said quietly, "Kevin followed her to a motel."

"Oh, that's right. Kevin parked his car at a restaurant next to the motel and went inside, where he waited until he saw Rhonda as she was leaving and then . . . you are not going to believe this . . . he saw a guy he knows from Carsonville leaving the same motel room." Taking another sip of coffee, she shook her head and remarked, "I thought she and Kevin had a happy marriage. Anyway, Kevin said Rhonda admitted she had been having this affair for some time and that she was in love with this guy." Priscilla leaned her elbows on the table, pausing for Sarah's response to this latest bit of gossip.

As casually as she could manage, Sarah said, "I think two people can put on a pretty good front and be miserable with each other at the same time."

"Oh, Sarah, you're always trying to be so philosophical about things. Don't you want to know who the guy from Carsonville was?" Priscilla asked with a tone of exasperation.

"Is it anyone I know?" Sarah avoided Priscilla's piercing brown eyes and looked out the sliding glass door, pretending to be either distracted or indifferent. She could feel the warmth of her flushed face.

"Who knows? Duane asked Kevin who he was, and Kevin said he'd rather not say. Kevin said this guy wasn't the first one to get involved with Rhonda and that he has had it with her running around on him. You remember at the dinner dance, how Rhonda even flirted with Jake, coming over to our table and asking him to dance the way she did."

"Yeah, actually, I do recall that incident." Sarah kept her attention on the view outside, hoping Priscilla would think she wasn't interested in Rhonda's affair.

"Sarah, I guess I'm really boring you with all this. I know

Rhonda's only an acquaintance of yours. It's just that Duane and I have been so shocked."

Sarah turned and looked at Priscilla for a moment before speaking. "Yes, I heard you. I'm sorry. I got absorbed in watching the morning sun hit those mountains. I guess the new will wear off, and I'll gradually take this incredible view for granted."

"Yeah, it sure beats the view from my breakfast table."

Sarah rose from the table and carried her coffee cup to the sink.

Priscilla padded after her. "Hey, we'd better get these dishes loaded in the dishwasher. I'm ready to hit the slopes."

"Why don't you go ahead and get dressed; I'll finish up here."

"Okay, if you insist." She raced up the stairs with an energy that always amazed Sarah, especially since Priscilla was about ten years older than she was.

Sarah's head was spinning from all that Priscilla had said. *Come on,* she told herself, *You have to steady your nerves. Don't jump to conclusions until you've talked to Jake. Would he admit to it this time, even if it were true? But it couldn't have been Jake. Jake loves me. He would never put me through that pain again. This time Rhonda was with another woman's husband, not mine.*

Having loaded the dishwasher, she stood at the kitchen sink, as if she were in a trance. She couldn't possibly bring the subject up to Jake until their friends had left. She knew how moody and temperamental he could be if he had something on his mind. She certainly didn't want Duane and Priscilla to think anything was wrong. To Sarah, married life was a private matter between two people. She went upstairs to change.

Pulling the hot pink turtleneck over her head, bits and pieces of Priscilla's conversation crowded in on Sarah's mind. She remembered that Kevin had said this guy was not the first lover in Rhonda's adulterous life. Sarah concluded that Rhonda must have become involved with someone else after her affair with Jake.

A tiny voice deep inside said, *Yes, but Jake left the house last Thursday for several hours. Had he been telling you the truth then?* Sarah looked at herself in the mirror and saw that in spite of the bright color of the ski suit, she looked pale. She put on more blush. *I'll give my best performance until they leave*, she promised herself. She joined Priscilla downstairs and found her sitting on the bench by the front door, putting on her ski boots.

As soon as they stepped outside, Sarah took a deep breath of fresh air. After a short walk to the rear of the complex, the two women prepared to enter Lonesome Trail.

"Wow, Sarah, this is unreal," said Priscilla. "Remember those times we had to lug our skis and poles from the parking lot up to the lift? I think this is the first time I've ever skied down a run to buy my lift ticket."

"I'm afraid we're going to get spoiled, but Jake says after we get our house built, we'll leave our skis in a rented locker at the base lodge. Of course, we'll have to drive down the mountain, which will be an inconvenience compared to this." Sarah adjusted her goggles. "Are you ready?"

"You bet. Lead the way. Maybe we can find those husbands of ours."

Sarah hoped they didn't find them right away. She needed some time to herself, to get her head cleared of the jumble of confusion.

Jake and Duane spotted Sarah and Priscilla from a chairlift. The two women had stopped to rest after their second blue run. "Hey, you two, wait for us at lift 3," Jake yelled, waving his ski pole in the air.

When their husbands joined them, Priscilla said to Duane, "Are you sure we can't move our real estate business up here? We could put up a Closed sign each day around noon and go skiing; in the summer we could play tennis in this fresh mountain air."

"Remember, Priscilla, you can barely tolerate a week of this cold and snow," said Duane.

"You know, I'm relieved that we'll have a chance to experience an entire winter season before we actually start building our house. Let's get in line. Duane, I'll let you ride with your wife this time."

Sarah was not prepared for this immediate moment alone with Jake. As they rode together up the mountain, she tried to concentrate on the scenery to distract her mind, but she wanted to tell Jake about Kevin's discovery, to hear his response. In spite of her longing to talk to her husband, she knew it would have to wait until after Priscilla and Duane left Sunday.

"I think it's time we showed them one of our more challenging blue runs. Let's take them down *Windsong*," said Jake. "Duane's had enough cruisers this morning."

"That's fine with me."

"You're in a bad mood this morning. What's wrong?"

She wanted to tell him exactly what was bothering her, but instead she said, "I'm just not awake yet. We were up so late last night."

When the *Prepare to Unload* sign appeared, Sarah was relieved to get away from Jake's questions.

The four of them stood a moment at the top of *Windsong* to appreciate the vista spread before them: snowcapped peaks with gunmetal gray spires of rock, the blue valley below with its ceiling of scattered white clouds.

"The view from up here is worth the price of the lift ticket," said Duane.

Surveying the run below, Priscilla said, "I can see I'll have to take my time on this one."

Duane said, "I'm ready to give this run a try."

After he had pushed over the edge, Jake and Sarah followed after him. Priscilla eased into her first turn and skied behind the others. Although the two men zigzagged down the narrow run a little ahead of Sarah, she soon passed them, keeping her skis in the fall line, the straightest run down the slope, picking up a speed that she seldom allowed. She reminded herself to reach down the mountain with her poles and run with her skis, not ride them. As she made the turn, she weighted the downhill ski, leaning her body into the direction of the turn without a second's hesitation. She felt an almost reckless desire for speed. Nothing mattered to Sarah except the run before her. For the first time in her skiing experience, she realized she was keeping up with her skis instead of letting them get ahead of her. The speed was exhilarating.

When she reached the small dip in the run where she usually

stopped to rest before the final descent, she didn't even slow down to observe the terrain below. Plunging over the edge of the dip, she felt the thrill of a child swooping down a big slide. She felt more connected to her skis than ever before. They responded to the slightest edging, becoming an extension of her legs. When Sarah reached the bottom of *Windsong*, she breathed hard and her knees quivered. Within seconds, Jake came to a skidding stop right below her.

Duane was right behind him. "Say, Sarah, that was good skiing."

Jake said, "Sarah, I've never seen you ski like that before." As if he were lecturing a child, he asked, "Were you out of control?"

Having caught her breath, she said, "No, I felt in control. You've been yelling at me all these years to pick up my speed."

"Yeah, I know, but you sure surprised me."

Priscilla was not quite down the run, so the three of them had a chance to rest. Although Sarah was tired, the tension was gone, and the morning's anxiety about Rhonda and Jake had vanished, at least for the time being.

Duane said, "Hey, Sarah, I bet in another year none of us will be able to keep up with you. If I know you, you'll be trying to ski four or five times a week."

"I have a lot of room for improvement, Duane." Sarah continued, "Here's Priscilla; let's give her a chance to rest, and then we'll take lift 5 up to Sprucetop for lunch."

Later that afternoon, when they were ready to return to the condo, they ended up on *Lonesome Trail*. Sarah had decided the name of the run was appropriate. The towering spruce trees lined the narrow trail in deep green for most of the way down, creating a lonely feeling. Standing knee-deep in the soft drifts of snow, the gigantic trees seemed to resent intrusion into their quiet world, thought Sarah. She wished the remainder of their friends' visit would pass quickly.

That afternoon they returned to the condo to have a drink and change into their after-ski boots. Jake suggested they drive up Timberline and take a look at their home site before dark. On the way he explained that eight lots had been sold. "We'll have to take prospective buyers to dinner, ski with them, that sort of thing." He slowed down and said, "This is where the entrance for Spruceland Estates will be. You should see the sketches for the stone entry."

"I think `pretentious' describes it," said Sarah.

Jake soon came to a stop by the side of the road. "Here's our lot. It already has a perfect clearing for a circular driveway. We're scheduled to begin construction in May."

"I wish you could have seen it in June," said Sarah. "There's a level place for about two hundred feet, and the rest of our property goes right up that hill."

"Duane, look at the view they'll have," said Priscilla.

Jake said, "You can see the country club off to your right. Cross-country skiers make good use of the golf course during the winter."

"Last summer when we were here, we had a shower every afternoon. You can't imagine how fresh everything smells in the mountains after a rainfall," said Sarah. "When the sun comes out, it gets nice and warm, but never hot like in Dallas. The best part is that no air conditioning is required."

"Jake, I believe your little PR lady is going to do a pretty good selling job for you," said Duane.

"That's true, but the beauty of this place will sell itself," said Priscilla.

"About ninety percent of our customers are looking for vacation homes, and the other ten percent will be year-round residents like Sarah and me."

With the darkness of the early evening dropping its black cloak around the mountain, he turned the Suburban around to head down Timberline Road to the Silverado Saloon in the village.

On Saturday, they spent the day skiing at Crested Butte Mountain Resort for old times' sake. The two couples had spent three ski vacations there, and it remained their favorite ski resort.

On Sunday morning, Duane and Jake started out the door with luggage and skis. "You and Priscilla should come in the spring when you can stay longer," said Jake.

"Thanks for the invitation, but we've made reservations at Snowmass for spring."

Before she followed after them, Priscilla looked at Sarah closely. "You haven't been yourself the last few days. Are you certain you're okay?"

"I'm fine." Sarah avoided looking at Priscilla's concerned expression. Before she got into the car, Priscilla hugged Jake and then Sarah. "You two take good care of each other."

They stood on the front deck, waving good-bye for a moment before they turned to go inside. Closing the front door behind them, Jake put his arm around Sarah. "I think Duane and Priscilla really enjoyed themselves. Aren't you glad they came?"

"Of course I am. It'll be hard to find good friends like them in Spruce Haven." Her mind was on the confrontation with Jake. She dreaded having to bring up Rhonda's name again, but the pressure was building.

"I have an idea." He turned her around to face him. "Why don't you come take a look at my office?"

Barely responding, she said, "Why don't we build a fire and relax? We can go look at your office a later." She wanted to bombard him with questions, but she wanted to find the right moment. Sarah felt she was reliving the first time she confronted Jake about Rhonda.

"Come on, Sarah, let's go now, before the storm blows in. When we get back, I'll fix us a big fire and we'll relax the rest of the day."

She gave in, knowing it was useless to argue with him and even welcoming an opportunity to put off the discussion a little longer. They drove down Main Street and turned left onto Evergreen Road. Jake pulled into the Evergreen Shopping Center, where his office space was squeezed in between Willy and Cliff's ski repair shop and a Realtor's office.

Leading Sarah into the office, he said, "Tomorrow we need to go to Gunnison to select office furniture and shop for a new computer."

He pointed to the wall map that showed the available home sites for Spruceland Estates.

"Here's Spruceland Drive, which will connect the country club to the mountainside homes. There's enough building to keep me busy for years to come." He indicated a lot that had been circled in red. "There's our lot. Our dream home will have a great view of the mountains."

With the words *dream home* echoing in her mind, Sarah stared at the spot on the map. She could drop the whole issue of Rhonda and concentrate on Jake's enthusiasm, but instead she turned around slowly to face Jake. "Did you see Rhonda before we left town last Thursday?"

"What in the hell brought up this closed subject?"

She began talking faster. "Priscilla told me Kevin and Rhonda are getting a divorce because he saw her and her lover leaving a motel last Thursday. Kevin told Duane about it, but Kevin wouldn't tell him the guy's name."

In an impulsive, frenzied gesture, Jake unzipped his parka and flung it in a chair. He strode to the window and looked outside. He couldn't believe Kevin had seen him. Jake had warned Rhonda about picking a motel that close to Carsonville. The idea that Kevin might tell someone else, if not Duane, enraged him. If Sarah found out, she would leave him for good the second time around.

Biting her lower lip, Sarah said, "I'm waiting for an answer." She hesitated and drew in a deep breath. In a strong, clear voice, she added, "And I want the truth."

His anger uncoiled. Spinning around with both hands on his hips, he leaned forward, straining his neck, revealing the prominence of his veins, and exploded, "Why don't you call Kevin and ask him yourself, if you doubt me so damn much?"

Sarah said quietly, "Jake, I'm asking you. Did you start up your affair with Rhonda again or not?" Color flushed her high cheekbones. With that old sinking feeling, she studied his reaction for a clue.

Jake paced the room, taking long strides and running his hands through his black hair. If he told her the truth, he'd lose her; if he lied, he'd destroy any hope of honesty in their marriage. He decided to adopt an arrogant, indignant attitude as his best defense. Continuing to pace and looking down at the floor, he asked, "Did it ever occur to you that Rhonda could have started seeing somebody new after me?"

"Yes, of course I've thought of that. Believe me, there's not much I haven't thought of since Priscilla told me about it Friday morning."

He stopped next to Sarah and seized her shoulders with both hands. His voice reverberated in the room, and the crescendo rose with each syllable as he yelled, "I want you to promise not ever to bring up her name again. Keep it up and you'll be the one to kill our dreams, to destroy our marriage, not me!"

Shaking herself loose from his grip, she backed away from him with a look of confusion and resentment. "The pain hasn't gone away, and it won't for a long time, if ever. Your affair hurt me a lot, Jake. I need time to myself. I want to walk home."

Leaving Jake's office, Sarah walked down Evergreen Road until she reached Main Street. Although she wore her after-ski boots and warm clothing, she half expected Jake to drive up beside her, insisting she get into the Suburban. She turned around and realized he must have decided to go to the club, which was a mile from his office in the opposite direction. Their argument had been no surprise to Sarah. She had prepared herself for one of Jake's temper flare-ups, but this time his anger had an almost violent edge to it. His words had been hateful. What concerned her the most was the haunting question as to whether or not the rage represented guilt. She asked herself if he were so angry because she didn't trust him, or was he upset that Rhonda's husband had seen them together?

When she looked at the sky to the northwest, she could see the snow clouds rolling in toward the valley. Dazed, she wandered aimlessly along Main Street, where shops and restaurants huddled in a cluster for protection from the cold wind. A party of skiers toting their skis and poles had to circle around her slow-moving form. She stopped in front of Rocky Mountain Gallery and looked in the window at the display of limited edition prints, but her mind was elsewhere. Had her breast surgery driven him back into the waiting arms of the seductive Rhonda with her perfect body? In fact, had he ever stopped seeing her?

Sarah decided to go in the Snowflower Restaurant for a cup of hot tea. Worn wood planks covered the floor, and glorious mountain seasons were painted on the walls. The cozy restaurant was filled with the aroma of bacon and coffee. Sipping her tea, Sarah thought how Jake had managed to turn the issue around so that she was the one who was guilty of destroying their marriage and their dream home in the mountains. How she resented him for that. The entire scene stirred memories of last May, a time she had been trying so hard to forget, but it was always there, beneath the surface, ready to emerge, ready to haunt her. How she wished she could shove that memory to the dark recesses of her mind.

These images spun around in her head like the swirling flakes of snow outside. *He lied to me before when I accused him*, thought Sarah, *even though he did finally admit the truth. However, I have to wonder if once again he's lying.* She admitted to herself that she had a huge problem in her inability to trust him again; in addition, she realized that her new insecurities about her body image played into the overall picture.

Has the surgery only made him feel obligated not to create more disappointment for me? Does he feel trapped, like a man who discovers his wife has a fatal disease and he couldn't leave her even if he wanted to? Is that what our marriage has become, an obligation? Sarah stood up and left the restaurant when it began to fill up with the noon crowd.

By the time she reached the end of Main Street, the snowstorm had hit in full force. Sarah thought how the fast-falling snow was a good metaphor for the whirling thoughts in her head. She pulled her ski cap down to cover her ears, but the relentless wind blew the flakes of snow into her eyes as she looked up the mountain at the shadowy ghosts floating down the runs. Through the snowy haze, she could see lift 1's covered chairs dangling from the cable above like ornaments on a Christmas tree. Since she was near Timberhouse, Sarah went in for a quick cup of hot chocolate to fortify her for the walk up the hill to their condo.

Entering the lodge, she found herself in the midst of a noisy, party-like atmosphere. The new snow had brought to the mountains a feverish excitement; skiers were predicting how many inches of fresh powder would be on the slopes by morning. After she had paid for her hot chocolate, she looked around the crowded room for a seat. The clumping of ski boots on the red tiled floor unsettled her nerves. *Even the most timid people gain a certain sense of authority in a pair of ski boots,* she thought. She could detect the familiar smell of damp wool socks, a characteristic trait of warming houses. Finally she found a seat at the end of a long table in the far corner of the large room.

A few tables to one side, she saw a couple of ski patrollers in their bright rust-red parkas with the white cross stitched on the back. When they stood up to leave, Sarah saw that the sandy-haired patroller was Clint Turner. When he glanced in her direction, she returned his smile and marveled at how such a simple expression could make one feel better in an instant. The patroller with Clint reminded Sarah of a lumberjack, with his large frame and heavy, dark beard.

Outside once again, she found herself in white gusts of wind. Relieved to see a shuttle pull up to the bus stop, she hurried to find a seat. When Sarah discovered that Jake hadn't returned home, she was almost relieved. In spite of the poor ski conditions, she made a quick decision to get on the slopes before the lift operations manager decided to close the lifts. She wasn't ready to face Jake yet. Opening her closet door, she selected her warmest ski outfit, a navy blue bib and matching goose-down parka. She changed quickly, afraid that he would return before she had a chance to leave. She wanted to disappear into the safe oblivion of a white haven outside, where these questions and feelings of doubt would disappear into the snowy haze.

efore long, Sarah was on the chairlift, riding by herself. She had been concerned that the lifts might be closed down because of the wind and heavy snowfall. She pulled the canopy down and adjusted her skis on the footrest. The snow was coming down at a steady rate, wrapping Sarah in a dense fog that made her feel suspended in space. She felt sheltered from reality, protected from the painful truth about Jake and Rhonda. She pulled up the wool gator that was around her neck and covered her chin and lips, offering more protection from the cold.

When she skied down the off-ramp, she headed for *Ponderosa Bowl*. Standing at the top, she hesitated a moment at the thought of taking off into the treeless, wide open expanse below. She eased into a traverse, letting her skis slide across the snow. Once she committed herself to that first turn, she welcomed the complete abandonment of disappearing into the snowy haze. But soon she had a sinking feeling when she realized she was in a whiteout and had lost her sense of direction. Here she was, alone, with no one to hear her frantic calls for help. Panic set in when she realized that Jake didn't even know she was on the hill. No one did.

Searching for another skier, Sarah needed a point of visual reference, but she couldn't see anyone or anything. *I have to get out of this soupy mess and get to the bottom*, she told herself. Her goggles began to fog up. She felt dizzy, lightheaded, moving in slow motion, drowning in a sea of white.

When she found herself on a steep pitched run, she knew she was on *Baby Doe's*, a short run of expert terrain. Managing to maneuver about a third of the way down the expert trail with its mounds of moguls, she avoided the middle of the run, trying to keep the shadowy line of trees in sight to guide her. She was tired, and she knew that made her situation even more critical. *If I fall and get hurt, no one will summon ski patrol.*

Her self-confidence began to slip. The wind was cold. She pulled her wool gator up over her lips, which were beginning to feel numb. *I can't wait here any longer.* Initiating a turn, she came around for the next one and fell forward, sliding over roller-coaster bumps, coming out of both skis. Grateful that she didn't seem to be hurt, she struggled to get up from the snow.

Oh, my God, I have to find my skis. She started sidestepping up the hill to look for her equipment. She managed to find her poles and one ski, but the other ski was nowhere in sight. By now Sarah was exhausted and at the point of tears.

The snow had started coming down even harder. *I have to find that other ski.* This was no time to lose her senses. Dragging her poles and one ski with her, she began the exhausting effort of sidestepping up the hill in search of her missing ski.

Looking up, she saw the shadowy figure of a skier at the top of the run. She wanted to cry out with joy as she waved her pole in the air and saw that he was headed toward her. The skier stopped to pick up her ski, and she saw that he was wearing a patroller's parka. As he skied down to where she was waiting, Sarah recognized him.

"Lose something?" asked Clint Turner as he placed her missing ski on the snow.

"I'm so glad to see you. I was about to panic because I was getting so tired."

He radioed for a snowmobile. "Sarah, you need to get to the bottom and get warmed up. You shouldn't be in this nasty stuff by yourself. We've closed the lifts, and we're sweeping the trails."

She was making an attempt to clean her goggles with a defogger cloth. The wind had died down, and only a light snow was falling. "I know better. I came on an impulse."

She looked up at him. He took off his glove and gently wiped traces of snow from her face. She was aware of his warm hand on her skin. It was a simple act of kindness, and Sarah accepted it gratefully. She heard the roar of the snowmobile, its engine cutting the silence like that of a speedboat on water. Clint helped her onto the backseat. "Put your arms around Brock's waist to hold on. He's a wild driver." He placed Sarah's skis and poles in the holder and patted her on the shoulder. "You need to have a cup of hot soup when you get to the bottom. Take care."

"Thanks, Clint." *Now,* she thought to herself, *I know what it feels like to be rescued by the ski patrol.* Snow sprayed out around the shiny black snowmobile as it blasted down the hill.

Clint stood there watching them speed away and wondered what sort of impulse had driven Sarah into the storm alone. It didn't add up. Sarah was a full-time resident, not someone on vacation trying to get in all the skiing possible. He shook his head and continued his trail sweep of *Baby Doe's.*

When Sarah opened the front door of the condo, she found it dark. The phone started ringing as she took off her boots. When she answered it, she heard a strange voice tell her Jake had been in an accident, but he was all right, a minor bang on the head.

"Where is he?" she asked.

"He's here at the clinic in town. We had to call a wrecker to get your Suburban out of the ditch, but the vehicle is okay. In fact, Jake can drive himself home."

When Jake arrived, he explained that he had gone to the club and that by the time he left, the snowstorm was so heavy that he had trouble seeing the road.

He put his hand up to his bandaged forehead. "Sarah, my head is killing me. I think I'll lie down here on the sofa for a little while."

She started telling him about her rescue, but Jake fell asleep. After covering him with a blanket, she made a nice fire and sat down to rest. Looking at his peaceful face, she made a silent promise that she would quit being the suspicious, jealous wife she had become. Jake was right. She would be the one to destroy their marriage because she didn't trust him or believe him anymore. Leaning down to smooth his dark hair from his temples, she thought of how the mountains surrounding Spruce Haven provided barriers to the outside world, insulating them from anyone or anything that could hurt their marriage. They would be safe here. They would find each other again and put the past behind them. She would never bring up Rhonda's name again.

SIX

The following morning Sarah woke early and lay in bed listening to the sound of explosives rumbling in the distant mountains, reminding her of a spring thunderstorm's deep-throated boom. The patrollers had disturbed her early morning tranquility with their avalanche control work. She thought of Clint Turner's assistance on the hill the previous day. He had been so kind to her.

"What time is it?" asked Jake, making an effort to get out of bed.

"It's seven fifteen. Do you think we'll still be able to make the drive to Gunnison after all this snow?"

Jake opened the blinds. "Sarah, get up and look at this. We must have a foot of new snow."

Grabbing her robe, she shivered in the morning chill. Peering outside, she gasped at the beauty of the white world where smooth drifts of snow had piled up against the condos across the street, and fleecy snowflakes had collected in the branches of the aspens, presenting nature's gentlest mood.

"Why don't we have breakfast," said Jake, "and get a snow report on TV. We have our four-wheel drive; I don't think we'll have a problem."

"Thank goodness the manager will have the driveway cleared in another hour or so."

"When we move, that chore will be up to me," said Jake.

As they were leaving the condo, Jake said, "Since I know you'd be bored shopping for office equipment, why don't I take you to

Crested Butte, and you can prowl around to your heart's content? It wouldn't be that much out of my way."

"Oh, Jake, I would absolutely love that. We haven't had a chance to go there since we moved here."

*W*hen Jake reached Highway 135, he turned right, following the road that ended in the old coal mining town named after Crested Butte Mountain, with its towering 12,162-foot-high peak. Located in a big valley surrounded by the Elk Mountain range, this small community had tried desperately over the years to cling to its legacy of a quiet, simple lifestyle. At the same time, the town had realistically accepted the challenge to be a good neighbor to Crested Butte Mountain Resort located three miles up Gothic Road.

When they arrived in town, Jake agreed to meet Sarah at five o'clock at the Wooden Nickel for dinner. Stopping to let her out on Elk Avenue, the town's main street, he said, "I'm sorry about yesterday . . . about losing my temper."

"It was my fault, Jake, pushing you to the edge like that." She leaned across the console and kissed him on the cheek. "Good luck finding what you need for your office."

He touched her arm as she opened the door of the truck. "Sarah, I love you."

"I love you, too. See you this afternoon."

Jake's declaration of love touched her, since he seldom felt called upon to say the words.

*F*eeling especially lighthearted, Sarah was determined to forget about the day before. Walking down Elk Avenue, she saw the familiar frame homes with a Victorian touch, many of which looked freshly painted. She wondered if people selected colors to contrast with the snow and whether the colors helped to lift their moods during the long winter months. She began to recognize the well-remembered shops, galleries, and restaurants, feeling a soothing comfort, like coming home again. Garlands of greenery with red ribbons decorated the street lamps of this quaint town, which was officially incorporated in 1880.

First she visited The Company Store, a renovated building that housed several gift shops. A cluster of quartz crystal caught her attention in one of the windows. When she went inside to price it, the owner of the shop explained that her husband's father had found the rock formation years ago, before the mines closed down. The woman had kept it on her mantel for a long time. "It's time for someone else to enjoy its beauty," she said.

Holding it in her hand, Sarah studied the way the light hit the many different shapes of the quartz crystal formation. She purchased it, thrilled to know she was the new owner of a small piece of Crested Butte history. Before leaving The Company Store, she stopped by another shop that had a huge collection of Christmas ornaments. With so many to choose from, she spent almost an hour trying to make up her mind. Finally, she selected two alike, one for Catrina and one for herself. The ornaments had been hand-painted with a depiction of the village of Crested Butte, surrounded by mountains.

When she left the shop, she crossed the street and continued her walk along Elk Avenue. She found herself in front of the Wooden Nickel Saloon, a false-fronted frame building, painted a deep maroon with a forest green trim. Many of the one- and two-story tin-roofed buildings used these false fronts that were so reminiscent of the Old West. She knew from her recent reading that this old saloon had originally been named Tony's Tavern and that it remained a favorite hangout for the locals. *Some things never change*, she thought.

Seeing the Wooden Nickel reminded her of the many ski trips when they had gathered around its mammoth fireplace opposite the bar, with its metal foot rail and row of bar stools. She looked forward to meeting Jake there, where they could feel a part of the warm, spirited atmosphere of the old saloon, as opposed to the new places in Spruce Haven.

As Sarah continued her stroll down Elk Avenue, she stopped at a jeweler's and selected a sterling silver chain with a pendant of deep blue lapis, intricately trimmed in sterling silver, for Catrina's Christmas gift. Pleased with her selections, Sarah decided to walk around town and take a closer look at the architecture of the original homes. Recently she had been thinking of writing a historical novel about the mining days of Crested Butte. For the first time, she would have time to devote to such a project, and she had a new computer that needed to be put to good use. She loved the idea of getting out her camera and taking interesting shots. The photographs would help with her descriptive writing later.

Making her way along Sopris Avenue, she found herself in front of a modest frame house, painted blue and trimmed in creamy white, with four slender columns supporting the roof for the tiny porch. The closed shutters that covered the two front windows were the closed eyelids of the drowsy home. Sarah remembered the time she and Catrina had chosen a Christmas tree from a selection of trees for sale in the front yard of a little home on one of the side streets.

It had been six years earlier, Christmas 1980, and the three of them had just pulled into town. Catrina had spotted the small Christmas tree lot, and she and Sarah had begged Jake to stop and let them buy a tree right then. As usual, he had given in to the two women in his life. Sarah remembered holding onto the tree with its top poking through the moon roof, snow showering the inside of the car. She and Catrina had talked often of that special time together. *Our minds seize those precious moments and store them away for safekeeping, never to be forgotten.* They had spent a wonderful Christmas Eve at Slogar Bar and Restaurant, where a small Victorian furnished parlor greeted guests, complete with a Christmas tree and old-fashioned ornaments.

Thinking of Christmases past reminded Sarah that she would be seeing Catrina and her new husband soon for the holidays. She missed her daughter's companionship, for they were also good friends. During Catrina's freshman year in college, the two of them spent a glorious spring break in Crested Butte. Jake had been too busy to join them and had insisted they go on without him. In the afternoons after skiing, they caught the shuttle into town and shopped until the stores closed. Trying to grab every possible minute, they almost missed their shuttle to the airport in Gunnison.

*I*t was time to meet Jake at The Wooden Nickel. As they sipped hot buttered rum drinks in front of the big fireplace, Jake told her about his accomplishments in Gunnison.

"The Suburban is loaded down with stuff for the office, but that's not all. Since J.T. told me to find a company vehicle, I went ahead and ordered a jeep. It'll be here in about three weeks."

Sarah was pleased to see that Jake's mood had improved. Seeing him make concrete plans for the project made her feel better about their future in Spruce Haven.

*T*he next morning, Jake left early for the office to prepare for J.T.'s arrival the following day. Sarah threw on her ski clothes, having decided to take advantage of the good snow conditions. Although she loved to ski with Jake, she cherished those times she went by herself. Skiing alone on untracked powder was a spiritual experience. For a brief span of time, she was a part of God's glorious creation, surrounded by deep blue sky and lovely old evergreens in their downy white coats. Sarah felt a keen sense of anticipation when she heard the familiar clicking sound of her bindings engaging her ski boots. She looked up at the summit, where the morning sun hit the higher slopes in a blinding halo of light.

As Sarah skied up to the lift line, she heard someone behind her say, "Mind if I join you?"

She turned around to see Clint Turner. "Good morning. No, I don't mind ."

The lift attendant greeted Clint by name and checked the season pass attached to Sarah's jacket. She wondered how lift attendants kept up such a friendly attitude throughout the day. She used her poles to ease her skis forward to the waiting point next to Clint. When the couple in front of them sat down, Sarah and Clint moved up to the loading position. With her poles in her left hand, she turned to grab the outside bar of the chair. "Have a good day," said the lift attendant. As the chair lifted, Sarah felt like a sea gull taking flight over a vast ocean of snow. The only sound was the soft whir of the cable moving overhead, giving them a slight jolt each time it crossed a pulley wheel.

"Haven't lost any skis lately, have you?" asked Clint.

"No, and I don't ever intend to go out in weather like that again."

"That's what's nice about living here. You can pick your days. We don't have much of a crowd on the hill today, but in a couple of weeks that will change."

Sarah felt comfortable talking to Clint. "How long have you been a patroller?"

"Oh, I've been in the ski resort business for about twenty years, not all of them patrolling. I started out really young as a ski instructor at Vail."

"Really? That's where I learned to ski about fifteen years ago. On the last day of lessons, our instructor had us skiing down this beginner run, and I was so tense and exhausted that I refused to go any farther. I skied to the edge of the run and collapsed in the snow. I told him to take the others on down, but I wasn't budging from that spot. He was a young man, probably around twenty-one; I remember his name was Jack. He took his skis off and joined me. He sat there and talked to me for a few minutes about the view. Soon I was ready to join the others and make it the rest of the way down. Funny how I can remember that as if it were yesterday." She was surprised to hear herself talking so freely to someone she barely knew. It wasn't like her.

"Yeah, they warned us in ski school to be on the lookout for crazy ladies like you," he said.

When Sarah saw the amused look on his face, she felt embarrassed. "I was impressed with the young man's patience. That was the point of my story."

"He didn't have much choice. They have a rule about leaving students stranded on the hill."

"Yes, but he dealt with the situation well."

"Right. He had to calm you down, make you feel you were making the decision to ski the rest of the run. The psychological element is important in teaching."

"I'm aware of that. I taught school for eighteen years."

"What subject?"

"English. I usually hesitate to tell people that, because they stop talking to me."

"Actually, I always enjoyed English; I was majoring in journalism when I dropped out of UCLA."

"What a drastic switch, from journalism to the ski business," said Sarah.

"Not really. You see, I wanted to be an editor or writer for a ski magazine, but I decided I'd rather ski than write."

When the off-ramp came into view, they agreed to take lift 2 together, since they were both headed for the top. Once they were on their way up the mountain, Clint said, "This is my favorite time of day. I love the peace and quiet of the early morning on the mountain, whether it's winter or summer."

"Where did you work before you came to Spruce Haven?"

"I was a patroller at Crested Butte. I miss that place, but when the job offer came along to be ski patrol director, I accepted it. It's taken me a while to get used to Spruce Haven, but I really think it has great potential."

"Jake and I are certainly hoping it will attract future home buyers. And I know what you mean about Crested Butte. My family and I love that place. I guess we've skied most of the major ski resorts in Colorado, but Crested Butte is our favorite. Of course, I've always been fascinated with the town of Crested Butte. I'm so glad it's stayed the same, unlike Aspen or Breckenridge. I spent the better part of the day there yesterday while Jake was in Gunnison on business."

"I lived near Crested Butte for about fifteen years; I have good friends still living there. Once in a while I ski The *Extreme Limits* on my day off."

"You mean those steep runs that's marked for expert skiers?"

"That's it."

"Didn't it used to be called *Outer Limits*?" asked Sarah.

"Yes, it was changed to *Extreme Limits* to eliminate possible confusion about out-of-bounds skiing."

"The *Extreme Limits* is not for me."

"Since you're living here, you ought to take a few advanced lessons, and someday you'll have to go there and give it a try. You wouldn't want to ski it alone, though. Believe me, you'd never forget the experience."

"If I lived to remember it."

"You'll become more self-confident after you've lived here for a few months."

Sarah decided not to bother him with any more questions, choosing instead to concentrate on the snow heaped in the tree branches, like fluffy balls of cotton. She felt comfortable in the quiet of the rest of their ride up the mountain, and she felt he did as well.

When the upper terminal came into view, Clint said, "I'm glad we had a chance to get better acquainted."

"Yes, me too. I hope you have a good day."

They skied down the unloading ramp and took off in opposite directions.

As he approached patrol headquarters, Clint thought of how much he had enjoyed talking to Sarah, whose straightforward manner was refreshing. When he entered the cedar wood frame cabin, he saw that Sam Bishop, his snow safety director, had just arrived. In charge of avalanche control work, Sam was Clint's best friend and his top advisor, a man whom he had learned to trust and respect during their years together at Crested Butte and Spruce Haven. Clint had been instrumental in hiring Sam to join him at Spruce Haven.

Sam sat on a wooden bench, looking down at the ice encrusted in the buckles of his shiny black boots, tiny beads of water covering the tops like raindrops on a waxed car. Clint saw him stroking his short, dark beard, a habit of his when he was in deep thought. Clint pulled up a chair opposite him and said, "What's on your mind, Sam?"

"It hit me earlier this morning when I was riding up. This is my last patrol season. This time next year I won't be here; I'll be running my dad's western boots store in Sweetwater, Texas, so he can take life easy. Man, I'm gonna miss the excitement around here."

"There's still the chance somebody will buy his business, and you'll be able to stay on here for a while longer. Maybe you'd even manage to get with the program and get new ski boots with these discounts they give us."

"Hey, there's nothing wrong with my old boots, but these old knees are starting to bug me."

"Come on, Sam. We all have bad knees. It comes with the territory."

"Hell, Clint, I'm almost forty-nine years old. You're younger than me and in a damn sight better shape."

"Our experience is worth a lot. You're one of the best snow safety guys around."

"You're a lucky man, Clint, and I don't even think you realize it. You have a lot of possibilities to keep you in touch with the mountains. You'd make a good mountain manager, and you could even write for one of them ski magazines."

"You're being sentimental this morning. You'll snap out of it. At least you have the whole season to look forward to." He felt unable to find the words to make his friend feel better. Changing the subject, Clint said, "I've been meaning to ask you. What's your impression of the new guy we hired from Breckenridge?"

"As for his personal life, I gather Brock has made the rounds of the available women. If we aren't careful, we'll have women trying to have accidents, hoping Brock will come to their rescue."

Clint said, "I'm talking about his professional life, Sam."

"I heard he did a good job bringing a young kid down *Jeopardy* yesterday. The boy had multiple fractures, and Brock sideslipped down that steep portion of the run. Ron King was with him on the tail, and he said this morning Brock did a hell of a smooth job picking a path through the moguls."

"Sounds as if he's had a chance to prove himself."

"Right. And you know what that run is like in the early morning, with a few icy spots to boot. You ought to brag on him in tomorrow morning's meeting."

"I'll be sure to bring it up."

"Yeah, we can all use a pat on the back now and then. I reckon I need to get to work." Sam stood up and adjusted his first aid belt.

"By the way, in my sweep report yesterday, I wrote down that we need to cut back on grooming *Bojangles*. We're getting too many over-confident intermediates who are skiing out of control."

"Yep, *Bojangles* is getting to be a real pain in the neck."

"Sam, why don't you meet me at the Pizza Parlor around six. I'm tired of my cooking."

"If you'd marry one of them gals that keep chasing after you, you wouldn't have to worry about cooking. I noticed Veronica had you cornered again the other night at The Silverado."

"That redhead is armed like an explosive, and I don't want to be the one to set her off. Besides, I haven't seen you rushing to the altar."

"You're damn right, and that's the way I intend for it to stay." Sam closed the door behind him.

Clint heard a call for a toboggan, midway on *Jeopardy*.

Grabbing his parka and belt, he told the dispatcher he was on his way.

That afternoon Sarah headed for the top to ski *Whippoorwill*, a blue run that merged with Lonesome Trail. After she had skied up to the next chair, the lift operator roped off the last lane for closing time, disappointing skiers behind her. As she prepared to get on the chair, she saw two patrollers behind her. Seeing them reminded her of that morning's interesting conversation with the soft-spoken Clint, whose sense of humor she enjoyed.

Before Sarah skied away from the chairlift, she stopped to adjust her boots. The patrollers behind her skied to the patrol building, where a few sat on picnic tables, waiting for the crowds to get started down the mountain. Sarah, too, waited, because she liked to have the mountain to herself as much as possible on the final run of the day. Jake had taught her that it was well worth the wait at the top in comparison to the crowds below, all skiing down at the same time. Pointing her skis downhill, she challenged herself not to stop until she reached the cutoff to their condo. The ski patrol would be sweeping the trail. If they had to wait for her to ski down, she would feel humiliated. Soon she was on Lonesome Trail and could see the rooftops of the Ridgepole condos.

With her season pass, Sarah could make only a couple of runs without feeling she had to ski all day to get her money's worth from an expensive lift ticket. She was happy to be making her home in

Spruce Haven, and she wanted to do her part to make J.T. proud of Jake and his work on Spruceland Estates.

When J.T. arrived at their condo on Wednesday evening, he was pleased to learn Jake had sold three additional lots for the larger homes. Dressed in a western-cut suit, he made himself comfortable on the leather sofa. "Our marketing consultant in Dallas says it's time to get started on those brochures we talked about last month. Do you have any good photographers in Spruce Haven?" He patted his thin gray hair as if to make sure it was still glued to his scalp.

"We have a couple of local photographers who take group pictures on top of the mountain. I'll check with them right away," said Jake.

"Let's go ahead and run that ad in the ski magazines for the first of the year instead of waiting until spring." J.T. leaned forward to pick up his drink. Sarah wondered if J.T. had ever looked at a ski magazine. He was not the least bit interested in skiing; Spruceland Estates was strictly an investment. Sitting next to Sarah on the sofa, J.T. reached over and took her hand. Reflexively, she wanted to pull away, but instead she glanced down at his fat fingers and his large diamond ring.

"Sarah, you sweet thang. I reckon you could go to the ski resort's executive offices and see if they have somebody in marketing who would help us out with summer pictures, people playing golf, riding horseback, that sort of thing. They're bound to have a collection of prints that ended up being rejects for their own brochures."

Flattered that he had that much confidence in her ability, Sarah agreed. At the same time, she knew he had used the same charm on her that he used on everyone. J.T. was one of those rare men who could pass for a TV evangelist one minute and a Vegas blackjack dealer the next.

He let go of her hand and stirred his drink with his index finger, an absentminded habit. "Hell, the owner of Spruce Haven Ski Resort and the owners of the shops and restaurants want to see our development succeed. They make more money if we bring more people to the resort. It's that simple. And that's what a ski resort is all about, isn't it? Money.

She couldn't put her feelings into words, but there was definitely something about J.T. that had bothered her since the first time she met him on the Vegas trip. He measured life itself in terms of dollars and cents. An even more dangerous quality about him, however, was his ability to sway people to his way of thinking. *And Jake is one of his most devout followers*, thought Sarah. She was relieved that Phoebe had been unable to come. Putting up with J.T. was going to be bad enough.

"You said on the phone you had a new slogan for Sprueland Estates," said Jake.

"I was waiting for you to ask about that. I wanted to see your reaction in person. I can't take the credit. It's what our marketing consultant in Dallas came up with last week. Imagine a fantastic shot of the snowcapped mountains with a cute family on skis; the caption reads 'Now you can have all that you deserve . . . Spruceland Estates.'"

"I like it, J.T. It has class," said Jake.

Turning to Sarah, he asked her what she thought of the slogan. She bit her lip to keep from saying that it certainly wasn't original. "I think it's appropriate for your audience."

"What we really need in that brochure," said J.T. "is a sexy gal sitting in one of those hot tubs at the club. Sex sells more than scenery."

Sarah tried to overlook his lack of tact in her presence.

Always eager to impress J.T., Jake said, "I have just the person in mind for a hot tub shot."

"See, I knew you and I thought along the same track." Holding up his glass, he said, "We even like the same drink. Tell me more."

"Yes, Jake, who is this gorgeous creature?" asked Sarah, raising her eyebrows

"Oh, I don't think you know her. She's a new ski instructor, a good-looking redhead."

"I'm certain she's the instructor I met the first time I skied the mountain."

"Yeah, don't you think she could add a certain interest to the brochure?"

"Of course that red hair would make a nice contrast with the snow," said Sarah.

Picking up J.T.'s empty glass, she offered to get him a refill and went into the kitchen. *Leave it to Jake*, she thought, *to meet the most seductive woman in Spruce Haven the first night in town.* Pouring the scotch, Sarah reminded herself she was no longer a jealous wife.

All the talk about promotion and advertising brought to Sarah's mind visions of slick magazine ads depicting ski resorts with those sophisticated people dressed in the latest fashion and sporting the newest equipment. *The ski industry has grown so fast that promotional gimmicks have crushed the simple enticement of skiing*, thought Sarah. She knew she was becoming a part of the very thing that could prove destructive to the sport. The cost of lift tickets and ski rentals was beginning to squeeze out the middle class, leaving skiing available only to those who could readily afford it. For no apparent reason, Sarah found herself wondering how Clint Turner felt about the prestigious Spruceland Estates. More than likely he wouldn't approve of the massive development sprawled across the western edge of Spruce Haven. She stirred J.T.'s drink and returned to the living room.

That night after Jake had gone to bed, Sarah looked at her reflection in the bathroom mirror before slipping into her nightgown. Her scars had begun to fade, and the tightness under her arms had improved greatly.

Overall, she was happy with her surgery. When she got into bed, she was surprised to find that Jake was still awake. "Honey, thanks for your support tonight. J.T. said I was lucky to have you, and I know he's right."

"Jake, I want to help you with this whole thing as much as possible, but sometimes I worry that we're getting in over our heads. This whole project is such a big undertaking, such a risk."

"I'm aware of that, Sarah, but this is a career opportunity that'll never come along again. I'd be a fool to pass it up."

"He better not call me *pretty thang* again. I detest that phrase."

"You have to ignore J.T.'s bullshit. You'll get used to it." Jake snuggled next to her and draped his long arm around her. "Sarah, you're not upset at me about that redhead business, are you?"

"I haven't given it a second thought," she lied.

"She came up to me in the bar that night and introduced herself and started a conversation. Most of those ski instructors are outgoing because they talk to strangers all day."

"Jake, I understand. Now let's go to sleep."

"One more thing. Would you mind talking to her about the advertising photos? I don't want her to think I'm coming on to her."

"I'll see what I can do tomorrow. Good night, honey."

"Sarah, thanks again for putting up with J.T. He's one of the richest men in Dallas, and I think he's going to help make us rich in the near future."

"By the way, what's her name?" asked Sarah, rolling over on her back, looking up at the skylight.

"Veronica something or other. I'm sure someone at the ski school can help you."

"Yes, I'm certain she's well known. And regardless of J.T.'s eye-catching theory, I think we need to keep the family concept in mind. A number of these people are grandparents buying vacation homes so they'll have a place to entertain the grandkids."

"I know that. I was trying to make J.T. happy. Let's go to sleep."

Although she wasn't looking forward to asking Veronica to be photographed, she was glad she would be the one doing the asking instead of Jake.

seven

A few days after J.T.'s departure, Sarah had a call from Kathy Castleberry from the Powder Hound Ski Shop. She and her husband wanted to meet Sarah and Jake at the Spruceland Club for cocktails that evening. They were interested in talking to Jake about the home sites in the new development. The second reason Kathy called was to see if Sarah would be interested in working part-time during the holiday season.

"We need someone right away to help us from now until the middle of January. We get most of our shoppers between four and nine in the evening. These are people who have just finished skiing or have just finished their dinner and want to browse. I thought you might be interested. In addition to an hourly wage, we can give you a nice discount on anything in the store."

Sarah immediately thought of Christmas gifts. She had planned to get Jake new skis and Warren a parka. "I'm interested in the job, Kathy, but there is one big problem. My daughter and son-in-law are coming the day after Christmas to spend three days with us. I couldn't possibly work during that time."

"Oh, that won't be a problem. We're open seven days a week; this is the resort business, but we'll be closed on Christmas Day. Neal and I have to take turns going skiing on days the village isn't crowded."

"When would you want me to start?"

"Day after tomorrow, if that's not too soon," answered Kathy. "We'll talk more about it at the club Saturday night."

Sarah thanked her for calling and raced into the living room to tell Jake her good news.

On Saturday night when the two couples met at the club, Jake did his best to interest the Castleberrys in buying a home site. "Come by my office and I'll show you a map of the different lots and a number of floor plans designed by our architects."

"I'm so excited," said Kathy. "We've been hearing about your development for years now. The condominium life is getting old."

Neal looked at Sarah and smiled. "We'll let Sarah watch the shop one afternoon next week, and we'll come to your office, Jake."

"Good," said Jake. "We can drive up Timberline Road and look at some of the sites. Roads for the larger three- and four-acre sites haven't been built yet, of course."

"Kathy and I are interested in the smaller sites. I know that land is costly," said Neal. "We'll have to take a long, hard look at the prospects of building a home."

"You may want to consider buying the lot now and waiting several years to build," said Jake. Selling home sites was a priority, since these early sales helped provide the needed cash flow.

"That's a possibility," said Neal. "We've been fortunate with our business. A lot of people find they can't keep up with the high cost of living in a resort community. We owned a ski shop in Colorado Springs before we moved here, but a ski shop located in a resort is much more exciting to own and operate."

"Neal's right," said Kathy. "There's a special energy you feel in Spruce Haven, a certain enthusiasm, especially during the height of the ski season."

That night when Sarah and Jake opened their front door, he said, "I'm glad to see you rounding up people for us to meet. I wish more of these locals could afford to live in Spruceland." He helped her out of her parka and hung it in the coat closet.

"Yes, but a number of people who live here are willing to make a sacrifice in order to enjoy these beautiful mountains."

"You know something, Sarah? You seem really happy since we've moved here."

"I am happy, and I'm looking forward to my new job. I know it isn't much, but somehow it makes me feel more a part of the community. This seems to be a place where people really care about one another."

"Let's go upstairs. I'm ready for bed," said Jake.

"I'm not really sleepy."

"Who said anything about sleep?" Jake turned off the downstairs light.

The following afternoon Sarah was about to leave for work when Jake came home from the office.

"I get my phones installed tomorrow. Then I'll feel like I have a real office."

"That's good to hear. I have to leave for work, sweetheart. Keep an eye on the stew, will you? I have it on simmer."

"I don't think I'm going to like this too much, your leaving as I'm getting home, or before I even get home."

"It won't be for long, and I like the idea of making extra Christmas cash." She put on her gloves and wool hat. "Yesterday I overheard two ladies talking at the post office about their waitress jobs, about how tips have been bad lately. And, Jake, they talked about how their husbands keep the children at night, while they work at the restaurant. I think I'm beginning to realize how much a number of people sacrifice to live here. I need to run. See you later."

Kathy was working on a window display when Sarah arrived.

"The display looks nice," said Sarah.

"A Christmas tree with blinking lights is original, don't you think," laughed Kathy. "Here, I'll show you how to operate the cash register. Most of our customers use plastic money."

After Sarah had helped a lady select a pair of goggles, she was proud of her first sale. When she saw a man trying on sunglasses, she approached him and asked, "Sir, are you finding what you need?"

He turned around to look at her, removing the sunglasses, and smiled. She was startled to see Clint Turner.

"Hello, Sarah. Actually, I'm killing time waiting for Neal to finish up. Tonight's our hot poker game. When did you start working here?"

"I started working this afternoon. I'm only part-time help during the holiday season."

Neal joined them and said, "Sarah, have you met our ski patrol director?"

"Yes, as a matter of fact I have."

Neal hit Clint on the shoulder. "Let's go. I feel like winning my money back tonight."

Clint said to Sarah, "Nice to see you again."

"Yes, it was nice seeing you."

When the two men left the shop, Kathy said, "Lucky Neal. Once a week he doesn't have to close because of his poker game. Did Neal introduce you to Clint?"

"Yes, he did, but I had already met him."

"Poor Clint experienced a terrible tragedy when he was a young man, and he's never remarried." Kathy stopped talking and said, "Oh, I really shouldn't have been blabbing on about his private life. He and Neal have become good friends, and one night Clint told him about something that happened a long time ago. I doubt if many people even know about it, except, of course, his best friend Sam Bishop. Clint is a private man."

"Kathy, I'm not going to tell anyone, but you have to finish. What terrible tragedy happened?"

"He lost his young bride of only five months when he was a ski instructor at Vail."

"What happened?"

"His wife, I think her name was Heather, was a nurse at Vail Medical Clinic. They met at a party at Vail, fell in love, and got married the next ski season at the white chapel in Vail. She was killed the following spring in a terrible accident. She was in an ambulance headed for Denver with a critically ill heart patient; the roads were icy, and the ambulance went off the road and plunged over the side of the mountain. There were no survivors."

"What a tragic thing to happen," said Sarah slowly.

"I didn't mean to get off on that." The front door bell jingled, and several people bounded into the shop. "Brace yourself for the evening lookers."

Sarah barely heard her. Her mind was still on Clint Turner's loss. She found it difficult to believe that behind his boyish smiling face there existed such heartache.

eight

$\mathcal{L}$ ocated above the Alpine Restaurant, Sam Bishop's apartment was the scene of Sunday night's poker game. After climbing the treacherous ice-and-snow-covered back stairs, Neal and Clint entered the small apartment where their friends were gathered around a table covered in blue and white checked oilcloth. Neal felt privileged to be included among this tight-knit group which included patrollers Damon, Gerald, and Jonathan, along with Sam and Clint.

"About time you two showed up," said Sam. "Okay, let's play poker."

"Hey, Sam, what happened to your Cowboys today?" asked Clint.

Jonathan, a short, muscular patroller who had come to Spruce Haven four years ago from Keystone, said, "Yeah, I heard LA rammed the Cowboys."

Disregarding the teasing from his friends, Sam said, "Like I said, let's play poker. I'll start the deal. Everyone gets ten dollars worth of chips, like always."

"What are we playing?" asked Damon, who at age thirty four was a senior patroller of thirteen years and the only family man in the group.

"Jacks to open, trips or better to win," Sam answered in a booming voice, picking up his cards.

The others studied their hands a moment. Jonathan asked, "Sam, aren't you going to offer us a beer before the game gets under way?"

"Yeah, after this hand. Let's play poker."

"Hey, I'm starved. Don't you have any chips or something to snack on?" questioned Gerald, one of Clint's assistants.

"What is this, anyway? I didn't know you ladies expected tea and crumpets," said Sam, still studying his hand, trying to ignore his friends' demands for food and drink.

"Sam, you know the rules," Damon persisted. "When the game's at your place, you're supposed to provide everything."

"Hang on to your britches. Larry is making us roast beef sandwiches. He said the roast beef is too old to use for tomorrow's customers. I'll go down in a minute and get 'em."

"Okay, boys, I bet a quarter," said Neal, throwing a blue chip in the middle of the table.

"And I'll bump you a quarter," said Clint.

The game continued until all the bets were down and Neal showed his winning hand, a full house, deuces over jacks. Raking in his chips, Neal said, "I told Clint I was going to win back some of the money I lost last week."

Gerald started shuffling cards. "Let's play Dr. Pepper."

"Hell, no. We don't want any of those wild card games. Let's play real poker," said Jonathan.

"Speaking of Dr Pepper," said Damon, "Do you have any, Sam?"

"Okay, okay, guys, help yourselves to whatever you can find to drink in the fridge, and I'll go get the damn sandwiches," said Sam.

Neal took off his wire-framed glasses to clean them and turned to Clint. "Kathy and I had dinner the other night with Sarah and her husband. We've been considering buying one of those smaller lots in Spruceland." He put his glasses back on.

"Business must be good," said Clint.

Damon said, "I heard that the new development is going to have some million-dollar homes."

Clint said, "Mansions like that belong in the cities, not up here in the mountains."

"I agree," said Neal. "Kathy and I would like a modest split-level house. The homes may be too expensive for us, but Kathy sure has her heart set on it."

Sam returned with the sandwiches, and they settled into their places.

"Yeah, women get these notions," said Damon. "My wife and I have lived in condominiums all our married lives, about seven years now. Course, Jill loves it up here as much as I do. She wouldn't trade places with her sister, who lives in Marietta, Georgia, in a fine two-story house on the country club golf course. But sometimes, she talks crazy, about how she'd like to build a small Victorian frame house."

Sam entered the room with a tray of sandwiches and beer. He said, "I leave you guys alone for five minutes, and I come back into a room full of gab about women and houses. Let's play poker."

The abrupt ringing of the telephone commanded Sam's attention before he could get the game started again. Reaching behind him, he heard the urgent voice of Bob Whitson, the mountain manager, even before he had the phone to his ear. It was an emergency call. "It's Bob," he said, passing the phone to Clint.

"What's up?" Clint made a mental note of the time, 6:18. He listened a moment and said, "We're on our way." He stood up.

"We have a missing skier. Grab a sandwich." He headed for the door with his parka half on, the others right behind him.

Following Clint down the stairs, Neal asked, "Can I come along to help out some way?" He wanted desperately to be a part of the action.

"Sure," Clint answered as he descended the last step. "You can help us round up personnel."

Approximately six minutes later in the patrollers' locker room, located at the rear of Timberhouse Lodge, Bob Whitson briefed Clint on the missing skier. The patrollers kept their ski equipment, parkas, and extra clothing needed for emergency rescues in this large room.

"Clint, I've already notified the chief of police. His guys are searching, but so far they haven't been able to come up with anything," said Bob. "I have the witnesses next door in the reception area of the clinic."

"Good, Bob. I'll talk with them in a minute."

"Clint, I've initiated our `A' alert. We'll have twelve patrollers on hand," said Sam, "and I radioed the snow cat foreman for the night shift to be on standby."

To Neal, who was standing nearby, Clint said, "Here, call these numbers and have them get down here right away." He handed Neal a list of numbers, which included the director of chairlift operations and the Spruce Haven switchboard operator.

"Okay, Bob, let me take a look at the profile." The pressure of making quick decisions had shifted to Clint, whose composed leadership always had a calming effect on everyone.

After obtaining routine information regarding name, address, weight, and height, Clint discovered that the missing skier was a twenty-one-year-old college student named Jeff Long from Western State College in Gunnison. Fortunately, the young man was wearing warm ski clothing and a ski cap, crucial to spending time in the mountains after sundown. Long's friends had seen him last around three thirty at the top of *Skyline*, a challenging intermediate run.

Clint entered the reception room and approached Jeff's friends. He introduced himself and started asking questions. A call from Sam interrupted Clint's interview. He told Clint that the police had checked all the bars and restaurants, and they had been unable to find a clue to the missing skier's whereabouts. Sam had alerted the county sheriff and the district forest ranger as well. They were on their way to the mountain center.

"When the sheriff and the others arrive, have them come to Bob's office. They can stay in contact with us there."

Clint turned to Bob and said, "Call the cable TV station and have them get out a lost-skier bulletin." Bob handed him the first page of his interview notes, which included a full description of the missing young man.

Directing his attention to the college students, Clint said, "Let's talk a bit about Jeff's skiing ability."

"Oh, Jeff is an expert skier, much better than either of us," said one of the friends. He paused a few seconds. "You probably need to know he sometimes left the trail on *Skyline* to ski through the trees, and he'd come out near the end of the trail. Usually, he'd ski down to the next chair and ski *Devil's Advocate* and *Risky Run*. The blue runs pretty much bore him. One other thing: he always stays until they close the lifts. We cut out around three thirty to go have a beer, so he was by himself."

After a few other pertinent questions, Clint asked, "Has Jeff seemed depressed lately?"

John said, "Jeff never seems to have a care in the world."

"I'm afraid he has one now. Thanks for your help. We'll need you to stay on hand here in case we have more questions. We'll keep you informed." Clint wanted to say something to reassure them. Their frightened faces were a pitiful sight, but long years of training had taught him never to promise what couldn't be delivered. Turning to John, he said, "Call your friend at the condo and tell him to call this number if Jeff shows up."

Joining the others in the locker room, Clint spread a large ski map on a table in the center of the room. To the other patrollers looking on, he said, "At least we have a number of clues to help define our search boundaries. I have a good idea he's somewhere here off *Skyline*, because he had a habit of leaving the trail to go for the trees, but we'll still cover all our bases."

The man in charge of lift operations entered the room. "Clint, which lifts do you want my crew to open up?" A heavy-set man, he was out of breath and red-faced from having rushed to the patrol room.

"Let's get lifts 1, 2, and 3 in operation right away, but run a check on all of them to be on the safe side."

The man hurried out into the cold December night to oversee his crew.

"Sam, go ahead and take four people on up to begin the initial search on Skykline. They need to look for tracks leading off the main trail. You'll be in charge of communications at headquarters. The rest of us will be right behind you." Clint reminded his patrollers that he had appointed Tina to be the search personnel registrar. Her duty involved making certain each patroller was accounted for at the end of the mission.

After everyone had left except Tina, Neal called Kathy and

asked her to come by the locker room after work to wait with him. "There's no way of knowing how long this could take. Since food service personnel are shorthanded, they could use our help. See if Sarah wants to come along, too."

*A*t lift 1, the patrollers loaded in silence. A snow cat crawled up a trail, grooming it for the next day, its occasional high-pitched electronic beep echoing like a submarine under water. The moon cast ghostly shadows across the snow. The colossal appearance of the mountain at night reminded Clint of a sleeping Goliath in the darkness.

When everyone had gathered at patrol headquarters, Clint announced team assignments. The patroller in charge of equipment made certain everyone had headlamps. Extra batteries were in their packs, along with compasses and flares.

The patrollers quieted down as Clint began his briefing. Looking at the faces before him, he felt an enormous sense of responsibility for his patrollers, who were risking their own safety in a dangerous undertaking. He took command in his quiet manner.

"We have a team looking for tracks leading off *Skyline*. We'll keep one team on hand here as a rescue team, and two teams will sweep ." The radio crackled; it was the initial search team. The time was seven fifteen.

"Patrol HQ, this is Jonathan. Over."

"This is headquarters. Go ahead."

"We've located tracks leading off *Skyline* near the top. We're doing a pretty good job of following them, but it's going to be slow work."

"Keep it up. Over."

After hearing the encouraging news, Clint felt a sense of both relief and despair. He was glad the team had tracks to follow, increasing the skier's chances of being found, but he was fearful of what could happen to him in that terrain of sudden surprises.

Before Clint had a chance to finish his briefing, Sam gave an update on the weather forecast, informing them of new snow predicted sometime for the late evening hours. "To make matters worse, we've got wind at fifteen miles an hour and a temp of fourteen degrees."

Knowing that precious minutes were ticking away, Clint hurried to finish his final comments. "Even though the initial team has located tracks leading away from *Skyline*, I want search teams two and three to go ahead and sweep the assigned trails in case the initial team doesn't find him. Check for tracks leading away from the trails. Most of you have participated in search and rescue before, but some of you haven't. Remember, don't overexert yourselves or take unnecessary risks in locating this guy. I don't want any of you getting hurt." He paused a few seconds and said, "Let's hit it!"

Search team two shoved off and skied in the direction of *Risky Run*, their headlamps shooting darts of bright light across the snow. Search team three veered off to the right in the direction of *Devil's Advocate*, skiing in a straight line and illuminating the snow before them as they disappeared down the mountain.

The initial search team continued to follow tracks that led farther away from the main trail of *Skyline*, each skier shining his light on the white cross of the one ahead of him. Tracking at night, even in good weather conditions, presented a challenge to the professional patrollers. When a low cloud cover moved in, it made their job more difficult. The beams of light from the headlamps were like those of cars on a dark, abandoned stretch of snow-covered road. Suddenly Jonathan, the team leader, stopped short. The tracks turned sharply to the left in the direction of a dense stand of tall trees.

Gerald, the youngest of the patrollers, said, "I guess this is where he decided the fun was over. He must have been trying to find his way back to *Skyline*."

"He had one slight problem," said Damon, the patroller with the most wilderness camping experience. "He missed that opportunity a long time ago. It would be impossible for a man on foot to climb out of here. He'd sink chest deep in snow."

Jonathan notified Clint of their position. He radioed back: "Proceed with caution. Over."

The patrollers had been calling out Jeff's name. Now they were silent as they ventured into the dark shadows of the trees. Jonathan didn't dare take his eyes from the narrow tracks that pulled him downhill in a giddy maneuver around shadowy tree trunks whose outstretched arms seemed intent on seizing him.

Around nine thirty, Kathy and Sarah entered the lower patrol room, their arms full of boxed cinnamon rolls that the Madisons had donated from their bakery. Neal poured them some coffee, and they listened to the patrollers' communication on Tina's radio. Hearing Clint's voice as he commanded the rescue operation made Sarah realize the gravity of his job.

When she had called Jake earlier to tell him it might be late when the Castleberrys brought her home, he had told her how foolish it was for her to get involved in something that had nothing to do with her. She hadn't been able to discuss the matter with him because Kathy could hear her conversation, but she had been upset that he wasn't more sympathetic with her desire to be helpful.

Sarah looked around the spartan locker room with its dark stained wooden lockers. Several pairs of bright red and orange ski boots were lined up neatly on top of them. A Coke machine with a small TV sitting on it was at one end of the room, and next to it was a large gray metal storage chest with a sign that read *Spruce Haven Ski Patrol Supplies*. A shelf near the door held a time clock with a wall-hung rack next to it for time cards. Also on the shelf was a black plastic holder where the patrollers' radios rested in their individual slots to recharge. Metal chairs were scattered about the room.

"I hope the young man is going to be all right," said Kathy.

"In cases like this, we never know," said Tina. "At any rate, he probably won't be on a pair of skis for a while."

"Of course, he won't be able to afford it either," said Neal, "after he gets through paying for the rescue charges."

"You mean he'll have to pay for this?" asked Sarah.

"I'm afraid so," said Tina. "It takes a lot of manpower and equipment. Not long ago a guy had to pay around twelve hundred dollars for a search and rescue."

"I guess it's only right," said Sarah. "He's in violation of the law." She started to sit down in a dilapidated chair.

"Oh, I'm sorry, but I don't think you want to sit there," said Tina.

"Pardon me?" asked Sarah.

Tina laughed and said, "That's Roxanne's chair. She's the year-old German shepherd pup that we're training for avalanche rescue."

"Really? How long will it take to train her?"

"Probably a couple of ski seasons. She even has her own ski patrol vest hanging up here," said Tina, motioning to a tiny rust-red vest with a white cross on the back.

"Tina, I think the three of us will go on upstairs and see about the food situation," said Neal. "I'll be checking back with you for an update."

Once the patrollers had made their way through the maze of trees, Jonathan suggested they rest a few moments. Skiing through the thick forest had taken tremendous skill and hard work.

Adjusting his backpack, Gerald said, "This would be a good time to catch our breath and get a second wind. The steep ravine isn't too far ahead. Even if the kid had wanted to climb out, the ridge over there with those steep cliffs would be way too difficult."

Jonathan had already started moving in the direction of the tracks, their tight S turns indicating the skier was following the steep fall line. Jonathan yelled to the others, "You're right; they're headed for the ravine. Come on. We're losing time."

The ravine was only about eighty feet long, but it was narrow and steep, giving the appearance of a dark gully. The patrollers knew they had reached the most dangerous part of their mission. Jonathan warned them to ski down one at a time. He was the first to ski down the narrow ribbon of white snow, avoiding the dark boulders protruding from either side like broken bones exposed through the earth's flesh.

When Jonothan reached the bottom, he found a crumpled body lying in the snow. Both skis had released and were lying beside him.

Jonathan called out, "Jeff, we're here to help you."

A weak voice answered, "I'm so glad to see you guys."

Stepping out of his skis, Jonathan opened his backpack to retrieve a blanket. He covered the young man and said, "Try to stay calm. Can you give me your full name?"

The young man was shivering and answered, "Jeff Long."

The other patrollers arrived. Damon quickly checked to see if Jeff was bleeding and placed additional blankets around him. Jonothan took his pulse, which was rapid but steady.

Jonathan asked, "Can you tell me where you're hurting?"

"My right leg . . . below the knee . . . hurts bad." Jeff became anxious. "I'm sorry about this . . . I got lost and I got really scared."

Jonathan said, "Don't worry about any of that right now. We need you to stay quiet and save your strength."

He radioed Clint to let him know they had found Jeff and to give their location. "He's conscious and injured, but he should be okay. Over."

"That's good to hear," said Clint. "Tell him to hang in there, and we'll be there soon. Out."

Clint said, "Sam, I'm going with the rescue team. We'll take a toboggan, and you radio for a snowmobile tow to wait for us at the base, directly below the ravine. You handle communications from up here. Radio for the two other teams to come back here on standby."

"Clint, you guys be careful. You know that slope from the ravine to the base is avalanche prone."

While waiting for the rescue team, Gerald took off his glove and put a warm hand on the patches of gray skin on Jeff's face, a sure sign of superficial frostbite. The patrollers knelt beside the injured skier, using their bodies to shield him from exposure to the unrelenting wind. The snow swirled about on the ridge above them.

When the rescue team arrived, Clint and another patroller who had accompanied him put a splint on Jeff's leg. Two others carefully lifted Jeff's body into the toboggan, making certain his legs were slightly elevated as a precaution against shock. They strapped him into place and covered him with additional blankets and a tarp. Clint notified Sam they were beginning their descent.

Sam's voice blasted on the radio: "Good work, boys. We got your tow waitin' for you at the base. Over."

"Ten-four," said Clint. "Rescue party is transporting."

It was almost midnight before the team radioed headquarters that they had reached the snowmobile tow. At that point, upper headquarters closed down, and the remaining patrollers skied down the mountain.

As they filed into the lower patrol room, Tina checked their names off the roster list. Grateful to hear that hot beverages and food were upstairs, the cold, hungry patrollers made their way around to the front of the base lodge. The initial search team and rescue crew were the last ones to enter Timberhouse. Brushing snow from his parka, Sam said, "It's a good thing it didn't start snowing again until an hour ago."

Clint started to respond, but the sight of Sarah serving soup caught his attention. "Sam, come here a minute. I want you to meet someone."

To Sarah, Clint said, "Looks as though Neal has you working overtime tonight."

She looked up and smiled. "I'm glad I could be a small part of this."

He introduced her to Sam.

As Sarah handed him his bowl of soup, Clint's cold fingers touched her soft warm ones. When she glanced up at him, he saw a look of tenderness in her eyes. She quickly looked down, busying herself serving food to Sam.

Neal approached Clint and asked, "What did the doctor have to say about the guy's injuries?"

"Fractures of both bones in his lower right leg, signs of shock, but he'll pull through."

"It's a good thing your people got to him when they did," said Neal.

"We were relieved to find him."

While Clint ate his soup, he watched Sarah move around the room, refilling coffee, serving cinnamon rolls and sandwiches. Her nurturing, calm spirit reminded him of Heather. Unexpected occasions such as tonight made him think of Heather in a way that brought grief rushing back into his heart.

"Attractive lady, that Sarah," said Sam. "You can't seem to keep your eyes off her."

He wasn't aware that he was being that obvious, but he knew Sam seldom failed to read his behavior. "Mind your own business," Clint said in a quiet voice.

"Yeah, and that's what you'd better do. I saw her wedding ring."

Before he left for his office in the Mountain Center to work on his report, Clint shook hands with Neal and Kathy and thanked them for their support. Then he walked in Sarah's direction and thanked her. "You're going to spoil my crew; they're not accustomed to such attention."

"You seem to have a fine group of people. I was surprised to see you have a few women patrollers."

"They're as capable of bringing a toboggan down as men."

"It seems to me that a toboggan could build up such momentum that the patroller could be pushed out of the way and lose control."

Clint grinned and said, "We have a saying in ski patrol: if you lose a toboggan, you'd better still have the handles in your hands."

"I hope I don't ever have to ride in one."

She watched him leave and thought how wonderful it was to meet new people like Clint and Sam, who were a part of this fascinating new world of mountains.

Sometime after two o'clock in the morning, Clint walked to his apartment complex, located two buildings over from Timberhouse. He was glad his patrollers had found the young man, and he was thankful that none of them had been injured. His boots crunched in the snow, making a rhythmic sound in the still night. He stopped to look up at the menacing mountain, partially hidden by the curtain of heavily falling snow, thankful its chilling wrath hadn't claimed another victim.

After he closed his front door, he removed his parka and boots and stretched out on the sofa. He remembered how surprised he had been to see Sarah earlier and thought of the electrifying touch of her fingers, radiating a warmth of spirit, his last thoughts as he drifted off in a deep sleep.

nine

*A*s Jake prepared to leave for work the following Monday morning, he suggested that Sarah meet him at the Silverado Saloon that evening to have dinner and watch a football game on the big screen. "I discovered this is where the locals gather on Monday evenings."

"Not that it's important, but who's playing?"

"The Seattle Seahawks and the Denver Broncos."

"Didn't you get enough football yesterday with the Dallas game?"

"I really don't care that much about the game. I'd like to mingle with people, watch a little football with them. You don't have to come by if you don't want to."

Sarah knew his tone implied that he was going there after work whether she joined him later or not. Not wanting to be left alone, she said, "Sure, I'll be there."

When Neal and Kathy closed the shop that evening, Sarah invited them to go with her to meet Jake.

"Sounds great to me," said Kathy. "It means I don't have to cook tonight."

"She must be desperate to endure a noisy football game," said Neal.

*W*hen the three of them joined Jake at the bar, the game had already started. The inside of the Silverado had a rustic appearance with a large stone fireplace. Old saddles sat astride the cedar dividers between the three sections of the bar and restaurant. They took their seats at a hand-hewn oak table, and Jake ordered a big tray of nachos along with a round of beers for everyone.

In the midst of the rowdy crowd, Sam Bishop came in the door waving a copy of *Ski* magazine in the air. "Hey, guys, take a look at this."

Several men gathered around a table, intent on the magazine spread before them.

"Those are my patrol buddies," said Neal. "I'm going to see what's so interesting."

"Neal can't stand to be left out of anything," said Kathy.

When he approached his friends, one of them said, "We found an article that Clint has written."

"That's great," said Neal. "I didn't even know he'd submitted an article."

"Clint likes to keep things quiet." said Sam. "In fact, he didn't tell me about it. I dropped by the drugstore on my way here and Don was putting the magazines on the shelf."

Seeing Clint enter the bar, Sam said, "There's our celebrity."

His friends motioned for him to join them. Sam shook Clint's hand and said, "Why didn't you tell us about this?"

Grinning at his friend, he said, "I was afraid it wouldn't get published, and I wanted to save myself the humiliation."

They all laughed and took turns shaking his hand.

Neal borrowed the magazine to show the others at his table. He explained what had happened and showed them the article with its full-page color photograph of an avalanche with thunderous clouds of white snow exploding upwards from the lethal mass of snow rolling down the mountainside.

"I can't wait to buy a copy," said Sarah as she stared at the title in bold black letters: "Avalanche Awareness."

"I had no idea that Clint could write," said Kathy.

"He never mentioned it to me, but Sam said something one time about an article Clint had written in a ski patrol magazine. Sorry, folks, but I had better return this to Sam," said Neal, getting up again.

Jake said, "That reminds me, Sarah; I've been working on a full-page ad for several ski magazines. I want to have it ready to show J.T. when I fly to Denver on the twenty-second."

She acknowledged his comment, but her mind was still on Clint's article. She remembered that he had mentioned his interest in journalism. Neal had taken the magazine away before she even had a chance to finish the first paragraph. She decided to get her own copy the next day.

"Jake, I'm sorry, but when did you say you plan to meet J.T. in Denver?"

"On the twenty-second. J.T's business partners will help us present the bank with updated figures. I'll just be gone overnight."

Neal returned to his seat. A Seahawks player fumbled the ball and someone yelled out, "He needs to go play for the Cowboys."

Jake swung his head around in the direction of the man who had made the sarcastic comment.

Sarah laid her hand on his arm and said, "Forget it, Jake. Remember, we have to live here." She tried to make light of the situation, knowing his temper was on edge in defense of the Dallas team.

Neal said, "Jake, I want you to meet a fellow Texan and a big Cowboy fan." He left the table and returned with a tall bearded man.

"This is Sam Bishop, our snow safety director. He's from Sweetwater. Sam, I believe you met Sarah last night. This is her husband, Jake Hansen."

"Am I ever glad to meet you," said Sam, pumping Jake's hand. He pulled up a chair to join them. "We Cowboy fans have to stick together."

"That's right," said Jake. "We ran into a streak of bad luck in yesterday's game with the Rams."

"You're damn right. I've had to take all kinds of kidding from my friend Clint, who's from Los Angeles. You can imagine the hell he's given me, but I've never deserted my Dallas Cowboys. You have to learn to keep a low profile on a day like today when the Broncos are playing."

Sam and Jake ignored the TV screen in the corner of the room and began to discuss the previous day's game, play by play. When

Sarah realized that Sam had the magazine with him, she asked to see it again. She and Kathy read the article together. After the first page, Kathy looked up behind Sarah and said, "I think we have company."

Sarah turned around and looked up at Clint. "Have I passed so far?" He asked.

She felt her face flush as her eyes met his. Although he was smiling, she saw that his face had a tiredness about it that could not be hidden.

"Hello, Clint." She turned to Jake and reminded him that they had met Clint when they visited Spruce Haven in June.

"Hey, Clint. Sure, I remember you. Sarah told me all about the rescue work the other night."

Sarah continued, "You must be proud of yourself; this is extremely interesting. I understand you've had work published before."

"Oh, a few articles, most of them in ski patrol publications."

The others made their congratulatory comments. Jake said, "Sarah's been on this kick lately about how the miners in the old days survived avalanches and hard times in the mountains. I told her she ought to write a book about it." Jake's tone indicated he hadn't taken her idea seriously.

Clint said, "It doesn't sound like a bad idea."

Sarah mumbled, "Oh, everybody wants to write a book." She didn't look at Clint. She was angry with Jake for even bringing up her idea in front of their new friends.

Neal said, "Clint, why don't you drag up another chair and have a seat?"

"Thanks, but if you'll excuse me, I'll leave you to your game. I'm heading home to get caught up on some shuteye."

"I'm sure you're exhausted," said Sarah, "after that missing skier incident last night. I had no idea so many people became involved in a search like that."

"It doesn't happen too often." He turned to Sam and said, "You had better get some sleep yourself . . . you've got an early day tomorrow."

"Yeah, I'm leaving in a few minutes. See ya in the morning."

Sarah ignored the football fans' cheers and the loud volume of the TV to finish reading Clint's article. He made a definite point about how the unexpected could always happen in the case of avalanches. The article indicated that many people who traveled in the back country on snowmobiles failed to heed the warnings about potential avalanche danger. He had recorded unusual experiences in the ongoing battle to control avalanches. When she finished the article, Sarah had a new respect for Clint Turner.

After Sam left, Neal ordered more appetizers and another round of beers. "Kathy and I would like to drop by your office tomorrow, Jake, to take a look at those home site maps. Would four o'clock be a good time?"

"Four o'clock will be fine. I have a three o'clock meeting with the mayor and the town manager to discuss a few utility problems, but it shouldn't take long."

"It's settled. We'll come by tomorrow afternoon," said Neal, "and Sarah can take care of things while we're gone."

Another couple from Spruce Haven joined them, and they finished watching the game. Pleased to see Jake happy, Sarah could tell that he had enjoyed the evening with their new friends.

*T*wo mornings that week Sarah signed up for private advanced ski lessons in hopes of improving her skiing by the time her daughter and son-in-law came for a visit during the holidays. She had told Jake that she wanted to surprise Catrina, who was an excellent skier, possessing a dancer's fluid movements.

On the second morning of her lessons, Sarah's instructor said to her, "You've really come a long way in a short time, but remember, you can't become a great mogul skier overnight."

"Tracy, I don't expect to become 'great' at any of this. I just want to be able to ski moguls."

"Practice it over and over until your body responds, rather than your mind. Eventually you'll find yourself developing a rhythm and turning automatically on each mogul."

Sarah thanked him and spent the next two hours practicing what she had learned for the past two days. Smiling to herself, she couldn't wait for Catrina to see that her mother could ski the bumps. She took *Snow Chief* down to the short black run on *Gambling Man*, where the patch of gigantic bumps had formed from the expert skiers' short linked turns.

As she began her descent, she could feel the exhilaration build. Using her legs as shock absorbers, she concentrated on keeping her upper body facing downhill. She could hear the instructor's words in her mind: *Be aggressive, attack each bump, keep your knees and ankles flexed.*

After completing a few turns, she felt her right ski slam into the side of a bump, causing her to lose her balance, losing both skis in the process. She managed to retrieve her skis and make it the rest of the way down without falling. She intended to keep practicing until she was ready for Jake to see her progress.

A week later, after Sarah and Jake had warmed up on an easy slope, they skied an expert run, where Jake discovered Sarah's vast improvement. "However," he reminded her, "with all the snow we've had lately, these runs are naturally easier than when we first got here. Don't get overconfident."

They had an early lunch at Sprucetop Restaurant, an octagonal building with a light pine ceiling that soared to a high pitch in the middle of the expansive room, surrounded by walls of windows. They sat at a round table that provided a view of the backside of the mountain with its virgin forest and untracked powder. Jake bought two wine coolers to celebrate Sarah's hard work on her skiing.

"Jake, I'm glad you're proud of my skiing."

"I've noticed another improvement besides your skiing," said Jake.

"Oh, and what is that?"

"Those new curves in your figure."

"I guess all this exercise is paying off." Sarah was glad that Jake had commented on her new figure.

They finished their lunch and skied until the lifts closed. When they arrived home, they sank down on the sofa, too tired to remove anything except ski boots and parkas. "Why don't we order a pizza?" said Jake. "After we eat, we can take a bottle of wine with us to the hot tub for a relaxing soak. I like what that warm water does to your body." He put his hand on her thigh with a firm pressure.

"I think that's a great idea."

When they came upstairs, towels wrapped around their glowing bodies, Sarah turned on a tiny lamp, allowing a soft light to reflect the deep rusts and golds of the room. She pulled back the comforter and turned to face Jake.

"Come here," he said, in a low voice. Loosening her towel and tossing it aside, he pulled her to him and whispered in her ear, "Like old times, babe." His long arms glided down her body. He wanted to show her that she didn't have to put on lacy lingerie for his benefit. He wanted to prove to her that he had accepted the change in her body. Most of all, he wanted to make love the way they had before her surgery.

They lay down together, hands touching each other's bodies with the familiarity of years. Their kisses became more feverish. He swept one hand along her hip, dipping in at her waist, moving up to her ribs, to her chest.

But then his body stilled. He rolled away from her, drew a tormented breath, and sighed, "I'm sorry, Sarah; it's no use. I guess the hot water took it out of me."

She lay back on the pillow and closed her eyes. "Jake, I know you miss my breasts. That's okay; so do I. I think it's time we shared our honest feelings, and then we can put it behind us and concentrate on other aspects of our lovemaking, like kissing. I think we've almost forgotten how sensual kissing can be." She took a deep breath and exhaled slowly, waiting for Jake to say something.

How can I tell her, thought Jake, *that I can't get used to seeing her chest and that I can't forget about Rhonda's sexy body?*

"Let's not talk this thing to death, Sarah." He got out of bed and yanked his robe off its hanger in the closet. "I'm going to catch the news." He left the room, feeling miserable for failing Sarah and for thinking of Rhonda.

As she walked to work the next day, Sarah reflected on the previous night and decided that she had attached far too much significance to the episode. She pulled up the fur collar of her parka for extra protection from the cold. *Jake needs more time to get used to the new me*, she reasoned.

The weather front had blasted its way into Spruce Haven with a swirling white intensity that blurred everything in sight, as if heaven had draped a wedding veil across the entire village. The storm showed no sign of letting up. Before she entered the shop, she stamped her boots to knock off the snow and brushed the white powder from her jacket.

Kathy met her at the door and exclaimed, "I know it's a mess out there, but we've had record sales today; people are shopping instead of skiing. In fact, Neal heard that the lifts up top have been closed down because of high winds."

"I don't doubt it," said Sarah, as she proceeded to hang up her things. When she returned, she said, "The wind blew a shutter loose on our place, and the banging sound kept me awake half the night. I called our manager first thing this morning, and he repaired it."

"Neal and I decided to make reservations for tonight at the club. We want to treat ourselves to an elegant dinner before the first rush of holiday skiers. Of course, our reservations have to be for nine o'clock. Why don't you and Jake join us?"

"We'd love to. I'll call Jake and make certain it's all right with him." She was glad to see that the Castleberrys wanted to develop a friendship. Sarah thought the couple had an appealing sincerity about them.

In fact, Sarah had found that Spruce Haven contained a number of sincere, interesting people who all shared one common trait: a sense of the present. They wanted to savor the simple aspects of life. In Carsonville, she had lived in an aura of urgency, an atmosphere of constant acceleration, where people she knew always seemed to be in a hurry to keep up with their busy schedules, to live in the future tense. When locals came into the shop, Kathy always saw to it that Sarah met them. Many of them owned their own businesses, like Kathy and Neal. Sarah especially liked the Madisons, who owned the bakery shop down the street. She often dropped by there on her way home to pick up sandwiches or fresh-baked bread.

Six days before Christmas, Sarah spent the morning shopping for a special gift for Kathy and Neal. She stopped in at Spruce Haven Treasures and browsed around, finally deciding on an unusual ceramic soup tureen. After she made her purchase, she turned to leave the store and saw Clint Turner looking at coffee mugs.

Walking up to him, she asked, "Are you about finished with your Christmas shopping?"

"Sarah, it's good to see you. I haven't been able to decide on anything for my sister and her husband. I need to get their present to the post office today, but all this stuff looks pretty fragile for the mail."

"Why don't you consider one of these unusual wind chimes? This one is a favorite of mine." She ran her fingers through the chimes, and the rich tones echoed in the shop. "Actually, I've had my eye on these, but I'll have to wait until we get the house built. I don't think our neighbors at Ridgepole would appreciate them as much as I do."

"Hey, Sarah, thanks for the idea. I think my sister would like this."

Glad she could be of help in making his decision, Sarah left the gift shop, feeling the joy of the holiday season in her heart.

Decorating the condo for Christmas occupied much of her time that weekend. A fresh garland of greenery with red velvet bows graced the fireplace mantel. A bunch of red poinsettias peeped out of a large basket sitting on the glass coffee table. A fresh wreath of pine boughs and pinecones, dusted with snow, adorned the front door. To complete the picture, Jake had searched throughout the village to find the tallest fir tree.

"Oh, it's perfect!" exclaimed Sarah when she entered the living room. Jake started stringing the tiny white lights on the tree while Sarah finished unpacking the decorations. As she hung her favorite ornaments, she turned to him and said, "Do you realize this is the first time you've ever helped me decorate a tree?"

"That's because you and Catrina always did such a good job."

"Actually, you were always watching a TV show and didn't

want to be interrupted. Have you noticed how seldom you watch TV since we've moved here?"

He put his arm around her and kissed her. When they had finished trimming the tree, Jake plugged in the lights, and they stood there admiring the seven-foot fir tree, all aglow with lights and ornaments.

"This is going to be the best Christmas season ever," said Sarah.

ten

The day before Jake was to leave for Denver, he and Sarah worked together on the layout for the brochures, spreading everything on the dining room table. He wanted to take the project with him to show to J.T. and the Dallas consultant for final comments, and the brochures would be ready for distribution sometime in January, as originally planned. Sarah had written captions for the pictures, and the photographer had done an excellent job on Veronica's ski shots. They presented a striking impression of motion, with her long, red hair blowing in the wind.

Placing one of the pictures in place, Sarah commented, "I bet ole J.T will love this hot tub scene of Veronica squeezed into that tiny swimsuit."

"Yeah, that's a fact."

She changed the subject to a more serious topic. "You've been so quiet the last few days."

"I have a lot on my mind with the Denver trip coming up. J.T. doesn't think he'll have any problem getting an additional loan. I'll feel better once the financing part is settled."

"You hurry back here Monday evening. Tuesday is Christmas Eve, you know."

"Speaking of Christmas Eve, have you made our dinner reservations at the club?"

"Yes, I took care of that days ago. I wish Warren and Catrina could have arranged to be here Wednesday for Christmas Day."

"I know, honey, but Thursday morning will be here before you know it." He gathered the layout copy to put in his briefcase.

"You're going to have to get used to the idea of Catrina having another family to consider when it comes time for Christmas and other holidays."

"You're right. I'm excited to see them. I can't wait to show her how I've decorated the condo for the holidays."

On the twenty-third, the day Jake was due home from Denver, another massive front swept across the Rockies, dumping heavy snow across most of the state. The storm had transformed the village of Spruce Haven into a sugarcoated fantasyland with snow piled on the rooftops like thick icing on a cake. The snow-drift outside Sarah's dining room window had completely blocked the view of the outside world. The complex manager kept the walkway cleared from the driveway to the front door, leaving a narrow path with snow piled shoulder high on either side.

Early that morning Sarah watched the news coverage that showed Interstate 70 with hundreds of stranded motorists, abandoned cars, and jackknifed trucks. Only one lane was open, and traffic moved at a slow crawl. A newscaster urged people to stay home except for emergencies. The TV camera zoomed in on a residential street, where a line of parked cars was completely buried in snow. They looked like a long procession of giant camels, their humped backs covered in white. Stapleton Airport announced that if the snow continued, the airport would be closed. Jake was scheduled to arrive at seven o'clock that evening in Gunnison, where he planned to catch the shuttle to Spruce Haven.

Sarah tried to concentrate on Christmas baking, but by noon she began to worry. Several airlines had cancelled all flights. As she was leaving for work, the phone rang. Sarah ran back into the living room and picked it up. "Hello," she said breathlessly, knowing it had to be Jake.

"Sarah, I guess you've heard the news. I can't possibly get a flight today, and they're saying it's doubtful for tomorrow."

"I know. I guess we'll have to wait and see what tomorrow holds for us." She tried to be brave for his sake, but she thought of how the two of them had never been apart on Christmas Eve. She could no longer keep her emotions under control.

"Sarah, don't cry. I'll call you from the hotel tonight to let you know where I'm staying. It's not the end of the world."

"What about J.T. and his friend from Midland? Did they get a flight?"

"Yeah, those lucky devils. They had a morning flight with Frontier, the last airline to cancel."

"I'll talk to you tonight."

They said their good-byes and she slumped into a chair, staring at the falling snow. She thought of the possibility that Warren and Catrina might not be able to get into Gunnison from DFW Airport on Thursday. She brushed these concerns aside and convinced herself that the next day would bring a brighter outlook.

That afternoon the excitement of Christmas shoppers filled the Powder Hound Ski Shop with a cheerful spirit. Sarah was thankful for the activity, because it meant she had no time to be sad about Jake's cancelled flight. Wishing complete strangers Merry Christmas gave her a warm holiday feeling.

The holiday mood was short-lived. The following morning Jake called with the dreaded news that no planes were leaving Stapleton that day. "They're optimistic about tomorrow, so we'll have to change our Christmas Eve dinner at the club to a Christmas Day Dinner."

"Jake, how awful for you to be stuck in a miserable hotel on Christmas Eve. I can't believe this is happening. The storm has upset a lot of people's plans."

"I know. Yesterday the news showed what the airport looked like. It reminded me of a war zone, with newspapers, trash, even broken bottles scattered all over the place, and some unfortunate people had to use it as a hotel."

"Yes, I saw it on TV. Jake, I miss you so much."

"Don't worry about me. I'll call you again tonight."

After she had finished talking to Jake, she unplugged the coffee pot and looked at the kitchen clock. The thought of staying home until it was time to leave for work was depressing. She called Kathy to tell her what had happened. "If it's all right with you, I'd like to come in now."

"That would be wonderful. We could use your help. By the way, Sarah, you could come with me this evening to attend Christmas Eve services in Crested Butte. I'm leaving around seven o'clock, but Neal is going to stay here until nine. We're having some friends come by for eggnog and snacks later this evening, and you can join us. No one should be alone on Christmas Eve."

"I'll think about it. Thanks for the invitation."

When Sarah arrived at the shop, she was amazed at the way last minute shoppers made almost random selections, giving little heed to prices. Gloves appeared to be the hottest selling item, but many ski sweaters also found their way into holiday gift sacks. The village Santa came into the shop and wished everyone a Merry Christmas. Neal told Sarah the same individual dressed up as Santa Claus each year and skied on Christmas Day wearing his Santa outfit. Although she felt sorry for Jake, trapped at his hotel, she was glad she could get away from the lonely condo.

"Sarah, did you decide to join me tonight for the Christmas Eve service?"

"Kathy, aren't you concerned about the two of us driving to Crested Butte after dark, especially with all the snow we've had?"

"Oh, I guess I forgot to tell you. Clint and Sam are coming by to pick me up. Neal wouldn't ever let me drive it alone, and they always go there, too. I grew up on a ranch between Gunnison and Crested Butte, and my parents always took my brother and me to this historic church in the town of Crested Butte on Christmas Eve. It's the one real tradition I've managed to keep."

Sarah paused to consider the choice of being alone or being among friends, and Kathy was being persuasive. "Is it the Union Congregational Church?" she asked.

"Yes. They have the most inspirational service, with a candlelight service and a choir. Nothing gets me in the Christmas spirit more than singing Christmas carols. You must come with us and after the service, we'll have snacks at our place."

"Okay," said Sarah. "You talked me into it."

When Clint and Sam dropped by to pick up Kathy, they were surprised that Sarah would be going along as well. She explained about Jake's situation.

"That's too bad, Sarah," said Clint, doing his best to sound as though he meant it. He was secretly glad things had turned out the way they had. He saw the look Sam gave him, and Clint ignored it.

By the time they arrived at the church, the snow was falling again. Clint had trouble finding a parking space.

"Looks like they have a crowd tonight," said Sam. "Sometimes more tourists show up than they expect. That's probably what happened tonight."

"Look how peaceful the church is with the soft light spilling out those arched windows. It looks like a Christmas card." They made their way up the steps and into the back of the church, where there was standing room only. Someone handed them four tiny white candles as they huddled together in the crowded sanctuary. The speaker was reading from the book of Luke, and when he finished, the choir began singing as the lighting of candles began from row to row, neighbor to neighbor.

Turning to light Sarah's candle, Clint looked into her eyes as she looked up at his. For a flicker of a second, Sarah felt an undeniable closeness to this man she barely knew. When they began singing "Joy to the World," Sarah felt tears well up in her eyes. Her heart was truly filled with joy. She turned to smile at Kathy as if to say *thank you for letting me be a part of this.*

The choir director asked the congregation to join in with "Silent Night" as they filed out of the church, stopping to blow out their candles and leave them behind in a container near the door. Sarah was keenly aware of the snowy, magical night.

Clint caught up with her, gently nudging her arm. "What did you think of our Christmas Eve tradition?"

"I'm glad I got to come. I'll always remember this night."

"Sam and I usually meet up with friends afterwards, but we're looking forward to the good eats at Kathy's place this year."

That evening at Kathy and Neal's, Sarah helped set out the food for the buffet.

She said, "Kathy, you've been cooking for days. You said eggnog and snacks. And you have meatballs, cheese logs, and all sorts of goodies."

Kathy laughed, "I only entertain once a year."

"Do I know anyone who'll be here tonight?" Sarah asked as she set the plates at one end of the table.

Lighting the red hurricane candle with fresh greenery around it, Kathy said, "You haven't met our next-door neighbors, but you know the Madisons." She went into the living room, where Neal was chatting with Clint and Sam. "Hey, you two, did you invite dates for tonight?"

"Negative, on both counts," volunteered Sam. Sarah began to feel slightly flustered, as if she had suddenly found herself in a social situation without her husband's comforting presence. Neal started passing around holiday mugs filled with eggnog. Several guests gathered around the fireplace while others stood around chatting and sipping their drinks. Lazy snowflakes floated down onto the huge snowdrifts on the deck, as if accompanying Dean Martin's "I'll Be Home for Christmas." Sitting on a huge ottoman near the fireplace, Sarah looked up from the fire when Clint took a seat next to her.

"So, do you think Jake will make it in tomorrow?"

"We won't know for certain until morning, but I hope so."

"Hey, I'm glad you could join us."

"Me too. However, I can't help but feel guilty to be having a good time with friends while he's there by himself." The sparks flying up the chimney occupied her attention.

After a short silence, he said, "So, have you been working on ideas for your book?"

Sarah turned and looked at him, feeling ill at ease that he had sat down so close to her. "Oh, I've been busy with the holidays, getting ready for a visit from our daughter and son-in-law. I wish they could be here tomorrow, but they'll be flying in the day after Christmas."

"Christmas at a ski resort lasts for weeks, not just a day." The reassuring tone in his voice made Sarah feel better about the holidays and her family.

She stood up and said, "I really need to get home now and give Jake a call."

Neal overheard her comment and said, "Sarah, I'd be glad to drive you home when you're ready, but I hate for you to rush off."

"Oh, Neal, don't be silly. I'm dressed for the cold, and I'll enjoy the walk home."

"Neal, there's no reason for you to leave your other guests," said Clint. "Sam and I'll see that she gets home all right. We have to get up early to meet our crew, so we really should be leaving now, too."

"After all," said Sam, "we might get a glimpse of ole Saint Nick gettin' ready to make his rounds." He winked at Sarah as he got up from the floor.

Sarah thanked Neal and Kathy for inviting her. Before the three of them started for the door, they told the other guests good-bye and wished them a Merry Christmas.

Driving down Main Street, they soon approached the Alpine Restaurant. "This is where I get off."

"Sam, You're joking. How can you live here?"

"Up there," he said, pointing to his apartment, where the drapes were pulled to display a small tree with colored lights twinkling in the dark. "The original tenants were owners of the restaurant, but they moved out last year, so I grabbed it for a decent monthly rent."

"Oh, how lovely," she said, although she felt the small tree seemed so alone, like Sam.

They said good night and continued down Main Street, which was lined with cars of vacationers dining at the various restaurants for their Christmas Eve celebrations.

When they reached Timberline Road, Sarah gave Clint directions to the condo. "We live in the last unit on this road."

When Clint pulled into the driveway and stopped, Sarah opened the door and thanked him for the ride. "Hold on, Sarah, and

I'll walk you to the door. I promised Neal I'd see you home safely, and that's what I intend to do."

She stepped out of the Blazer, and he took her arm to assist her. They made their way up the front walk. The snow had stopped, and their whole world seemed muffled in a quietness that made them conscious of heartbeats and breathing in and breathing out, their vapors filling the air before them. They had conversed freely up to this point, and now neither of them spoke.

When they reached the front door, she shook Clint's hand. "Now you can tell Neal you did your job like an honorable patroller."

Still holding her hand, he said quietly, "I volunteered because I wanted to."

His steady gaze penetrated her soul. "Merry Christmas, Clint," she said quietly.

She let go of his hand and put the key in the lock, no longer trusting herself to look into his eyes, afraid of what she might see, terrified of what she might convey. She closed the door behind her and took a deep breath before going into the kitchen and calling Jake. She apologized for waking him and explained where she had been for the evening. He told her he had a noon flight the next day.

As she climbed the stairs to bed, she scolded herself for reading anything into Clint's words about volunteering to bring her home. *You're a married forty-five-year-old woman who's not accustomed to such attention. Besides, he was just being a kind neighbor who might have been carried away with the holiday mood.*

eleven

*H*aving landed at Gunnison County Airport that afternoon, Jake found himself lost in thought during the hour-long shuttle ride to Spruce Haven. Like an obsession, Rhonda had come back into his life. She had been calling him at the office for weeks; finally he had agreed to meet her briefly in Denver at his hotel. He had given in to her sexual attraction just as before, finding himself irresistibly drawn to her curvaceous body and sophisticated style. A moment of hurried sex had turned into two days, for they seldom left their room, an arrangement brought about by the snow gods who saw fit to dump an avalanche of snow across the Rockies. *Here I am*, he thought, *once again allowing this woman to come into my life and destroy any hope of restoring my marriage.*

As the bus neared Spruce Haven, Jake squared his shoulders and faced the undeniable fact: he wanted both Sarah and Rhonda. He could imagine neither a life without Sarah, the woman who gave his life meaning, nor a life without Rhonda, the woman who gave his life excitement. Jake Hansen knew he was hopelessly lost. He and Rhonda had even planned another rendezvous in Denver for the following month, when he would be there for a meeting with his engineer. He realized that Rhonda reminded him of the lifestyle he had left in Dallas, where the stimulation of a big city made him feel a powerful energy.

At first the whole idea of living in the mountains had been new and exciting. He and Sarah had seemed to find much of what they had shared in the early years of their marriage. But now the reality of living through the hard winters had begun to weigh on his mind.

He saw the endless white landscape of the valley, knowing that Sarah would find something beautiful about a scattered herd of Hereford cattle and a few isolated old barns with a blue-green river running alongside the highway. Jake envied Sarah the happiness she had found in the mountains. At the same time, he wondered how he could possibly shatter that happiness. He felt ashamed and defeated.

The closer he got to Spruce Haven, the more he felt trapped, snow closing in on him from every direction. He could see Crested Butte Mountain looming on the horizon ahead and knew that before long he'd be home. The other passengers were jubilant skiers on their way to spend a Christmas holiday at a ski resort, but Jake's thoughts were on Dallas, where freeways were clear of snow and the pulse of the city made his heart race. Soon he could see the peak of Spruce Haven Mountain, the wind blowing plumes of snow in a slow-motion swirl of white, like a dancer's billowy skirt. The bus pulled into Spruce Haven Village and stopped at the transportation center on the corner of Main Street and Evergreen Road. Jake collected his suitcase and called Sarah to come get him. When he heard her cheerful voice on the other end of the phone, he loathed himself.

At the club that evening, the two shared their delayed Christmas Eve celebration. Throughout dinner he made grumbling remarks about the inconvenience of all the snow.

"Sarah, don't you ever miss being able to push a grocery cart across a dry, paved parking lot instead of shoving it across ice ruts?"

"Jake, you've been looking for negative things tonight because the snow kept you from getting here on schedule."

"No, it's not only that. It's more. The snow governs everything we do. For instance, you can't even get dressed up in a sexy dress to go out to dinner. I may go crazy seeing you in pants all the time."

"Can we please change the subject? We're supposed to be celebrating our delayed Christmas Eve dinner."

"I'm sorry. I guess I'm a little on edge. What time are we expecting Warren and Catrina in the morning?"

"Around eleven o'clock. Maybe it'll seem more like Christmas once we're all together again."

"By the way, did you enjoy yourself at Neal and Kathy's get-together?"

"Oh, yes, of course, I felt sad because you and I missed a Christmas Eve together." She told him about going to Crested Butte for the Christmas Eve service, but Jake didn't appear to be listening to anything she said. She took a sip of her wine, and her mind returned to the magical stillness of the night before, when Clint had walked her to the front door. She concluded that he was an unusual man with a unique combination of sensitivity and strength.

"Are you ready to go?" asked Jake, getting up from his chair.

Startled out of her thoughts, she felt guilty for thinking about Clint Turner. Gathering her gloves and handbag, she said, "I think what you need is a good night's sleep in your own bed, so you won't be such an old grouch tomorrow."

As they neared the lobby, Jake said, "Wait here and I'll get the truck warmed up."

When he opened the heavy entrance door, a gust of chilly night air forced its way inside. Sarah felt chilled. Because Jake had been in such a bad mood ever since his arrival from Denver, she was worried that he was keeping something from her about the meetings with the bankers. For the first time since their move to Spruce Haven, Sarah felt concerned for their future.

Warren and Catrina's visit brightened the holiday mood for Jake and Sarah, providing the essential element of family warmth, with gift exchanges and a constant stream of chatter. The day after their arrival, they prepared to spend the first day skiing together. Dressed in her new black stretch pants and ski sweater, Sarah came down the stairs, pleased to hear Jake's whistle.

Catrina said, "Mother, those pants look really nice on you. I've tried to get you to buy a pair of those for years." Turning to Warren, who was wearing his new navy and red parka from Sarah and Jake, she added, "And doesn't my husband look handsome in his new jacket." She hooked her arm in his, her soft brown eyes lit up with pride.

That afternoon on the hill, Jake said, "Why don't we try *Jeopardy?* It's the shortest black slope we have."

Catrina said, "That's fine with us, but if Mother tries that one, her life will be in jeopardy all right. Daddy, there are a lot of fast skiers zooming down this run. They'll kill her."

"Oh, I think I can get down *Jeopardy* without too much trouble," said Sarah, eager to show Catrina that her mother's skiing had improved.

"Mother, getting down and skiing down are two different things. You shouldn't be on a black run."

Warren, pointing with his ski pole, said, "You could take that blue run and meet us at the bottom."

"I know, Warren, but Catrina always told me to challenge myself. Jake can wait for me if I have any trouble, and you two can go on ahead and ski some other runs. We'll meet you at the condo later if we should get separated."

With that understood, they took off for *Jeopardy* with Jake in the lead. When they reached the top of the run, Catrina peered over the lip. "Mother, you'll never make all those moguls. I'll go ski an easier run with you, and the guys can ski this one."

"Catrina, you have no faith in your mother," said Sarah. She pushed off, anticipating her path through the bumps laid out in a uniform pattern like buried Volkswagens in the snow. The others watched for a moment, giving her a good head start, but they soon realized she didn't need it.

"Daddy, when did she learn to ski like that?" asked Catrina in disbelief as she watched her mother execute her quick, calculated turns.

"You'll have to brag on her, because she's been taking advanced lessons and practicing on these moguls for weeks."

They followed her down the run. When Catrina reached her mother at the bottom, she said, "Mother, I can't believe you skied that."

"You really had us fooled," said Warren. "I wiped out, and you kept up your controlled pace." He brushed the snow from his navy stretch pants.

Sarah laughed and said, "Catrina can tell you I used to be petrified of moguls. Two years ago I wouldn't have skied near that run, much less down it."

"No kidding," said Catrina. "Two years ago she took off her skis and tried to walk down the side of a mogul patch."

On the next lift, Catrina and Sarah rode up together. "Mother, you're looking absolutely terrific. How's the tightness under your arms?"

"Much better, but I still have to keep working at it," Sarah responded.

"I think I'd be afraid to ski for fear of falling on my chest."

Sarah laughed and patted her daughter's knee. "You can't be afraid of what might happen and let life pass you by. Besides, I talked to the doctor about skiing."

"Mother, I can tell you love it up here, but I'm not so sure Daddy is that sold on it."

"He's having to make a few adjustments," Sarah said slowly. "I think when the snow begins to melt in the spring and construction picks up momentum, he'll be much happier."

"It seems the two of you are happier than you were last May before my wedding. I felt that I was the one to blame, because things were so hectic."

"Oh, it wasn't your fault. You must believe that." Sarah was silent for a moment, searching for the right words to ease her daughter's mind. *Parents protect their children from the truth,* she thought. *Then when the children become adults, they try to protect their parents in the same way.* "It was just that your father was working extra hard, and I was trying to finish my teaching year. I was pretty burned out by the end of May. Then we had all those last-minute details to take care of for the wedding."

"I'm glad you and Daddy are living up here. I can't wait to see that new house you're planning to build. Your future grandchildren will love coming to visit you."

"Oh, are you trying to tell me something?"

"No, Warren and I want to wait a few years before we start a family. He wants to be more established with the firm, and I want to finish my degree."

"That's a wise decision. I think the two of you need to get adjusted to each other before you consider a third party. Do as I say, not as I did," she laughed.

"You know something, Mother? I've really missed our long talks. It's not the same over the phone."

"I know what you mean, but I'm glad we can stay in close touch."

"Mom, you got carried away buying me this necklace, but I do adore it. It means a lot to me because you got it in Crested Butte."

"I'm glad you like it."

On the following day, Catrina suggested they all ski Crested Butte, since Warren had never been there. Jake had two prospective clients, so he couldn't join them for skiing, but he agreed to meet them for dinner at the club. Warren had rented an SUV at the airport, so transportation was not a problem.

Once they had purchased their lift tickets at Crested Butte, Sarah suggested they take the Silver Queen lift first. The three decided to ski *Paradise Bowl* and then take *Ruby Chief,* a good blue run, all the way down to Paradise Warming House. "If we get separated, we'll agree to meet there and have a hot cocoa break."

The three of them gathered at the warming house. Catrina and Warren, their faces glowing from the fresh air and exercise, said they didn't need a break and they wanted to ski the East River runs, saying they would return in less than an hour.

"You two go on and have a good time. I get to ski whenever I want to, so I'm going to sit here and relax in this glorious sun," Sarah told them.

Sarah was happy to see Catrina and Warren having such a good time. She climbed the stairs to the deck, sat down on the bench of a picnic table, and propped her ski boots on the opposite bench. Removing her goggles and ski cap, she shook her thick chestnut-colored hair free, the sun catching the metallic gleam of gold and copper. She felt herself starting to drift off into a nice nap.

"Are you comfortable enough?" she heard a voice say.

Startled, Sarah straightened up and saw Clint standing beside her. "What a surprise to see you here."

"Remember, I told you on my days off I sometimes come here to ski the *Extreme Limits*. Are you here by yourself?"

"Oh, no. I'm waiting for my daughter and son-in-law to get back from the East River runs."

Two men joined them and one of them said, "Hey, Clint. Why don't you introduce us?" Clint introduced Sarah to two of his Crested Butte ski patrol buddies, who were also enjoying a day off from the rigors of their job.

About that time, Catrina and Warren walked up. "Hey, Mom, we're starving. Want to join us for lunch?"

"Yes, I do, but come here first. I want you to meet some people." Sarah stood up and made the necessary introductions, explaining to Catrina and Warren that Clint was the Spruce Haven ski patrol director.

Clint shook their hands and said, "I know Sarah has been looking forward to your visit. Are you having a good ski day?"

Warren said, "Oh, yeah, totally awesome. This is my first trip here. Sarah, maybe I shouldn't say it, but I like this mountain much better than Spruce Haven."

Clint and his friends laughed heartily. Clint responded, "Warren, you don't have to worry about hurting my feelings. I completely agree with you, but to be fair to Spruce Haven, it's just getting started in terms of adding lifts and new trails. Believe me, Crested Butte had its share of growing pains."

Removing her mittens and attaching them to the hook on her jacket, Catrina said, "All I can say is that moving up here has really improved Mother's skiing ability. All I used to hear was 'Catrina, wait for me.' Now I have to work hard to keep up with her."

Wanting to let the patrollers get back to their day off, Sarah hastily said, "You three go have fun. We're on our way inside for lunch."

Clint smiled his usual grin. "Yeah, I guess we're ready to hit it again. I'm really glad I got to meet both of you, Catrina, Warren. Maybe I'll catch you on the hill before you leave." Turning around, he added, "Sarah, it was good to see you." With that, the three patrollers took off in the direction of their skis.

As they went inside, Warren said, "Man, I should have asked

them if I could tag along. Maybe I could have picked up some free skiing instruction."

"Warren Bailey," Catrina began "Are you crazy? They're on their way to the new North Face lift to ski those double black diamonds."

"Oh, I didn't realize what they were talking about," said Warren. "Yeah, I'm too young to die." The three of them had a good laugh.

That evening after dinner at the club, they all returned to the condo. Sarah brought out the house plans to show Catrina changes they had made. They spread the plans on the dining room table. Warren and Jake were in the living room, watching a sports channel.

"What do you think of adding a skylight right here over the whirlpool?" asked Sarah.

"Perfect. Maybe you should add another one here in the master bedroom." They continued to study each room, commenting on the changes Sarah had made in the past few months.

In an unexpected show of energy and emotion, Jake stood up and whirled around, facing Sarah. "Can't you leave those plans alone for one night? We have talked about that house until I'm sick of it. Who knows? We may end up staying here where some other sucker can shovel snow off the roof."

With four long strides he was at the dining room table, rolling up the plans. The rubber band snapped into place with a finality that made Sarah feel as if a giant rubber band was wrapped around her chest, cutting off her air. She was shocked and embarrassed by Jake's behavior. He normally reserved such outbursts of temper for her alone. She watched him sweep up the roll of plans and put it in a bottom drawer of the built-in hutch. Sarah stood there speechless.

Warren said, "Catrina, we have to get up early in the morning. We need to leave here by nine. Do you have all our stuff packed?"

"Of course not, but you can come upstairs and help me." She gave her mother a sympathetic glance and a quick hug and followed Warren upstairs.

When Sarah heard the bedroom door close, she stomped into

the living room to confront Jake. "I didn't want to add to the ugly scene you made in front of Catrina and Warren, but I would like to know what is wrong with you. Ever since you made the Denver trip, you've been unbearable to be around."

"Taking care of a house up here in the winter will be a constant hassle with the snow. I'm beginning to doubt if we'll ever build that house. Living here at Ridgepole, all we have to do is call the manager if we have a problem. We don't have to worry about the snow piled on the roof or the driveway."

"If you have concerns, then the two of us need to sit down and calmly talk about them, not suddenly blow up in front of others. We'll discuss it tomorrow after Catrina and Warren leave. Are you coming to bed now?"

"No, I'm going to watch the game. I'll be up later."

Sarah sighed and started up the stairs. She had to face a glaring reality: he was losing interest in the mountains as well as in their new home. However, at the moment, she concluded, her biggest problem was the possibility that he was losing interest in her. Once again, that old heavy feeling invaded her heart, filling it with dread, replacing the happy feelings of the past several days.

After Warren and Catrina left the following morning, an atmosphere of gloom settled over the condo. Sarah fought a compelling urge to take down all the Christmas decorations, which suddenly seemed fake instead of festive. Christmas had fallen short of her expectations. After an unsuccessful attempt to discuss matters with Jake, she suggested they take a walk in the unusually warm December weather, but Jake wanted to work out with his weights in the garage.

Having decided to go for a walk by herself, Sarah closed the front door behind her and breathed in the fresh morning air. Instead of choosing a walk through the village or around the base of the mountain, she headed up Timberline Road, where she always found a sense of peace and solitude. Tiny pine trees, babes of the forest, stood on either side. Seeing a small cluster of pine cones, Sarah was tempted to collect them, but her better judgment warned her of the deceiving depth of the snow. Their lot was located about a mile and a half from the condo. Walking uphill at that altitude helped to ease her tension.

Breathing hard, Sarah found herself standing in front of their lot. The acre of spruce trees no longer held the wonder for her that it once did. The morning sun beamed its harsh rays on the tree branches, releasing melted snow. She thought of her conversation earlier that morning, when she had tried to tell Jake that the house didn't matter; what mattered most to her were the mountains. When she told Jake the condo had become home to her and she would be happy to stay there, he had become withdrawn and said, "Let's put everything on hold for right now."

She turned around to look across the valley below, at the lazy smoke drifting up from the chimney of the country club, at the antlike size of a lone cross country skier, moving slowly across the snow. "Great," she said aloud. "My life is on hold for right now."

Recalling the scene from the previous evening, Sarah remembered how Catrina's face had gone pale, her brown eyes wide in disbelief at her father's words. When she left that morning, she whispered in Sarah's ear, "I hope Daddy gets in a better mood for your sake." Sarah wished Catrina lived closer.

She was glad she'd be at the Powder Hound that afternoon. Her job let her escape Jake's moodiness. With only a few weeks left at the shop, she began to realize that she would miss being around her new friends. However, with a friendship established, Sarah decided to keep in touch by issuing dinner invitations. She prayed Jake would be more open with her and share his feelings. Keeping her marriage together was important, but, at the same time, she reasoned, Jake had to do his part. She couldn't do it all alone.

The New Year's Eve dance at the Spruceland Country Club was an event Sarah looked forward to, for Jake's mood had improved in anticipation of a party. He had arranged for them to join another couple, Philip and Joan Norton. Philip was editor of the *Spruce Haven Reporter*, and his wife operated the cross-country ski school. Philip had been helpful to Jake in promoting Spruceland Estates with articles and advertisements.

As she dressed for the party, her spirits lifted. To complement her black crepe pants she wore a black silk angora sweater with a deep V neck, trimmed with gold beads. She put on her dressy black leather high-heel boots to complete the outfit. Unaccustomed to seeing herself dressed up, she felt glamorous, and she hoped Jake would think so too. She clipped on her chunky gold earrings, added a touch of Diva at her wrists and throat, and picked up her evening bag. She turned toward the stairs and saw Jake waiting for her in the foyer.

When Jake saw Sarah, he set down his drink and came towards her and embraced her. "Sarah, you look great." He kissed her neck and said, "You smell good, too." He helped her into the crystal fox jacket that he had given her for Christmas. "It's about time I could afford to buy you a fur. You look real classy, Sarah. I'm sorry it's taken me so long to buy you nice things."

"Don't be silly. I love the jacket, but clothes have never been a priority for me." She looked at him closely. "Jake, how many drinks have you had already?"

"Just enough to get in a good party mood, so don't go and spoil it."

When Jake and Sarah arrived at the club, they found balloons and streamers floating from the ceiling, party hats and horns piled on tables, and the main room already crowded with Spruce Haven locals and visitors. Kathy and Neal waved at the Hansens as they made their way around the room to the table where Philip and Joan Norton awaited them. Sarah found their new acquaintances to be an unusually interesting couple, although getting to know them in the midst of the noisy confusion of people and music proved difficult. They had to strain to hear one another.

"Jake mentioned your writing project to me the other day," said Philip. He leaned toward Sarah. "I have a book that should be helpful to you. It's a history of the various mining camps in Colorado. I bought it because the author writes about the early newspapers in the twenties and thirties."

She wished Jake hadn't told Philip Norton about the outline she was working on. "Thank you for your offer." At this point she had no idea if she could actually write a book. "I'd like to borrow it sometime."

"It's at my office. I'll give it to Jake in the next day or so. What you really need to do is visit the Denver Public Library. You could dig up all sorts of information."

"Thanks, Philip. I'll keep that in mind."

Joan said, "Your project sounds interesting."

Wanting to divert the attention away from herself, she turned to Joan and said, "I've always thought cross-country skiing would be fun, but it looks like a lot of hard work."

"Cross-country doesn't have to be rigorous. Why don't you come over to the school one day soon, and I'll personally give you a beginner lesson, no charge. It would be my way of welcoming you to town. I'll have you catching on to the basics in no time. It's like dancing, all a matter of rhythm."

"I may take you up on that, Joan. Thanks for the offer," said Sarah, smiling.

"Speaking of dancing," said Jake, "I think it's time we give it a whirl." They made their way to the dance floor. "You're the prettiest woman here tonight." He pulled her closer.

As they moved together in unison, a feeling of contentment engulfed her. Jake's attentive behavior was a welcome change.

After their dance, they stopped by Kathy and Neal's table and chatted before returning to their own table. Sarah recognized a number of familiar faces and decided to introduce Jake to more of her acquaintances. He would be proud of her effort to be social. The band played a slow song, and Jake suggested they dance again.

"I'm so glad to see you having a good time," said Sarah as they danced.

"It's a great party. We needed to get out like this and meet people. I like seeing you in fancy clothes for a change."

When they returned to their table, the Nortons introduced Sarah and Jake to another couple. She thought that the party was serving a real purpose, a way of helping her and Jake become a part of Spruce Haven. While she was visiting with one of Joan's friends, she looked up to see Clint and Veronica enter the room. Sarah was surprised to see him with the noticeable redhead, for she didn't seem his type. Veronica's hair cascaded around her shoulders like a waterfall in a tumbling, frenzied descent. Continuing her conversation, Sarah had difficulty paying attention when Clint nodded in her direction and smiled. She thought how unusual it was to see him all dressed up in his black slacks and jacket with a cream-colored turtleneck. In spite of his refined appearance, however, she saw that his rugged outdoor look prevailed.

Later in the evening, he asked Sarah to dance. Before she could even respond, he turned to Jake and said, "That is, if you don't mind."

He looked surprised but quickly said, "No, by all means, go ahead."

"Well, Sarah?" Clint looked down at her, waiting for a response.

Realizing she didn't have much choice, she stood up from the table. When they began dancing, she struggled to find something to say. "Your date is striking. I've met her before; in fact, she's going to be on the cover of our brochure."

"Yes, believe me, she's told everyone about it. Actually, she's a date, nothing more."

Looking off in the direction of Jake's table, Clint said, "Don't look now, but Veronica is getting even with me for abandoning her. She's asking your husband to dance."

Instinctively, Sarah turned to look at Jake and saw him taking Veronica's hand and leading her to the dance floor. Sarah's knees weakened, and she felt the pressure of Clint's hand as he pulled her closer to him.

"Are you okay?"

"Yes, it's just that I was suddenly reminded of another place, another time."

"I think that means you'd rather I didn't ask any more questions."

She said nothing, relieved that he had given up trying to make small talk. Dancing close to Clint made her feel safe. She reasoned that it was only because he had come to her aid on the afternoon of the terrible storm when she was stranded on *Baby Doe's*. When the dance ended, she looked up at him and said, "Happy New Year, Clint."

"I hope yours is a happy one, too, Sarah." He returned Sarah to her group.

Jake, too, had rejoined the others. Soon it was twelve o'clock and the clamor of tooting horns and the strains of "Auld Lang Syne" rang out as the waiters served trays of champagne-filled glasses. Jake leaned forward and kissed Sarah. "I'm about ready to get you home to really welcome in the New Year."

She smiled. "Yes, I think it's definitely time for us to go home, and don't even think about driving." Sarah had become concerned about his sudden increase in drinking. Jake had always been a man to control his liquor; she had never seen him the least bit drunk. Taking a sip of champagne, she saw Clint at a nearby table. He looked at her and raised his glass of champagne in the gesture of a toast. In response, she smiled and did the same. For the most part, the evening had seemed full of promise. Sarah hoped the upcoming year of 1987 would fulfill her expectations for a new life in the mountains.

twelve

The weekend following the New Year's Eve celebration attracted record-setting crowds to Spruce Haven, which made it a busy time for ski patrol. A major front had moved in early Friday afternoon, bringing with it frigid Arctic air and a drastic drop in temperature and leaving behind sixteen inches of new snow. Clint's Saturday morning began well before dawn when he and Sam met at lift 1 to begin their avalanche control work. Shivering from the frigid morning air, they pulled the plastic canopy down to protect them from the cold wind and positioned their feet on the bar below.

"Damn, it's colder than a well digger's ass this morning," said Sam.

"I can't believe it. You mean the Bear is actually admitting he's cold?"

The off-ramp came into view, and they skied down to the next lift, which would take them to headquarters. They rode in silence the rest of the way up, as they usually did on early morning rides.

Clint thought about the dance the previous night. He had felt somewhat guilty for accepting Veronica's invitation, because the only reason he went was his hope of seeing Sarah there. Sarah had been on his mind ever since he took her home on Christmas Eve. Remembering how unnerved she had been when she saw Veronica asking Jake to dance, he sensed that her reaction had indicated far more than a simple case of jealousy. Jake's past behavior could be the reason for Sarah's reaction.

Once he was at headquarters, his duties for the day took precedence over any thoughts of Sarah. He told himself for the tenth time that he needed to forget about her. Having gathered their weather data, Sam and Clint began their battle plan, based on understanding which slopes had taken on the most snow.

When all the patrollers had gathered at headquarters, Sam reviewed their various routes, cautioning them to be on the alert for certain changes in snow conditions. Everyone gathered their avalanche backpacks, which contained collapsible probes, avalanche shovels, igniters, and hand-thrown explosives, each weighing two pounds. In addition to their radios, each patroller carried a Skadi avalanche transceiver, which emitted a beacon to a fellow patroller's transceiver in case of an avalanche accident.

Sam and Clint had determined that a particular route needed additional help and supervision. Sam, Clint, and three other patrollers skied from headquarters to the east side of the mountain, where a steep slope high above *Snow Chief* continued to be a hazardous slide path.

When the five reached the top of the run, they attached climbing skins to the bottom of their skis for traction in the deep snow. After a long hike to the ridge, high above the lifts and trails, the strong Arctic wind lambasted them, making their movements appear to be in slow motion. The avalanche zone high above *Snow Chief* had shown a tendency to slide early in the season, making it dangerous for the trail below. The control team threw four bombs into the large concave shaped slope, which was rounded inward like a bowl. The charges boomed with a deafening blast that rumbled across the mountainside. Apparently there was no weakness in the snowpack, for no release occurred.

The patrollers made their way down the side of the bowl and threw additional two-pound charges, each detonating with a deep throated rumble. Still, there was no action from the mountain, which indicated a safe slope. They heard other control teams calling through the trees, and they picked up on radio responses. It seemed that the other patrollers were having a relatively quiet, routine morning of avalanche control work. Years of working together as a team afforded them a relative degree of safety as they made certain the trails below were protected.

"Let's ski cut this baby and give it a test," said Sam. Years of experience had taught him that sometimes both techniques of throwing explosives and ski cutting were essential to make certain an avalanche path was safe.

Preparing to ski cut the path, he shoved off at the top of the bowl and rapidly traversed or crossed to the opposite side at about a 45 degree angle, arriving at the edge of the steep slope. Lifting his downhill ski on its tail, he pivoted the ski in the opposite direction, completing a kick turn, so that he was turned facing the other side of the bowl. Picking up speed, he traversed to the opposite edge, well below the others. The other patrollers followed one at a time, dropping down at least several feet below the previous skier's tracks. Clint was the last of the group to ski cut this portion of the avalanche path. He did a kick turn, and when he reached the other side, free from danger, the entire slope slid, fracturing about a hundred feet above him, spreading some fifty feet to either side.

The deadly mass of avalanche debris grew in size and intensity as it crashed down the slope, carrying with it boulder-size chunks of snow and shooting up a spray of snow dust high into the air with a roar like a jet engine. The avalanche stopped about three hundred feet below Clint The strong winds soon cleared the cloud of snow dust.

The five patrollers who were positioned above Clint skied down to join him.

"Hey, Clint, that could have been a nasty ride," yelled Sam.

The other patrollers teased him about it, but they knew their job required the skill to pick up momentum to carry the skier off the moving slab if, indeed, it did fracture above. They returned to patrol headquarters and prepared for another ski day.

A few hours later, Clint skied down *Red Bird*, an intermediate trail that had a long stretch of moguls. On most of the blue runs, the grooming crew kept the moguls knocked down, but the mountain manager wanted *Red Bird* left alone for the mogul lovers.

From a bench on the hill, Clint spotted two beginners who were having difficulty maneuvering their way down. They had managed to get down the roughest part, but apparently they had slid most of the way. They eased around the mound of packed snow, and after the turn they picked up speed in the trough, fell, and slid. Without being too obvious, Clint skied to within fifty feet of the middle-aged couple. The man had fallen again, and when his wife got up, she said, "Honey, stay there; I'll ski over to you and help you up!"

As she traversed toward him, the man managed to stand up, steadying himself with his poles. He faced his wife, who skied straight into him, her right ski sliding between his skis, her arms and poles flung out as if to embrace him. The impact of her body knocked her husband down, sending them both sprawling in the snow.

Clint skied down to help untangle the intertwined mass of skis, poles, and bodies.

"My God, Cynthia, Are you trying to kill me?" asked the man.

"May I offer you folks some assistance?" asked Clint, trying his best to suppress a smile.

The lady replied from her reclining position with goggles and hat knocked askew, "Oh, really, we're fine," but she reached for Clint's extended hand just the same. He made certain they got safely down and encouraged them to build up more confidence on the beginner runs.

That afternoon he stopped in at headquarters and found Sam and another patroller named Lucinda taking a short break to grab lunch. Sam had returned from making a toboggan run to the clinic.

"I'll be interested in seeing how many lift tickets we sold today. I've never seen the mountain with this many skiers on it."

Winking at Lucinda, Clint said, "Of course, it would help a lot if all those crazy Texans had their own mountains and snow. They account for more than half of the winter invasion every year."

"That's right," said Sam. "It's those so-called crazy Texans that keep southern Colorado resorts in business."

From the control room they heard the dispatcher's loud, crisp voice: "Hey, you three in there. Kilgore has an unconscious victim— Upper *Windsong*—possible head injury."

The three patrollers sprang into action, gathering the necessary equipment.

When they approached the accident scene, marked with crossed skis, Clint skied directly down to John Kilgore, the patroller who had made the assessment and had radioed for assistance. While John informed Clint of the patient's vital signs and the circumstances involved in the accident, Lucinda positioned the toboggan and quickly stepped out of her skis, placing them in the snow. She used the skis for support to brace the toboggan. Sam put the cylinder of oxygen in the snow near the patient and grabbed the cervical collar out of the toboggan.

Clint had learned that the patient was a sixteen-year-old girl who had hit an icy track while skiing fast. Her father, who had been skiing with her at the time, explained that his daughter Kate had come out of both bindings and had flipped forward two or three times in a somersault fashion down a fairly steep slope. When he reached her, she was unconscious, lying on her back. Kneeling in the snow near his daughter, the father wanted answers from Clint that were impossible for him to give. Checking her pulse and the pupils of her eyes, he told the father they would take all precautions in case of serious injury.

Clint's mild manner and conversational tone seemed to calm the father. Nevertheless, the distraught man never took his eyes from his daughter as the patrollers prepared to apply manual cervical traction in case of a neck injury. Placing one hand on either side of the patient's head, Lucinda managed to keep the patient's head and neck in a neutral position while Clint slipped the rigid cervical collar in place.

Sam had the backboard ready. With Lucinda maintaining neck traction, Clint and John slid the board underneath Kate and strapped her into place. Positioning their hands in the handholds under the backboard, the four patrollers painstakingly lifted her into the toboggan with her head in an uphill position. While the others covered her with blankets and a tarp that had to be secured into place, Sam began to administer oxygen. Lucinda placed the girl's skis and poles in the toboggan, and Clint radioed for a snowmobile to take the father to the clinic.

Having put on their skis, the patrollers prepared themselves and their precious cargo for a long, tedious journey to the bottom with an absolute minimum of movement. John picked up the handles of the toboggan as Clint gathered up the tail rope. The father's eyes filled with tears at the sight of his bundled-up, unconscious daughter. "Be careful with my little girl, guys."

Sam said, "She's in good hands, sir. I'll wait here with you until your ride comes along."

John turned to Clint and gave a nod to signal their descent. Lucinda was to ski alongside the toboggan to monitor the patient. As tail man, Clint's job was to keep the rear of the toboggan properly positioned with a tail rope and help John with the braking motion as needed. If John ran into any problems, it was Clint's job to control the toboggan. He hoped that the girl had simply sustained a hard fall, causing her to lose consciousness, but without any significant damage. On the other hand, if she had sustained a serious injury, he was confident that she could be transported safely by helicopter to the hospital in Denver. As the toboggan slid smoothly over the packed powder, Clint was thankful for the good snow conditions, which provided optimum braking control. John followed the fall line down *Windsong* in a fluid, consistent motion.

When they reached the clinic, located on the lower level of Timberhouse Lodge, John stepped out of his skis and pulled the toboggan up the ramp onto a platform. Attendants assisted the patrollers in lifting Kate, attached securely to the backboard, onto a gurney. Clint, gesturing to the others to go on without him, followed the patient inside to fill out the necessary accident report and to talk to the anxious father.

When Clint left the clinic, he skied to lift 1. Before he knew it, he found himself looking for Sarah. She was crowding in on his thoughts more and more. Sarah was the first woman who had made such an impact on him in a long time. Being alone hadn't been an issue until Sarah arrived on the scene.

Clint admitted to himself that after losing Heather, he hadn't wanted to become seriously involved in a relationship for fear of going through heartache all again. *How did all those years pass so quickly?* he wondered. Here he was at forty-seven, starting to realize how empty his life was except for his passion for the mountains and his patrol work. He wondered if the day's events had influenced his state of mind. He stopped to consider the early morning's avalanche experience, an emotional father's concern for his injured daughter, and the death of a young skier on the hill. *I want to start making the most of my life*, he decided.

As Neal started to put the "closed" sign on the door, Sam Bishop entered the shop, his six-foot frame filling the doorway. Sarah had her parka and gloves in hand, ready to go home.

"Hello, Sam," said Neal. "We've been hearing all sorts of rumors today about a death on the hill."

"I'm afraid it's no rumor. I've seen it happen a few times," said Sam, leaning on the counter, rubbing his right hand across his beard slowly. "The accident happened a little after two o'clock. Young guy, about twenty-one. Ran into a damn tree. Up until then, we'd had a fairly typical day, although we had an unconscious teenage girl on our hands—that could have been serious. I dropped by the clinic to check on her; the doctor said the X-rays came out fine. I sure wish that other kid could have been as lucky."

"Most of these young guys give up that kind of risk-taking skiing when they hit thirty." Neal adjusted his glasses and said, "For me, it was even earlier."

"Was he out of control?" asked Sarah, bewildered by the day's tragedy.

"He was skiing on his own equipment," answered Sam. "It was the best money can buy. He was a strong, experienced skier, according to the report, but yes, he evidently got out of control at a high speed and couldn't avoid the tree."

"Sam, let's go have a drink," said Neal, putting his hand on Sam's big shoulder.

"Thanks, Neal, but I'm bushed. I think I'll head on down to the corner, grab a pizza, and eat it at home. It's been a long day."

Sarah put on her parka and gloves. "Come on, Sam, we can walk together."

"You've got a deal," said Sam. Neal unlocked the front door for them.

"Sometimes, I have to admit," said Sam, "I miss not being able to drive through one of them fast food places and pick up a burger and fries, but our town council won't let fast food places build here. Even Vail has a McDonald's."

"I know what you mean about the convenience of a drive-through place," said Sarah, "but it's nice not to have the golden arches to remind us of the real world. However, right now, I'm afraid Jake would welcome a taste of good old suburbia."

"Hey, Sarah, it's too soon for cabin fever. February is the month for those symptoms. Is Jake already that miserable up here?"

Sam's abrupt question took her by surprise. "Let's just say he hasn't found the happiness in the mountains that I've found." They arrived at the Pizza Parlor. Sarah glanced in the windows at the crowded restaurant with its Tiffany lamps and dark wood tables.

"Sarah, Jake will get used to it up here. He'll adjust, especially with a woman like you to encourage him."

"I hope so. I love it here. Thanks for listening, Sam. I think I'm just depressed about what happened to that young man today."

"Yeah, me too, Sarah. A damn shame, that's for sure."

Walking home in the chilly January air, Sarah reflected on the dark mountains around her. She considered how the mountain could destroy a person who didn't keep up a constant guard, yet the mountain could offer a person peace if he accepted it on open terms. Jake seemed unwilling to reach any sort of compromise with his environment. His mood the day after the New Year's Eve party had taken another downward swing, partly because of his horrible hangover. For the past several days he had continued to be sullen and withdrawn. She decided to talk to him about returning to Texas.

When she approached the condo, she saw a new jeep parked in the driveway. As soon as her key turned in the front door, Jake was there to open it.

"Sarah, I've been waiting for you to get home so we could take a ride in the new jeep," he said, ushering her out the front door.

"Jake, calm down a minute and let me catch my breath. Who drove you into Gunnison to get it?"

"Philip Norton," he answered as he opened the jeep door for her. "I stopped by the newspaper office around noon to see if he wanted to have lunch, and when I told him I had received a call on my jeep, he insisted on driving me to get it. He also sent that book with me, the one you wanted to borrow." He closed her door and rushed around to climb in on the driver's side. Sarah had wanted to tell him about the fatal accident that was on her mind, but she didn't want to spoil his carefree spirit.

As he settled himself behind the wheel, he continued his story. "Philip had business to take care of in Gunnison, so it worked out great." Inserting the key in the ignition, he asked, "How do you like it?"

"It looks . . . uh . . . durable, and it smells new." As he backed out of the driveway, she asked, "Why didn't you come by the shop to show us?"

"I wanted to wait and surprise you. Now get ready. This is going to be a lot rougher riding than in the Suburban." Jake proudly shifted the gears, and the jeep lurched forward.

"You're telling me! I don't think I can ever learn how to drive this thing, and I'm not convinced you've learned yet."

Jake headed up Timberline Road, leaving the village and the condos far behind. The instrument panel lights cast a soft glow in the jeep, enough for Sarah to see the hint of a smile on Jake's face. She was pleased to see him excited about something again. She decided the talk about moving back to Texas could be put off, perhaps for good.

"Jake, why don't we wait until daylight to take this road? We could have car trouble and get stranded up here."

"Sarah, where's your spirit of adventure? This baby is a real machine. Man, I love it." The narrow snow-covered road twisted and turned, climbing higher and higher. A few miles farther on, he slowed and said, "There's a good place to turn around."

He drove down the mountain road, lined with tall trees standing like sentinels keeping their silent vigil. Sarah knew he was teasing, but his comment forced her to take a closer look at herself. After all, she had always chosen the safe route. She wondered if it were time, here in these rugged mountains, to try living life with a little adventure.

thirteen

At the close of the holiday season, Clint stopped by the Powder Hound on a Sunday evening. Sarah looked up from behind the counter when he entered the shop. Neal was busy fitting someone with boots in the next room, and Kathy had left the shop early.

"Hello, Sarah. I understand you'll be leaving the shop in a few days."

"That's right. I guess you and Neal have your poker game tonight. He's with a customer now."

"Good. That'll give me some time to talk to you. I wanted to let you know that my sister was crazy about the wind chimes. I told her a friend with good taste helped me choose them."

"I'm glad she was pleased."

"By the way, I haven't seen you on the hill lately. In fact, I guess the last time I saw you was at the club on New Year's Eve."

"I guess I've only been skiing about three or four times."

"Does that mean you've been working on your novel?"

Sarah looked up at him, startled that he had brought the subject up again. "I've been reading and taking notes. I've written a few pages."

"I'm glad to hear you're making progress."

Neal's customer left the store, and he joined Clint. "I'll be right with you, Clint. I need to grab my jacket."

"Sarah, Sunday nights won't be the same without seeing your smiling face," said Clint.

Neal returned and said, "It's all yours. See you tomorrow."

"Have fun, you two." She caught Clint's smile, and she smiled in return. He had that effect on people, she reasoned.

When Sarah's job ended, she helped Jake mail the Spruce-land Estates brochures, using a list of real estate firms in both Colorado and Texas. With that major task accomplished, she turned her attention to her book. She made a trip to the college library in Gunnison and gathered material for her research.

One evening, while she was curled up on the sofa working on her notes, she interrupted Jake's newspaper reading and suggested they take a day off together and go to Crested Butte to ski.

"We've been intending to go there to ski ever since we moved here, but there's never been a good time. Besides, it would do us good to take off and have some fun. You've been working seven days a week."

"Sarah, you go ahead if you want to, but I'm getting a number of good responses from our advertising, and I can't afford to leave the office. Besides, now you have the Suburban all to yourself, so take off when you want to."

She sighed and asked, "Are you certain you don't mind if I go tomorrow?"

"No, you go ahead. The roads are in good shape. Jake positioned the newspaper in front of him again, as if he were intent on reading some article. He had a meeting with his engineer in Denver on Friday of that week, and he had purposely avoided telling Sarah. He had arranged to spend Friday night with Rhonda and fly to Gunnison the following morning. Above all, he had feared that Sarah might want to join him. He knew he couldn't avoid the subject of the upcoming trip any longer. Having already decided to use the excuse that he needed her to cover for him at the office, he brought the topic up.

When she heard his plans for Friday, she put her notebook on the coffee table and said, "You know I've been wanting to go to Denver so I could go the library and collect more material for my book. I wish I could go with you."

"Sarah, this project is more important than your book. We can't afford to miss potential buyers."

"All right, I'll take care of the office, but why are you just now telling me? You've probably known about this trip for weeks." She began clicking the top of her ballpoint pen in a gesture of frustration.

"I never thought of it while we were talking. Look, I'll get away soon and take you skiing at Crested Butte, if that's what you want." He headed for the kitchen to mix another drink.

When he returned with his scotch, she said, "The point here, I think, is that we don't seem to spend any more time doing things together in Spruce Haven than we did in Carsonville. Isn't that ironic? We moved here for a slower paced lifestyle, yet you manage to be just as busy as ever."

"Sarah, let's not argue. Damn, don't you understand how much energy and time it's taking to get this thing off the ground? Slick brochures and magazine advertisements aren't enough. And if this project falls flat, the moneylenders in Denver will be after me. I'm under a lot of pressure that you don't even know about, because I try to let you have your mountain fantasy."

"Jake, don't be so unfair about my so-called mountain fantasy. In the beginning, I distinctly remember this whole idea of moving up here was your idea. What's happened to you . . . to us . . . to all our dreams that we never talk about any more?"

"Look, if you're going to keep bitching, I'm going to the club."

"It won't be necessary. I was on my way upstairs to work on my book." She gathered her pen and notebook.

"Great. You always have your nose stuck in a book."

"If you have a better suggestion, I'm listening."

"Drop it for tonight, Sarah." He got up to turn on the TV. "I'm going to catch the news."

He was aware of her presence at the bottom of the stairs for a few moments. Jake realized their problems were mainly his fault and that it was unfair to make her feel guilty. He knew Sarah felt confused, and he tried to convince himself that in time he would find a solution to his predicament.

He finished his drink and began to think of the pleasures that lay ahead of him Friday night in Denver with Rhonda. He was like a drug addict looking forward to his next fix.

*T*he next day Sarah decided to spend the day skiing at Spruce Haven. A ski outing at Crested Butte would have to wait until Jake could take a day off from the office. Spending quality time together had been her original intention when she asked him to join her. Jake had managed to create a distance between them, not unlike what had happened in Carsonville. She resented his threats to go to the club when he wanted to avoid a serious talk. Pushing negative thoughts aside, she decided to enjoy the day that lay ahead. That was what Sarah loved most about the sport of skiing. No matter what she might have on her mind, once she clicked into her bindings she entered another world.

The weather was unseasonably warm. She reached for her dark glasses to protect her eyes from the bright snow that glistened like tiny pieces of glass reflecting the sun. Leaving the condo behind, she skied down *Lonesome Trail* to lift 1 and on to lift 2 to the top of the mountain. She rode up by herself, glad that no other skiers were in the lift lines. Looking down, she marveled at how empty the mountain appeared. The holidays had come to a close, and the next big rush would be spring break. Sarah felt the warm sun on her face and saw how the delicate shadows of the aspen trees below her looked like arteries and veins sketched lightly in pencil across the white canvas of snow. Looking off to her left, she could see the snow-capped mountains that looked like frothy ocean waves spread on an oil canvas.

*A*s she started to shove off for another run down *Whippoorwill*, she heard someone call her name. She turned and saw Clint skiing towards her. Seeing that he wasn't wearing his ski-patrol uniform, she knew it was his day off. His friendly face lifted her mood for the first time in days.

"Wait up and I'll ski with you," he called to her.

They skied together, keeping the same rhythm in their fluid, connected turns, never stopping until they reached the bottom.

"Hey, Sarah, let's grab this lift to the top and go ski *Chancy*. I skied it earlier, and the snow conditions are perfect."

"Clint, that is a hard black," said Sarah. "I've heard people say it should be marked a double diamond because it's so difficult."

"Sarah, I've watched you ski. Trust me, you can handle it. Besides, if you don't challenge yourself, you'll become bored living up here. And what better time to try it than when you have a ski patroller with you? See, you're in safe hands."

A slight shiver ran up her spine when she registered the word *safe*, realizing that was part of her attraction to him. Yes, she concluded, she did find herself drawn to him after dealing with Jake's moodiness of late. *Still, we're just two friends enjoying a day of fantastic skiing. What possible harm could come from that?* she asked herself.

"Okay. I give in, but you better not run off and leave me stranded up there."

On the chairlift ride up the mountain, Clint started the conversation. "How's the book coming along?"

"Actually, I only have about twenty pages on my computer, so don't laugh. At this rate, it'll take me years and years." She appreciated his interest in her writing.

"Listen, I'm impressed you're trying for it. That's the first step. Who's the main character in your book?"

"I'm planning to have three, all women, representing three generations of the same family. Two-thirds of the book will portray the hardships of mining camp life from a woman's point of view. I'd like to bring it up to the present by showing how the third generation woman inherits her grandmother's house in town. She, too, wants to make Crested Butte a permanent part of her life."

"Sounds interesting."

"Thanks for the encouragement. Jake compares my writing to working crossword puzzles, both a waste of time." Wishing she hadn't shared something so personal, she hurriedly changed the subject and said, "I guess your job is easier, now that the crowds are gone."

"Things have slowed down some, but we hope to keep a steady flow of skiers for the remainder of the winter. After spring break in March, there won't be any lift lines."

"The village was so crowded during the holidays. The shuttle buses were filled, and the restaurants were crowded. Even shopping at the grocery store was a nightmare. Worst part of all, I always had trouble finding a place to park when I had errands to run."

"You're beginning to sound like a real local."

"Oh, but living up here is worth any small inconvenience," said Sarah as she prepared to get off the chairlift.

Standing at the top of *Chancy*, Sarah said, "Clint, that looks too tough for me. In fact, I think I'm getting dizzy."

"There you go again with that negative attitude. We're really going to have to do something about that. Look, you don't have to worry about some idiot running into you. There's no one here this morning. You'll never get a more perfect opportunity. Don't feel rushed. I'll stay right behind in case you fall, not that you're going to, mind you."

"Oh, I can't believe I'm doing this," said Sarah as she turned her skis toward the slope. The terrain was the steepest she had ever skied, except for a few short blacks, but she knew one thing for certain—she mustn't hesitate on the turns.

She began her descent.

She felt as if she were flinging her body off the mountain into nothingness.

She was a high diver waiting to hit the water.

Her mouth was dry.

Breathe, she told herself. *Breathe. Weight the left. Weight the right.*

An endless expanse of white stretched before her. Her muscles ached.

If I fall, I'll never stop.

She caught sight of a bench ahead, a leveling-off place. *If I can make it there, I can stop. Or will I be able to?*

I'm on a runaway train. *I can't stop! Can't stop!*

Just before she reached the bench, Sarah fell, rolling forward twice, losing her cap and sunglasses first, then her skis and poles.

Clint skied to her, picking up her cap and sunglasses on the way. "Sarah, are you okay?"

"Yes. I got a mouthful of powder and humiliation."

"You were doing great." He stepped out of his skis and helped Sarah make her way down to the level spot. Clint handed her the ski cap and sunglasses she had lost. Putting his skis on, he side-stepped up the hill to retrieve her skis and poles.

Once he had returned, he took his own skis off and planted them in the snow in order to help Sarah into her skis. She shook the snow from her ski cap and started to put it on her head.

"Wait a minute; your hair's still full of snow."

He took off his gloves and brushed the snow from her hair. With his other hand, he lifted her chin. She looked up at him, and their lips came together with the lightness and quickness of a soft brushstroke. He encircled her in his arms, holding her a few moments, and tried to kiss her again.

She put one hand up to his chest and pushed him gently away. "No, I shouldn't be here with you. I shouldn't even be on this black run. I want to get my skis on and go home."

"Don't be upset. I didn't plan this, although I have to admit it's been on my mind."

"Please, Clint, don't say any more."

When they were both ready to ski again, he said softly, "Sarah, you've been doing fine. Look at what you skied."

"You must be kidding. All I want to look at is the bottom of this run." She peered over the edge and found that it looked even steeper than what she had just skied. Two young men came flying past them, snaking their way down in tight, short S turns. They never once hesitated at the small dip in the mountain where Clint and Sarah stood. "The longer I stand here, the steeper that run looks. I'm going to shove off."

Taking a deep breath, Sarah sighed, admitting to herself that she had always chosen the predictable path. Here she was willing to take a new course, a risk. When she spotted *Lonesome Trail* ahead, she continued skiing with an almost reckless abandon. Once she reached the bottom of *Chancy*, she came to a stop and turned to see Clint close behind her.

"Sarah, that last half you skied is more difficult terrain than the top half. Aren't you glad you did it?"

"Yes, but I won't be skiing this run any time soon."

Clint edged his skis closer to Sarah's and said, "I realize you think I got you up there so I could take advantage of you."

"Clint," she interrupted, "I'd rather not talk about it."

"Sarah, please hear what I have to say. I wish I could say I'm sorry, but the truth of the matter is, I'm not, and I don't think you are either."

"Look, Clint, I crossed the line here," she began.

Clint interrupted. "Maybe Jake has given you a reason to cross that line."

"Good-bye, Clint. Let's pretend it didn't happen." She pointed her skis to the safety of home and shoved off, upset at herself for getting in such a predicament in the first place.

Her mind was in a whirl as she skied down *Lonesome Trail*, which would lead her home. Somehow the entire episode seemed like a blurred picture: the skiing, the fall, the fear, the excitement, and the quick, unexpected kiss. Fearful of where this new friendship with Clint could lead, her hands shook when she tried to put the key in her front door.

Record high temperatures prevailed for the remainder of January. Although Jake's sale of properties was better than he had hoped, his disposition remained touchy, and detours at the club on his way home from work became more frequent. In an effort to get him in a better mood, Sarah gave a dinner party, inviting the Nortons and the Castleberrys, but Jake was unusually quiet the entire evening. Their guests left early, and Sarah felt her efforts had been nothing short of a social failure. She suggested they return to Texas if it would make him happier, but he insisted that he needed to prove himself with the Spruceland project. Sarah resumed work on her novel, avoiding discussions with Jake about their future in Spruce Haven, hoping that in time he would quit locking her out of his world. Blocking the image of the instant, light kiss with Clint was becoming more and more difficult.

One afternoon in the first week of February, Sarah took her notebook with her to Timberhouse to work on her novel. She took a seat on a sofa in the spacious lounge, where a large window wall rose two stories high to provide a view of the downhill skiers scattered across the runs like water bugs scurrying for safety.

A new front had blown in the night before, as if to remind everyone Old Man Winter was back in control, flexing his muscles with vigor. The temperatures remained mild, but the gusty winds brought in new snow that fell steadily, like flour being sifted through a sieve.

After the lunch crowd had cleared out of Timberhouse, Clint stopped in for a bowl of minestrone before taking another routine run. Having finished his lunch, he headed for the front doors, but he stopped at the sight of Sarah. Not a day had passed that he hadn't looked for her on the mountain or in the warming houses. He could see that a notebook in her lap held her complete attention. He joined her and said, "So this is how you've been occupying your time." He sat down on the sofa next to her. "Mind if I join you for a little while?"

"Actually, I was leaving," she said, closing her notebook, avoiding eye contact with him. "I came here to see if this marvelous view could inspire me. So far I haven't had much luck. This whole idea is probably just a big waste of time—at least that's what Jake keeps telling me. I don't work on it if he's around."

"Have you been thinking of a title?"

"Actually, I have. I'm thinking of using *Refuge in the Rockies.*"

"I guess *refuge* means that your characters feel safe or find a home in the mountains."

"That's right. Once they're here, they don't ever want to leave. I guess I can relate to that."

"So, Sarah, why don't you let me take a look at what you've written so far, and I'll give you my honest opinion."

She opened her notebook and took out about five printed sheets. "Here, you can scan the first chapter, but I'm giving you fair warning; don't expect too much. It's a rough draft, and I need to gather more research and fill in the details."

He took them from her, folded them, and placed them inside his parka. "I have to get to headquarters. I'll read them tonight and return them to you tomorrow, same time, same place." He grinned when he saw the shocked look on her face and stood up to leave.

"Clint Turner, you thief, give those to me this instant." She stood up and reached toward him, but he had already backed away from her.

"Tomorrow, Sarah," he said over his shoulder. He knew he was taking a big chance, but he also knew she'd be there the next day. Every time he was with her, she seemed to fill an emptiness that he didn't know was there. He enjoyed her keen perception of everything around her. Today, however, she seemed different. She was sad, and he wondered why.

That night, after Clint settled in for the evening, he began to read the first page of Sarah's first chapter.

Sarah Hansen
Refuge in the Rockies

Chapter 1

The shrill whistle coming from the Big Mine in the town of Crested Butte broke the stillness of a bitter cold March afternoon in 1897. Two women hanging out their laundry stopped to stare at each other, knowing in their hearts what it could mean. Leaving their piled baskets of laundry behind, they gathered up their long skirts and wrapped their heavy shawls more tightly around their shivering bodies.

"Hurry, Pearl," Miranda called to her sister-in-law as she headed down White Rock Avenue, her long dark brown hair flying in the wind. She kept telling herself, "Please, dear God, don't let it be my Joseph."

As the two women made their way through the heavy snow, clusters of other women joined them. No one spoke, each lost in her own fear of what lay ahead. Approaching the mine, a group of miners held up their hands as if to indicate that the women could come no farther.

"Ladies, bear with us. We don't know exactly what's happened or who's missing."

The women huddled together in tight circles to protect themselves from the cold and to comfort one another. Their dainty lace-up boots provided little protection from the deep snow. Some had their heads bent in prayer, and some were openly weeping. All were filled with dread, anticipating the news to come.

They waited patiently, standing defiant against the harsh wind that had picked up speed. Then the swirling snow started coming down in a dizzy mass of white. Miranda pulled the shawl up over her head, her dark lashes sprinkled with tiny flakes of snow. The final whistle for the day sounded, piercing the women's hearts a second time, signaling the end of another grueling day in the deep, dark mines, where men sometimes ventured six or seven miles into cramped, smelly quarters. The ever-patient, hard-working mules always stood ready to pull heavy carts of coal out to the light of day. The carts were hauled to the tipple, where the coal was dumped into the waiting railway cars. The system worked most of the time, but there were days like today, when something went wrong, always a possibility in the back of every miner's mind.

The miners filed out, carrying their tin lunch pails, looking for the worried faces of their wives. Some women broke from the tightly knit circles and called to their husbands by name, their relief audible in the muffled sound of the new snowstorm.

Getting nervous because they had not seen their husbands, Pearl said gently to Miranda, "We must brace ourselves for whatever we must face. No matter what, we'll get through this together, like always."

They held to each other tightly when one of the bosses made his way toward them. Tipping his hat, he nodded and began telling them the horrible news. "We're missing the brass life checks from the board for Joseph Salinek and for Thomas Lichner and his two sons, Frederick and Carl. Do these menfolk belong to you ladies?"

The wails coming from Miranda and Pearl gave the answer he suspected. They were the only wives left, so he knew they were still waiting for news of the missing miners.

He continued, "You ladies need to head on home where

it's warm. It'll take us a good while to find them, but we'll send you word when we do." He found out where they lived and tried to offer them some hope. "They could still be alive, but I'll be real honest with you, it doesn't look good. We had some heavy timbers cave in, and, well . . . you know how that can turn out." He shook his head and walked toward the mine, where the rescue men were waiting for instructions.

Miranda remembered that her eight-year-old daughter would be waiting at home, frightened that her mother and aunt were not there. The streetlights cast a soft glow to help guide them home. Miranda knew the coal was running low in the parlor, but Abigail was capable of going tto the shed to get more. With heavy hearts, the two women made their way along Second Street and down to their house on Sopris Avenue.

Before they reached home, Miranda cried out to Pearl, "I don't know what I'll tell Abigail."

"The truth," Pearl answered. "That's what we do here. We have to face the possibility that they're dead or else badly injured." She muffled a sob and said, "Oh, my poor, sweet boys. The other day, I told Thomas that at ten and twelve they were too young to be working in that mine."

They made their way up the front walk. Miranda turned to Pearl and said, "We have to keep hoping until we get the final word. Let's go inside and pray with Abigail that God is protecting them this moment and the rescue men will find them soon." She wiped the tears away and squared her shoulders to face her daughter with the bad news.

As it turned out, the heavy timbers that had caved in on them had crushed all four. Three days later, the two widows stood at the cemetery outside the town. Dressed in black, they stood straight and solemn as their minister from the Union Congregational Church finished addressing the small, huddled crowd. Many of their friends could not come, because they were working in the mines. Miranda thought how cruel it was to be back in the cemetery just three years after they had buried their young son Jonathan, who had died of scarlet fever. The tears rolled down her face as she remembered her sweet child and thought of all the many infants and young children who had been buried there. Miranda looked up at the towering, rugged butte before her, drawing strength from its massive display of endurance down through the years.

She remembered the first time she laid eyes on Crested Butte Mountain when she and her handsome new husband had pulled into town on the train in 1887 after a five-day journey from New York City. Joseph and Miranda had left Croatia and their families behind to begin a new life in this little mining town. Now she was all alone with the responsibility of a daughter looking to her for care and protection. Abigail favored her father, with the same warm brown eyes.

Miranda reminded herself that many women had lost their husbands in mining accidents, and the brave ones stayed and managed to provide for their families. Leaving the cemetery that gloomy afternoon, she resolved to find a way to stay in Crested Butte.

A week later, Miranda came in the back door carrying a heavy bucket of coal for the big stove in the kitchen. When she went into the parlor to check on the stove there, she was startled to see Pearl emerging from the bedroom carrying two big suitcases. Her face was puffy, as though she had been crying, and her usual bright blue-gray eyes were dull.

"Pearl, what on earth are you doing? I thought you were going to wait to hear from your sister in Kansas before you made a decision about leaving."

"Miranda, I'll tell you the honest truth. Yesterday, when we realized the roof was going to cave in if we didn't get up there and shovel the snow off, I made a decision right then and there to pack this morning and catch the afternoon train. I feel terrible about leaving you like this, but this town has taken everything that was dear to me, and if I stay here, I'll turn into a bitter old woman. Besides, Miranda, we're not going to make it by taking in sewing and laundry. There are no jobs available anywhere in town. You know that."

Taking a seat in the rocker by the stove, Miranda sighed heavily and said nothing for a few moments. "Pearl, you have to do what you feel is best for you."

"You and Abigail could come later on and join me. My sister and her husband have a huge old farmhouse, and they would welcome the extra help. They have a daughter about Abigail's age."

"No, Pearl, we're going to stay here, but I do appreciate the offer."

"How are you going to make it here by yourself? How will you pay the rent, buy groceries, keep the snow shoveled off the roof, not to mention the shed, the outhouse, the front walk? It's too much for you to do alone. Abigail is too young to be of much help."

"Since you've decided to leave, I'll take in a couple of boarders—you know, miners who are waiting for their families to come and join them. I could do their laundry, ironing, cooking, patching. They would pay the rent and help me shovel snow in the winter and cut wood in the summer."

"Miranda, you'd have the whole town gossiping about you. It wouldn't be proper for a widow to be taking in complete strangers."

"Maybe that would be the case in some other town, but not here in Crested Butte. Everyone here pulls together to help each other in tough times."

"But, Miranda," Pearl persisted. "what about Abigail? You need to consider what's best for her."

"That's just it—I am thinking of Abigail. She loves her school here. If we went with you to live in Kansas, think how isolated she would be. We have neighbors here, friends, our church, a feeling of community." She paused to take a breath and stood up, smoothing the wrinkles from her skirt. She looked Pearl squarely in the eye. "This is where Abigail and I belong. This is our home."

Pearl hugged her sister-in-law, knowing it was useless to try and convince her to leave Crested Butte. Besides, she thought to herself, as she took a look at petite Miranda with her dark brown hair neatly braided in a tight bun at the nape of her neck, you probably won't be on your own too terribly long. You're young enough to get married again and have more babies.

When Clint finished reading the last page of Sarah's first chapter, he was pleasantly surprised to see that she was serious about trying to write a novel. Since few women lived alone in the oppressive, harsh environment of a mining town, the reader immediately became apprehensive about this young woman's future. He found himself looking forward to seeing her the next day with an interest that was beginning to concern him. The incident on *Chancy* had caused him to wonder more than ever about her marriage. That moment they had kissed, it seemed like the most natural, irresistible thing to do. He was slowly realizing that he yearned for the companionship and intimacy he had known with his first wife. Superficial women like Veronica had been a disappointment to him for a long time. He enjoyed the company of several female friends who worked for the resort, but he hadn't been seriously involved with anyone in a number of years. And now there was Sarah.

The next day when Clint looked for Sarah at Timberhouse, he saw her standing in front of the window, watching the skiers. He felt ridiculous about being nervous, but he didn't want to say the wrong thing and harm their tenuous friendship. He felt like the captor of a wild, exotic creature that might dart away from him at any moment.

"Sarah, are you still speaking to me?" asked Clint in a quiet voice.

"Hello, Clint," she said, turning her attention from the scene before her. "I feel as if I'm watching a giant movie screen without audio. Tell me, did my writing put you to sleep last night?" She reached out to take the folded pages from him, but he shifted them to his other hand and shook her outstretched hand instead.

"Congratulations on a good beginning. I look forward to reading more about these characters., and I'm not saying that to get you to be nice to me." He handed her the first chapter. "Thank you, Sarah, for sharing this with me. Jake must be proud of you."

"Jake hasn't wanted to read any of it. He says he'll read it if it ever gets published." She shrugged her shoulders. "And that probably means never."

Again, Clint sensed her changed attitude, a resigned demeanor that had replaced her earlier vitality. "Don't think about the publishing part right now. Keep writing every day. Can I buy you a cup of hot cider?"

"No thanks. I'm meeting Jake on the deck; we're taking clients skiing. It's the first time Jake has had a chance to ski in weeks."

"Funny, isn't it? I mean we're both in the same line of business in certain ways; both of us are working on PR, helping to improve the image of Spruce Haven."

She smiled and said, "Our involvement is more mercenary, I think." The sarcasm in her voice was unmistakable.

"How are sales going?"

"The sale of lots is slow. Jake keeps saying this recession of the eighties can't last forever."

"I guess once the development takes hold, the trees on Timberline will be facing execution."

"Please don't sound so macabre." She glanced down at the folded pages in her hand and then at Clint. "Thanks, Clint, for the encouragement on my writing. I'm mainly in the note-taking stage, outlining plot ideas and developing characters in my head."

She said it with such sincerity that he was momentarily taken aback. He watched her start to walk away, but before she got more than a few steps from him, he called after her. "Sarah, I have an idea to help you on your novel."

She swung her head around, her full hair in motion, and gave him a quick, curious glance. "What is it?"

"Let me drive you to Crested Butte and introduce you to

an old-timer who remembers the mining days. And I know the historic sites you need to see. Remember, I used to live there." He waited for her reaction, pleased to see her hazel eyes light up with enthusiasm.

Her full lips parted in a wide smile. "Clint, that would be really helpful, to interview people who could give me that sort of information—an inside, personal touch, a way to breathe a life into the historical facts." She took a few steps toward him. "Of course, I've thought of doing it myself, but I don't know the people to see. When would it be convenient for you?"

Surprised that she had agreed so readily, he said, "How about tomorrow, my day off?"

"Okay. I'll see if Jake wants to come with us, although I seriously doubt it. Why don't we meet here? What would be a good time?"

"Let's say around one o'clock."

"Great. See you then." She turned and left through the big double doors on her way to ski with Jake and his clients. He was pleased that Sarah wanted to go with him, and it was nice to see a happy expression on her face. He hoped Jake wouldn't go with them.

At the end of the day, Clint and Sam were the last ones in the patrol locker room. "I forgot to mention that I'll be at Crested Butte tomorrow," said Clint as he closed his locker door.

"Tell the guys hello for me." Sam hung up his patrol parka and reached for his heavy sheepskin jacket.

"I'm not going up to the mountain. I'm taking Sarah Hansen to town, to introduce her to Leo Graziano, who can give her background for a novel she's started."

"Are you trying to convince me or yourself?"

"What do you mean by that?"

"Just the two of you going . . . alone?"

"I hope so. Jake may come along. I won't know until tomorrow morning."

"Clint, I like Sarah, but I don't want to see either one of you get hurt. Nothin' good can come from a man being with a married woman, and an unhappy one at that."

"What makes you say 'unhappy'?"

"Her husband doesn't like living up here. She mentioned it to me not long ago, although I don't reckon she meant to tell me as much as she did. You best watch your step."

"Sam, I don't need a lecture."

"I'm not so sure about that. Don't go losing your head over a married woman. It don't fit your character."

"You're one to be talking about character. I thought you were the confirmed bachelor around here. You've been having dinner at the Alpine almost every night. I don't suppose that would have anything to do with the waitress you've been seeing lately."

"Hey, leave my personal life out of this."

"That's exactly what I'm trying to tell you, Sam."

They left the locker room and went their separate ways.

On his way home, Clint gave a great deal of consideration to what he had learned about Jake. If he wasn't happy living in Spruce Haven, it could be just a matter of time before they left. Clint understood most of Sarah's sadness, but he knew there was more, much more. He intended to make it his business to find out the next day, if Jake didn't go with them to Crested Butte.

fourteen

Jake wasn't the least bit interested in spending the next day in Crested Butte.

"I think you're getting obsessed with that book, Sarah. Actually, I think it's a pretty stupid idea to impose on Clint like that. I don't know why he'd want to take the time."

"The trip wasn't my idea, Jake. He was the one who offered to introduce me to a man who grew up in Crested Butte during the mining days and to show me around. You don't understand how much I need that exposure for my research."

"Damn it, Sarah, I don't understand why you're working so hard on this project of yours. You're getting as wound up in writing this book as you were in your teaching."

"That's not true. For the most part, I only work on my book when you're at the office."

"Speaking of office, I think you forget I have a business to run. If you want to go, then go. Leave me out of it."

That night she went upstairs and found Clint's name in the phone book. She picked up the phone to tell him she couldn't make the trip, but instead of punching in the number, she hung up, determined to go without Jake. Angry with him for not taking her writing more seriously, she swung open her closet door and grabbed a pair of black wool pants and a lavender ski sweater to wear to Crested Butte the next day.

On the way to the old mining town, Sarah stared out the window of Clint's older model black and silver Blazer at the whitewashed landscape with occasional houses, barns, and live-stock flashing by her like fast-forward images on a videotape. Clint was lost in his own thoughts. He had removed his heavy goose-down parka when he got into the Blazer, and Sarah saw how much a part of the mountains he appeared, in his traditional Norwegian sweater with its intricate yoke of tiny white checks. Opening the notebook in her lap, she focused her thoughts on her research and looked over the questions she wanted to ask.

"I see you've been doing your homework," said Clint, glancing at her. "When you get these people started talking, you won't need to ask questions. Be prepared to jot down as much as you can."

"I brought this along so I wouldn't miss anything," said Sarah, reaching into her purse and bringing out a tiny tape recorder.

"*H*ave you ever wanted to try writing a novel?"

"No way. I like writing about real events and issues, not fiction. That doesn't mean I don't respect what you're doing, though."

"You mentioned that you started out as a journalism major. Have you ever thought about writing a novel based on a real event?"

"I don't have enough self-discipline to tackle an entire book."

"I find that hard to believe, considering that your job calls for a great deal of self-discipline. What made you decide to be a patrol-ler?"

He related the story that Kathy had told her earlier about his young bride's death.

"Heather wanted me to train for ski patrol; she didn't feel that being a ski instructor was challenging enough for me. She saw the ugly side of skiing that most people don't ever consider. She always said working at the Vail Medical Clinic was like being backstage in a theater. The average skier sees the glitter of Vail Village; she saw the people with broken limbs or bad sprains or those suffering from high altitude sickness or a heart attack. The waiting room was filled with friends and relatives with strained faces. All this was a part of her resort world. Not exactly the travel brochure picture."

Hypnotized by the rhythmic sound of the windshield wipers as they swept away the fast falling snow, she imagined the scene that

Clint described. "I never stopped to think about those aspects of the sport."

"No, most people don't. I didn't intend to get carried away. It's just that Heather often wished she were a better skier so she could be a patroller."

"And after her death, you decided to become a patroller," said Sarah, turning to look at Clint, his windblown hair touched with golden streaks of the sun.

"No, not right away. I had a hard time dealing with losing her. I went on with my instruction and started teaching private lessons that paid better. A couple of years later, a friend of mine called me from Crested Butte and wanted me to train with him to be a ski patroller. I was reluctant to leave Vail at first because there was so much there that made me feel connected to Heather. At any rate, I needed a new direction in my life . . . a purpose. So I headed for Crested Butte, and it was the best decision I ever made."

"I'm sure she would be proud of the work you're doing now," Sarah said softly.

For a second he took his eyes off the road and turned to Sarah. Looking ahead again, he said, "I didn't tell you that story to gain your sympathy."

"I know you didn't."

"Few people know that much about my past. It was a long time ago, but for some reason I wanted you to know the story."

Sarah said, "I'm glad you told me." Changing the subject, she said, "There's that jagged crest of the butte. It seems to be reaching for heaven itself."

"I know what you mean."

And she felt that he did.

Their first stop was the home of Leonardo Graziano on Sopris Avenue. Clint knocked on the aluminum storm door of the modest light yellow frame house. An elderly man with thick white hair appeared, using one hand to push open the door and leaning on a cane with the other. He motioned for them to sit down on the sofa, and he sat in a sturdy oak rocking chair with gold cushions. A rug of faded cabbage roses covered the uneven wood floor.

"Mr. Graziano," Clint began, "I really appreciate your letting us come on such short notice. As I mentioned last night, I used to work with your grandson when I was a ski patroller here at Crested Butte."

"Oh, sure, I remember you. Now, you two call me Leo. That's what everybody around here calls me. Clint, I remember Robert used to bring you by here sometimes. That boy is still good about checking in on me every other day or so."

"That's good. You tell him hello for me." Turning to Sarah, Clint said, "This is Sarah Hansen, the lady I told you about on the phone. She'd like to ask you a few questions about the mining days for a book she's working on."

Leo appeared pleased to have company. He explained that he lived alone since his wife passed on a few years earlier. Clint helped Sarah out of her parka, for the wood-burning stove in the corner of the room had overheated the small parlor. A gray cat suddenly appeared out of nowhere and jumped on Leo's lap. He stroked the cat as he talked, and Sarah looked at his large, knuckled fingers— the hands of a hard-working man. Old family photographs of stern men and women hung on the walls.

Sarah placed the tape recorder on Leo's antique end table "Leo, do you mind if I record our conversation?"

"Oh, I don't mind at all."

"You can talk in your normal tone of voice," added Sarah.

"Why don't you tell me what you remember most vividly from living in Crested Butte in those early days?"

Leo stroked the cat's back for a moment and said, "I remember when I was a kid my father always had to strap on those darned old snowshoes when he went outside in deep snow, which was most of the winter. We didn't have the means of clearing what few roads we had."

"Was your father also a miner?" asked Sarah.

"Yes. My father and mother were Italian immigrants, came here in winter of 1894, and my father got a job with the CF and I Company. You know that CF and I stands for Colorado Fuel and Iron, which, of course, owned the Big Mine. Some years later my father liked to brag that a thousand tons of coal a day came out of that mine."

"Tell me, Leo, how did your mother feel about living here?"

"Oh, my. She hated the winters . . . hated the cold. She was always a sickly woman. We had one of the bigger homes in town, and my family took in as many as five or six boarders at a time. A number of the miners stayed at the Elk Mountain Lodge. You might want to go take a look at it. Course, it doesn't look the same today. Mama prepared the boarders' meals and did their laundry. Mainly she perked up in the summer, and she loved her garden. Her flower beds were filled with delphinium. I always think of her when I see delphinium blooming. We lost her in 1921—she died of influenza. Lots of folks did." He went silent, lost in clouded memories.

Gently, Sarah said, "I've seen the cemetery on Gothic Road. I suppose many of those markers represent the loss of young lives."

"Oh my, yes. I lost a brother and a sister, just young things. We had many epidemics. Scarlet fever and diphtheria took the lives of babies and young children. We didn't have doctors and we didn't know what to do for the children when they got so sick."

Changing the subject, she talked about transportation. Leo explained how isolated the town of Crested Butte had been in the early days once winter set in, making the road to Gunnison impassable. The train from Gunnison to Crested Butte provided the only means of transportation to and from the town in the winter months.

"Do you remember mining stories of your father's?" she asked.

"Oh my goodness, yes. He used to tell about the year 1902, when they had a bad snow slide. A number of miners lost their lives. I believe the camps close by, Gothic and Irwin, suffered the greatest loss of lives. My father used to tell the story about a tramway at one of the mines that got swept away and some of the miners with it. After that year, my father said Mother always told him good-bye when he left in the mornings, because she was afraid she might never lay eyes on him again."

"Leo, with those long, hard winters, what did you do for entertainment?"

"Oh, we had Saturday night parties, usually polka dances. Many nights we men would go to the hardware store and play games, mostly checkers. It was one of the warmest places to be on a cold night, with that huge coal-burning stove." He smiled in Sarah's direction. "Believe it or not, young lady, we were never bored. We all had it rough, but we had good times, that's for sure. Be sure you put that in your book."

Sarah smiled, and after asking Leo a few more questions, she thanked him and stood up, turning off the tape recorder and dropping it into her bag. They shook hands with Leo and walked out to the Blazer.

"Clint, what impressed me most about that kindhearted man was his peaceful outlook on life."

"Yes, I would say Leo Graziano is a contented man, but, perhaps that's what living up here in the mountains is all about—at least I've always thought so."

"You mean living a simple life and working hard?"

"Something like that. And feeling fulfilled. It's hard to put into words. But I think the people who live here today aren't so different from the early settlers."

"I know, and that's what I want to convey in my novel."

Clint parked the Blazer near Old Town Hall on the corner of Second Street and Elk Avenue. They walked across the street to the Forest Queen Hotel, a two-story frame structure, painted gray with a striking combination trim in rust, forest green, and white. Other than the unique paint job, the building, with its small window-panes upstairs, looked like a hotel in a western movie. They stood on the pedestrian bridge that crossed over Coal Creek, watching the stream below. Sarah grabbed her camera and started taking pictures.

"In the early days, this hotel's second floor had a reputation as the red-light district in town," said Clint, breaking the silence.

"Prostitutes were a colorful part of life in those early boom town days. I guess my book wouldn't be complete without at least one or two prostitutes."

"There's a legend about a lovely lady of the evening named Little Liz, who jumped from one of those upstairs windows into the creek below."

"And what made her commit suicide, according to the legend?"

"Oh, something about being jilted by a no-good gambler." He smiled at Sarah. "Let's get back in the Blazer and I'll take you to see the Old Rock Schoolhouse."

This old building housed the first permanent school in Crested Butte. Made of fieldstone with a tin roof, the two-story structure had a cupola and a bell, giving it a quaint appearance. Naturally it was locked, but Sarah could imagine the noise and laughter of high-spirited children. She took several pictures of the historic school, knowing it would find a place in her novel.

"Oh, Clint, I have a great idea. The many times we've been here, I've begged Jake to pull in past that old cattle guard that leads into the cemetery. Could we drive over there so that I can walk around and take pictures of the headstones?"

"Sarah, we've had entirely too much snow for that today. You need to go over there this summer and spend the afternoon to really appreciate the history of the place. It's actually much larger than it appears from the road."

"I guess you're right," said Sarah. "Summer would be a better time, but I've always felt intimidated by that cemetery. I feel as if I'd be stepping onto private, sacred ground."

"I've been there a few times, once to bury someone that I knew through an acquaintance of mine. He was the uncle of a former ski patroller."

She glanced at her wristwatch. "We've run out of time. Let's stop by the church and I'll take a few last pictures."

They pulled up in front of the church, and Sarah got out to photograph the white frame church with its soft yellow trim. The unusual belfry presented a memorable appearance with the mountains in the background. She walked up the steps and read the historic marker. The church had been erected in 1883.

Clint came up the stairs quietly behind her. They found the double arched doors open, which surprised them. Inside, hazy light filtered through tall, narrow arched windows. Neither spoke as they admired the simple, understated beauty of the small sanctuary. They stood behind a pew quietly taking in the scene before them. Sarah didn't feel it was appropriate to take pictures of the inside, a place of such solemn reverence, with its rich history. She remembered the Christmas Eve service, when the small church had been overflowing with all those happy people. Sarah spoke softly. "Talking to Leo today and being in this old church reminds me of my sweet grandfather and the church I knew as a young girl. Spruce Haven has that one nondenominational church, but it's contemporary . . . rather cold, actually. We went to services there once."

She removed a glove and ran her hand along the marble smoothness of the pew in front of her and asked, "Why does the past always appear so much less complicated than the present?"

"The present doesn't have to be complicated, Sarah . . . it's up to us. It depends on the choices we make." He covered her hand with his.

For a few seconds she stared down at their hands. She withdrew her hand and put her glove on. "Life isn't that simple—it's not just a matter of choices. One has obligations, commitments."

"But is your husband as committed to you as you are to him?"

She whirled around without looking at him and hurried out of the church. Over her shoulder, she said, "That isn't any of your concern."

Outside, gray clouds covered the village.

Feeling a mounting apprehension about being alone with Clint, she said, "I have enough information for one day. Let's go."

On the way to Spruce Haven, Sarah pretended to be absorbed in her notes, but her mind replayed the scene that had just taken place in the church. The innocent gesture of covering her hand with his had ushered in all those defenseless feelings from the day she had skied the black run with him. Once more, the undertow was tugging at her emotions. Sarah knew she must never be alone with this man again. She felt an undeniable attraction to him.

The awkward silence was more than she could bear. Fearful that he would bring up the subject of her unhappy marriage again, she tried desperately to think of a topic of conversation.

"Clint, I plan to have an avalanche scene in the novel. Would you mind if I turned on the tape recorder and asked you some general questions?"

"Fire away."

"I've been reading how the early settlers used twelve-foot iron rods as probes to locate victims. I also read that a few of the mining towns were buried in avalanches."

"Yeah, I think Aspen was one of the towns that was practically buried."

"I've read that hard-slab avalanches are deadly, but suppose I have a character who is buried in an avalanche, and he's able to breathe in an air pocket of some sort. What are his chances for survival?"

"Survival depends on depth as well as time. If he's more than six feet below the surface, he's pretty much a goner. But then again there's the time factor. He may be only two feet deep, but after thirty minutes, only about half of all avalanche victims have a chance of making it."

"Does it ever bother you to work on avalanche control?"

"What do you mean by *bother*?"

"Isn't there always the fear that you might get caught?"

"I wouldn't call it fear exactly. I think respect is a better word. We learn through experience what to look for, and we do our job, like a lot of other people in risk-taking professions."

"I guess patrollers have lost their lives in avalanches."

"It rarely happens, but yes, there have been some unfortunate cases."

"I'm sorry. I didn't mean to sound so depressing."

"You really know how to bring a guy back to reality."

They had little to say the rest of the way home. When they reached Spruce Haven, she said, "You can let me off at Jake's office in the shopping center up ahead. That's his place with the black jeep parked out front."

He pulled up in front of Jake's office. "I hope you got some good material."

"I'm sure it'll be helpful. I appreciate your taking the time to do this for me."

"Sarah, I want you to know I'm sorry about being so pushy with all the questions. You're right. It isn't any of my business."

As she got out of the Blazer, she turned to look at his serious expression. "I know you meant well, Clint, but I appreciate the apology just the same."

When Sarah opened the door to Jake's office, the icy breath of the late afternoon air followed her inside.

"Hey, Sarah, it's about time you got here. The Davidsons are waiting on us at the country club. They were in this afternoon to look at the smaller lots."

"Sure, Jake, give me a few minutes to freshen up a bit," she responded. She looked at herself in the bathroom mirror and tried honestly to answer the question whether she had allowed her interest in Clint to grow just to even the score with Jake. She had never been one to play games. Had she started now? She felt emotionally drained and too confused to understand how she felt about anything at the moment. Clint's question about Jake's commitment to her continued to haunt her thoughts.

Sarah's behavior that evening was an embarrassment to him. Her mind seemed to be a million miles away, and she had made no effort to help him keep the conversation centered on the positive aspects of Spruce Haven. Another reason for Jake's anxiety was Rhonda. Since he didn't have any trips to Denver scheduled, he didn't know when he'd be able to see her again. When they had met two weeks earlier, she had pressured him about asking Sarah for a divorce. She wanted him to move to Dallas, where, as she put it, he could start to live again. He didn't know if his feelings for Rhonda involved love or lust, but he did know he wasn't willing to give her up.

To make matters worse, he was finding it increasingly difficult to maintain any kind of intimacy with Sarah. She had tried to talk to him about it, but he managed to avoid the issue. He knew he couldn't make his home in Spruce Haven, and he hated deceiving her about a future for them in the mountains, or, for that matter, a future for them at all.

fifteen

A few weeks later, Sarah was in the grocery store, pushing her cart down the aisle, mechanically selecting items from the shelves. When she saw Sam, she stopped to chat a moment.

"On my days off I always make a point to do my grocery shopping in the morning," said Sam. "After the lifts close, it's a zoo in here with all the tourists who can't afford to eat out or who are tired of eating out. They'll run over you, trying to get to the checkout counter first."

"I know," laughed Sarah. She saw that his grocery cart contained primarily canned items, including Spam, tuna, beans, and soup.

That afternoon when she opened the oven to take out the pot roast, she thought of Sam and his grocery cart full of canned goods. Jake had called to tell her he needed to entertain a couple who had to leave town the next morning. This time he didn't ask her to come to the club, and she had no desire to join them and struggle to make small talk with complete strangers. *I'll put some of this pot roast in a foil pan and take it to Sam's*, she thought. She called first to see if he would be home.

Sam invited Sarah in and offered to take her coat. "Thanks, but I'd better get home."

She handed him the pan. "You can keep the container."

"This is mighty nice of you. Thank you."

"You're welcome." As she turned to leave, she heard Clint call her name.

"Sarah, don't go yet."

She shot an accusing look at Sam.

"Sarah, don't go getting mad at me. I'm real sorry. Clint dropped by, and when he found out you were coming by, I couldn't get rid of him."

Clint appeared in the doorway behind Sam. "Sam's right, Sarah. Come in out of the cold. I need to talk to you, just for a little while."

She stepped inside and said matter-of-factly, "I don't mind telling you two that I know when I've been set up."

She directed her next comment to Sam. "There's no need for you to let your dinner get cold. And as for you, Clint, whatever you have to discuss with me can wait until another time." She turned to leave.

Grabbing his jacket off the hook by the door, Sam said, "Sarah, maybe the two of you need to talk. That was real sweet of you to bring me dinner. If Clint behaves himself, I may share it with him. I won't be gone long." Sam gave Clint a nod as a warning to keep his end of the bargain and slipped out the door, closing it behind him.

Sarah stared at Clint in disbelief. "Sam has to wonder what in the world is going on between us."

"Here, let me take your coat."

"No. I'm only staying a few minutes, so you'd better start talking."

"Sam knows how I feel about you, and that's all he knows, or for that matter, all he needs to know." He took a few more steps toward her, as if he were walking a tightrope and dared not look down.

She held up her hand, a sign not to come closer. "Don't you see, Clint, my feelings for you may be the reason my marriage is in trouble. I need to stay away from you."

"I think your marriage had problems long before I came on the scene."

"Clint, forget about me, about us."

He took a chance. He stepped forward quickly and wrapped her in his arms. In a whisper, he said, "All I can think about is you."

Instead of struggling to free herself, she stood perfectly still.

Unable to control the emotions she had reined in so tightly, she lifted her face to his. He kissed her with a passion that she met freely. She felt the exciting closeness of his body pressed to hers.

With his arms still around her, he looked down and said, "You can't deny you feel something for me."

She freed herself from his arms and walked toward the door. With her hand on the doorknob, she said, "No, I don't deny it." She felt her body tremble as she tried to steady her nerves. "But that doesn't change the fact that I'm married."

"I think I'm falling in love with you. Can't you see that?"

She tried to avoid his eyes, but they were locked onto hers. In a pleading voice, she said, "We can't keep having these moments together."

"Answer me one question." He moved closer.

"That depends on the question."

"How happy are you with Jake?"

"I don't want to talk about that with you."

"Let's get a few things out in the open. I saw you fall apart at the New Year's Eve party when Veronica asked Jake to dance."

"It reminded me of another time, that's all."

"A time when Jake was involved with another woman?" He paused to give her time to respond. "Sarah, let go of the doorknob and look at me."

Her hand fell limply at her side. She looked away from him.

"Yes, Clint, if you must know." Her eyes met his again.

"So . . . you and Jake came to Spruce Haven to leave it all behind. Only it's not working out as you had planned. Isn't that true?"

"What is true here is that getting involved with you would only complicate matters. Besides, it wouldn't be any different from what Jake did to me. He betrayed me. He betrayed the trust in our marriage. I don't want to be unfaithful to my husband. I don't want to hurt him."

"Sarah, you're talking in circles. You still haven't answered my original question."

"Look, Clint—" she paused a moment. "No, we haven't been as happy as I hoped we'd be." Her eyes filled with tears. "At first it seemed to be working pretty well, but ever since the Christmas holidays Jake has been so moody. I've never seen him like this. Clint, a marriage takes hard work. You can't look for the easy way out and make excuses for your actions." She took a deep breath, trying to decide whether to tell him about the major problem in their marriage. "There's much more to our problems, and it's too personal to go into."

"Go ahead. I'm a good listener." He folded his arms across his chest and leaned against the wall. "You might feel better if you talked about it."

Sarah sighed and brushed the tears from her eyes. "Not long after we came home from Spruce Haven last summer, I was diagnosed with pre-cancerous cells in my breasts. I had my breasts removed and had reconstructive surgery. The entire ordeal has been an added burden on our marriage." She searched in her shoulder bag for a tissue and wiped her eyes again.

Unfolding his arms, Clint took a step toward her. "Sarah, I didn't mean to make you cry or to invade your privacy."

"Jake can't deal with the scars . . . or with any of it."

He kissed her gently on the forehead. "I'm sorry for all that you've been through."

"Did you understand anything I said?" asked Sarah, exasperated that she had been pushed to the point of revealing so much about herself and her marriage.

"Yes, I understand far more than you think I do." He closed the space between them and took her in his arms again. "Sarah, there are physical scars and emotional scars. Both of them take time to heal. I thought I'd never get over the emotional scars of losing my wife."

Releasing her, he reached around and opened the door. "I'll let you go for now, but I think it was important that we had this talk."

Sarah held on to the railing to steady herself as she walked down the stairs to her car. The evening had started out as an innocent gesture of goodwill for a neighbor and had turned out to be a reality test on her marriage and her feelings for Clint Turner. Having revealed so much to Clint that was so personal and private had completely unnerved her. Her willingness to meet his advances was even more disturbing. At the same time, having shared her heartache with someone else did make her feel better. Being held in his arms was the most comfort she had felt in a long time. She promised herself she would try harder to bring Jake into her life again, if only she could think of a way.

sixteen

One evening the following week, Sarah called out to Jake from the upstairs landing, where she leaned over the railing in a red nightgown. "I bet you forgot tomorrow is Valentine's Day. I thought I'd give you a reminder."

Jake looked up at her. His heart ached when he saw her attempt to get his attention. He gave the plastic surgeon credit for providing Sarah with breasts that looked downright sexy in the red lace lingerie she was wearing.

"With a reminder like that, I don't think I could forget."

And he didn't. The next day he sent her a dozen red roses with a card that read, "You have been the best." Jake was late getting home that evening. When he arrived, Sarah teased him about the message, asking why he didn't say "You are the best."

He took her in his arms and held her for a long moment in an embrace that was not like him.

Still holding her in his arms, Jake said, "It's not working out, is it, Sarah? I mean with us, here in Spruce Haven."

She pulled away from him and searched his expression, but he let go of her and slumped down in a chair in the dining room. Running his hands through his thick hair, he sighed and folded his arms on the table with downcast eyes. The red roses, most of which were still tight little buds, were in a glass vase on the table in front of him. She sat down opposite him. Jake hesitated, searching for the right words. He had closed up like the rosebuds before her.

Sarah broke the silence and said, "I think my surgery has totally turned you off. I remember the doctor saying that some husbands can't deal with it. You turn away from me every time I start to get close to you."

"Your surgery doesn't have anything to do with our problems," he lied. "Lately it seems like we're either fighting or going for days on end barely speaking."

"Jake, I think the real problem has to do with your job, with living here."

He wanted to go ahead and ask her for a divorce. Instead, he decided to break some other news to her. They could discuss divorce later, when he had more courage.

"Sarah, I've been trying to find a way to tell you, but there hasn't been a good time. I sold our lot."

"You sold our lot? When?"

He turned away from the hurt look in her eyes. "Two days ago, to a couple from Houston."

"Why didn't you talk to me first?" asked Sarah. "You know I would have agreed to sell, but it would have been nice to be included in such a major decision."

"I know that was wrong of me, and, believe me, Sarah, I am sorry . . . sorry for so many ways I've been a disappointment to you."

"Jake, we can move back to Texas and you can get into your construction business again."

He wanted to tell her it was pointless to work at their marriage any longer. He looked at the bewilderment on her face. "I think you'd be happier staying in Colorado."

"Are you trying to ask me for a divorce?"

"I didn't say the word. You did." Jake stood up and walked to the stairs. "I'm sorry I've been such a disappointment to you, Sarah."

Jake walked up the stairs without looking back. Sarah was devastated, unable to fully comprehend what he was telling her. She lay down on the sofa and closed her eyes, but sleep wouldn't come. Unlike their usual arguments when Jake lost his temper, this one had been different. He had seemed withdrawn and sad. The rage was missing, along with the usual dramatic behavior. His reference to her staying in Colorado meant only one thing: divorce. He had been unable to verbalize what was really on his mind, and she hadn't wanted to hear the words.

For the first time she began to wonder if she were being fair to Jake by clinging to their marriage with such tenacity. Was it because she thought no one else could ever love her again with her new body? *No, that's not it at all,* thought Sarah. *I want my marriage to work out because I love Jake and I can't bear to lose him.*

In the early hours of the morning, she slipped off the sofa and made her way to the kitchen to make a pot of coffee. She glanced at the dark red roses and flinched at the sight of them. The tiny rosebud faces seemed to ridicule her for thinking their beauty represented Jake's love. He had sent the roses out of guilt . . . guilt that he had sold the lot without talking to her about it . . . guilt that he hadn't tried harder to make their marriage work. She had a sudden impulse to fling the bloody red things out into the snow and let them freeze, the way they had frozen her heart. She grabbed the vase, slid open the glass door, and flung the roses one by one into a snowdrift on the deck. She closed the door and tossed the vase into the kitchen trash. Then she carried a steaming cup of coffee to the living room and curled up on the sofa, tucking her bare feet under her.

Trying to reason how she had failed Jake, she wondered if she ignored him too much because of her writing. *No, it's something much more serious. Is he seeing someone else? Am I being stupid for a second time? Am I being deceived again?* Her relationship with Clint had escalated to the point where she wondered if he was more of a threat to her marriage than she was willing to admit. She suddenly thought of the times she had allowed herself to be alone with him, and she was overcome with guilt. She winced when she remembered how much of her personal life she had shared with him.

Placing her mug on the coffee table, she went to the fireplace and started a fire. The blue and orange flames instantly made her feel better. She opened the blinds to see if it was still snowing; the expanse of whiteness before her made her blink until her eyes adjusted to the brightness. The snow was coming down harder now. She was glad the roses would soon be buried under a blanket of white.

Returning to her original place on the sofa, Sarah decided to concentrate on something pleasant that would help her fall asleep. Her mind traveled back to the previous week, when she had gone to Crested Butte with Clint. The peaceful old church with its softly lit sanctuary had given her a warm sense of bygone days. The thought lulled her to sleep as dawn broke.

A few hours later Sarah heard the front door close when Jake left for the office. He had put a blanket over her on the sofa, and she soon drifted into a deep sleep.

The following week, Sarah had no desire to ski or even to see anyone. Her writing occupied much of her time. Choosing to become absorbed in a world of her own creation, she sat for hours at the computer. Her fingers moved lightly across the keyboard as her imagination developed the character of the second generation, Abigail Selinek. Leaning back in her chair, she realized that she had been working for several hours. Reluctantly her thoughts returned to the real world. Each day brought more tension in her marriage. She avoided any serious discussion with Jake, afraid that their talk would lead to a conversation about divorce. Holding on to her marriage was like being under water, holding her breath. The ringing of the telephone interrupted her thoughts. It was Kathy, calling to invite Sarah to lunch the next day. She accepted gladly.

In the bright afternoon sunshine on a quiet day in the village, Sarah walked to the Serendipity Restaurant on Aspen Road to meet Kathy. Getting outside had lifted her spirits. When she arrived at the Austrian restaurant, the waiter led her up the narrow stairs to the dining room, where burlap lampshades decorated with silk flowers and ruffles hung from the low ceiling. Kathy waved at her from a round booth with seats upholstered in a fabric that coordinated with the peach and blue flowers on the wallpaper.

After the waiter had set their vegetable quiche before them, Kathy said, "Before I forget it, Clint is planning a surprise birthday party for Sam. He wanted me to be sure and invite you and Jake the next time I saw you."

"When will it be?" asked Sarah, trying to hide her anxiety.

"It's a week from today, March 3. Clint insists on having the party at his place, although it's going to be pretty crowded. Of course, he's not inviting the entire ski patrol; it'll mainly be his poker buddies and their dates or wives." Kathy set her glass of white wine on the table.

"I appreciate the invitation, but we don't really know Sam that well."

"You're from Texas, and that makes you special in Sam's book. He's always asking about you two when he comes into the shop. Sam doesn't take to just anybody."

Sarah knew it was pointless to keep making excuses, so she agreed that she and Jake would go to the party.

"Good. I'm glad we have that settled. We'll count on seeing you on the third. It's been ages since we've seen you two. Did Jake tell you that Neal and I have bought a lot?"

"No, he didn't mention it."

Her doll-like blue eyes opened wide. "You mean he didn't tell you we're going to be neighbors?"

"Actually, I guess Jake's been too busy lately to discuss much about the development." When Sarah looked up from her plate, she saw the hurt look on Kathy's face.

"Sarah, you can be honest with me. If it's upsetting to you that we've chosen a lot next to yours, please tell me."

"Kathy, don't be ridiculous."

"Something's bothering you. That much is obvious."

She had caught Sarah in a weak moment when she was tired of pretending that everything was going smoothly in her life. "Kathy, Jake has sold our lot. We've decided to stay where we are for right now. I'm sorry for acting like such an idiot, but things have been confusing lately."

Kathy took a sip of her wine before she spoke. "Forget it. I can imagine how upset you are."

"I know you'll keep this private. It wouldn't exactly be good advertisement for Spruceland," said Sarah, wishing she hadn't confided in Kathy, but at the same time relieved that she had. "He doesn't want to be responsible for a big house on an acre of land.

He likes our condo lifestyle. Actually, the move up here has been a real adjustment for Jake."

"I'm certain he'll see things differently once he's experienced our glorious summer and fall months. The first winter is always a shock to people who aren't accustomed to the mountains." When the waiter left the bill on the table, Kathy took care of it. "This is my treat today. Your turn next time."

"We'll have to do it again soon. I've missed seeing you."

"I'd better get back to the store before Neal thinks I've abandoned him for the afternoon."

Sarah went to the Rocky Mountain Gallery next door and bought Sam a small framed print of horses grazing in a green valley with Crested Butte Mountain in the background. She thought it would give a nice touch to his rather dreary apartment. On her way home she thought how awkward it would be to see Clint at Sam's party, but in a community the size of Spruce Haven Village, people were bound to bump into one another. The evening at Sam's two weeks ago had been the last time she had seen Clint. She had avoided skiing for fear of running into him on the slopes or in one of the warming houses. Sarah decided that she and Jake would make an appearance and not stay long. *How could anything happen at a birthday party?* Sarah asked herself.

seventeen

During the first week of March a new storm moved in across the Rockies, spreading its dark gray tent of clouds across Spruce Haven like the big top of a traveling circus. Sarah worked on Monday to help Jake with a backlog of paperwork. He hadn't brought up the subject of divorce, and Sarah was hoping for a miracle that could bring them together again. Before leaving the office, she reminded Jake of Sam's surprise party that evening. When she went outside to get into the Suburban, she found it covered in a thick layer of snow. With her gloved hand, she brushed the snow from the windows.

When she turned onto Main Street, she decided to stop in at the Powder Hound to get directions to Clint's place. Dreading the party, she was about to use the excuse that she and Jake were entertaining clients that evening.

When Kathy saw Sarah enter the shop, she rushed toward her. "Oh, Sarah, I'm glad you're here. I wonder if I could impose on you?"

"Of course, what do you need?"

"I need you to fill in for me and take the cake to Clint's place and prepare the punch for the party. Clint took care of ordering some party trays. I just got a call from him; the mountain manager called a meeting on short notice, and Clint didn't know how long he'd be tied up after trail sweep. We've been swamped since the doors opened this morning," continued Kathy, out of breath. "And now that the lifts will be closing down soon, it'll only get worse.

Of course, we'll have to close early for the party. He left me a key to his place."

Sarah tried to think of a way to get out of Kathy's request, but she couldn't think of a logical excuse. "I'll do my best, but you'll have to tell me how to get to Clint's condo."

"He lives in that second complex, the other side of Timber-house; it's called Hilltop, and his unit is in the second group; the number is here on the key." Handing Sarah the key, she said, "The punch ingredients are in the refrigerator. I'll go in the back and get my punch bowl and the bottle of Southern Comfort." With that, Kathy whirled around and disappeared only to return with the two items. "Here's the recipe; you can't go wrong. The cake is at the Madison's Bakery, and Clint has already paid for it."

Looking at the written instructions, Sarah said, "What about chipped ice?"

"Clint said he bought two bags of ice last night. They're stored on the deck. We can add ice before Sam's arrival.

"If I have any problem, I'll call you."

"Thanks, Sarah. I can always depend on you," said Kathy.

*O*pening the door to Clint's apartment, Sarah felt like an intruder. She carefully balanced the boxed cake in one hand and retrieved the key from the lock with the other. Making another trip to the Suburban, she retrieved the other items. After she had closed the door behind her, Sarah smiled to herself when she saw the balloons tied to the light fixture above a small oak dining table.

Setting the cake on the table, she took a moment to observe the living room, where a well-worn beige tweed sofa greeted her. Although he had obviously cleaned for the party, a certain casual look remained. Objects strewn around revealed clues to the personality of the occupant.

Before turning to the kitchen, Sarah noticed a pair of old snow-shoes, with splintered, racket-shaped forms and worn strips of leather, hanging on the wall above the fireplace mantel. A number of framed photos and snapshots were positioned across the mantel. A much younger Clint and Sam, wearing shorts and brightly colored

Hawaiian shirts with their ski boots and skis, leaned forward on their poles and grinned into the camera with their sun-burned faces. Another picture was a faded old photograph of a man and woman—his parents, she guessed. Another snapshot anchored her attention. Clint, dressed in a blue Vail instructor's parka had his arm around a beautiful dark-haired girl, who was wearing a beige ski outfit. Sarah knew the woman must have been Clint's late wife, Heather. *How young they both look*, she thought. Heather couldn't have been much older than Catrina. She ran her hand over the smooth, cool riverbed stones of the fireplace.

Scolding herself for trespassing in Clint's private domain, Sarah hurried into the kitchen and began locating the ingredients for the punch. Clearing a work space at the serving bar, she moved a paperback novel by Larry McMurtry, a box of pretzels, and an empty Coors bottle to a nearby counter.

Minutes later, just as she was about to slide the heavy glass punch bowl onto a shelf in the refrigerator, she heard the muffled sound of boots stamping on the threshold outside. Startled, she forced the bowl into place, spilling punch in the refrigerator. *Oh, no*, she thought, *he's here early*. The front door opened. Her heart beat faster as she heard Clint step inside.

Clint rounded the corner into the kitchen. "Sarah?" he said, obviously surprised.

Sarah hastily finished wiping up the spilled punch with a paper towel before she straightened up to face him. "Hi. I thought you had a meeting that was supposed to last until six."

"Yes, I thought I'd be running late, but Bob had to cancel the meeting at the last minute."

She closed the refrigerator door and turned around again. "Kathy asked me to pitch in for her; they've had so many customers today." Wiping her hands on her black corduroy pants, Sarah said, "I just finished the punch, and the cake's on the table, along with your house key. I'll run along and change for the party." She marched past him toward the front door.

"Wait. I'd like to talk to you." He took off his black parka and hung it on the back of a chair.

Looking at her watch, she said, "It's already a little after five.

I really have to go." She reached for her parka on the rack by the door.

"I know about the trouble you and Jake are having. Neal told me he sold the lot."

Sarah spun around. "He had no right to tell you." She swept the bangs from her dark eyebrows impatiently.

"He let it slip. He said Kathy was concerned about you the other day, that you seemed upset."

"Clint, I really have to leave and get ready for the party." As she started to put on her parka, she said, "I hope Sam will be surprised."

"Sam also told me you confided in him that Jake misses Dallas," Clint continued. "The pieces of the puzzle are starting to fit together."

"Really, Clint, this isn't a good time to talk." She was still struggling with the sleeve of her parka.

"You know how to avoid the subject better than anyone I know. Can't you at least talk to me about what's happening in your life . . . as a friend?"

She drew her parka around her as if for protection. She looked out the window at the encroaching shadows of the evening. "Jake hates it here, and I think he wants a divorce." Looking up at Clint, she added, "The bottom line is, he's not happy living here, and he's not happy being married to me. There—does that answer all your questions?"

Not taking his eyes from hers, he said, "I'm sorry for your pain, and you know I'm here for you. I always have been."

In that instant, Sarah knew she was falling in love with Clint. She managed to get her other arm into the dangling armhole of her parka.

She felt weak as she turned to open the door. "Sarah." Gently, he took her by the shoulders and turned her around. "I've let you run away from me too many times. Not now . . . not this time." He slowly removed the parka from her shoulders, sliding first one arm out and then the other.

Not wanting to make any attempt to stop him, her eyes fastened on his. The last bit of resolve slipped away, leaving her vulnerable to this sensitive, caring man. They kissed each other with a kiss that made her unaware of anything except the moment. His right hand slipped under her red cashmere sweater, caressing her bare back, thrilling her senses with his touch. Responding, she put her arms around his neck and welcomed more kisses, each one becoming more passionate.

She felt like a small twig being rushed along a fast-moving mountain stream, swirling around eddies, disappearing momentarily, then bobbing up again for the journey ahead.

Clint murmured softly in her ear, "You know I want you." She could feel his warm breath on her neck.

"No, I can't." But Sarah knew the journey had already begun.

He took her hand and tenderly pulled her with him toward the stairs that led to the loft. She gave in to the rushing current inside her, knowing it was moving her closer to the white waters ahead. As soon as they were upstairs, Clint pulled his turtleneck off and then reached out to Sarah and helped her lift the sweater over her willing arms. His eyes held hers as he finished undressing her slowly in the dimness of the small loft. There was no turning back; she was in the frenzied white water rapids.

After they made love, Sarah felt like a tiny twig, floating serenely into calm waters. Wrapped in the safety of his arms, Sarah felt complete and desirable, but most of all she felt loved. In her heart she was falling in love with this man who had rescued her in more ways than one.

In the next instant, the powerful jolt of betrayal hit her, forcing her to acknowledge her actions. She freed herself from him, starting to get up, but he took hold of her arm. "Sarah, don't start regretting what happened. It was inevitable."

She broke away from him and began grabbing her clothes in a panic. "I have to rush home to a husband who's waiting for me. How do you think that makes me feel? And we have to come here for the party. Clint, how can I even look at you?" She finished dressing.

Clint zipped up his pants and reached out to take her hand.

"Sarah, will you calm down? I'm not giving up on you. This was not an afternoon fling. I want you in my life." He kissed the palm of her hand and took her hand in his.

"I've never been so confused. When I'm with you, I can't even think straight. Maybe I am falling in love with you, but the problem is, I still have a husband." She pulled her hand from his and rushed down the stairs. She stopped to grab her parka and hurried out the door.

Getting through the rest of the evening was going to be impossible, she thought as she drove away. By violating her own code of ethics, Sarah felt she had betrayed herself as well as her husband. She did not know this brazen woman who had tumbled into another man's bed.

*A*n hour later, as she and Jake waited for Clint to answer his front door, Sarah wished she had come up with an excuse at the last minute. Seeing Jake at home had been almost intolerable, for she had never kept anything from her husband. She now knew how it felt to be guilty of betrayal.

When Clint opened the door, wearing jeans and a crisp denim shirt, she did her best to avoid eye contact. How had she managed to get herself in such a mess, she wondered. *Like Hester Prynne,* thought Sarah, *I feel as if all eyes are on my visible* A. But most of the other guests had already arrived, so the chatter of voices and laughter helped make the situation less uncomfortable.

Clint asked Kathy to help him carry the coats upstairs to the bedroom. Just then more guests, carrying presents and trays of food, knocked on the door. Kathy said, "Don't worry, Clint; Sarah and I will get these out of the way."

Before Sarah knew what was happening, Kathy was handing her an armload of parkas. She followed Kathy up the stairs and piled the jackets on the bed. It was hard to believe she had been there with Clint not long ago. She felt like a criminal returning to the scene of the crime.

As the two of them went back downstairs, Clint called for everyone's attention, asking them to get quiet so they could be ready for Sam's arrival. He glanced up the stairs at Sarah and Kathy, but his gaze rested on Sarah. Their eyes met with the unabashed candor of lovers. The doorbell rang, and Clint opened the door for Sam. Dressed in jeans, a sheepskin jacket, and a dark brown cowboy hat, he beamed with surprised pleasure when his friends started singing "Happy Birthday." When he saw the huge cake decorated with a rust-red patrol parka, his eyes glistened with tears.

"Hell, I ain't ever had a surprise party. Y'all have been purty sneaky. I thought Clint was going to treat me to a steak dinner."

Everyone laughed, and most of the men slapped Sam on the shoulder. Kathy took Sam's heavy jacket and cowboy hat and hung them on a coat rack by the front door. The snacks were on a table off the kitchen, and the huge punch bowl and plastic cups were on the bar. Everyone started helping themselves, and the party was under way.

Soon Clint announced that it was time to cut into the birthday cake, and he lit one big candle. "Sam, we thought we'd make it easy on you. Surely you can blow out one candle."

Before blowing it out, Sam looked across the table at Lois, pleased that Clint had thought to invite her to the party. Sam's wish involved a future for the two of them in Texas. Divorced when she was only twenty-three, Lois had worked hard as a waitress in various Colorado ski resorts for the past fifteen years. Sam had met her at the Alpine Restaurant about six months earlier, and now they had secret marriage plans. They had even talked of Lois coming to visit Sam in San Antonio for a summer vacation. He had told her that Sweetwater wasn't much to look at, but that he'd be proud for her to see the romantic city of San Antonio, with its famous River Walk.

Kathy sliced the cake and served it to the guests. Then Sam opened his presents and thanked his friends for making his birthday special.

When Sam saw Gerald tuning his guitar, he said in his deep, booming voice, "Don't tell me we have to listen to you play that damn guitar of yours."

"Sam, I've been working real hard learning the words to your favorite Willie Nelson song, 'No Place But Texas.'"

"Hell, Gerald, I've never heard you play anything on that guitar except 'Whiskey River.' I reckon I ought to be impressed. If the others can stand it, I can too."

"Don't worry, Sam," said Gerald's girlfriend, "I brought along the real thing in case he runs into trouble." She held up a Willie Nelson CD, and everyone laughed. Gerald began playing his guitar. The lyrics flowed across the room in a slow, melodious tune about how a cowboy loves the bluebonnets and wide open spaces of Texas.

Gerald stopped a moment, and he said, "There's a second stanza, but I haven't learned the words yet."

Everyone clapped at Gerald's good intentions, even though he was a little off key.

"You did a damn sight better than I woulda thought," said Sam. Although he loved the mountains and had made Colorado his second home, the lyrics had touched his sentimental side. His heart was swelling with pride for the Lone Star State and for a friend who had cared enough to learn the song in order to play it for his birthday.

Clint put on some Bob Seeger music. The guests stood around in small groups, talking loudly to be heard above the music. They were enjoying an opportunity to break loose from rigorous work schedules and the dead-of-winter blues.

Later in the evening Sam realized he hadn't had a chance to talk with Jake and Sarah. He saw them standing near the kitchen, talking with Gerald and his girlfriend, and he moved toward them. "I guess you two enjoyed Gerald's song as much as I did."

"You can say that again," said Jake. "It made me miss those wide open spaces."

Sam noticed that Jake's speech was slurred when he talked. He decided Jake didn't need any more Southern Comfort punch.

"What I don't miss about the part of Texas where I come from," said Sam, "are the damned rattlesnakes and the scrawny ole mesquite trees."

"Oh, that's right," said Sarah. "You're from that town where they have that rattlesnake roundup in the spring."

"Yep, the Sweetwater Rattlesnake Roundup. It's a good thing they have it, or else the countryside would be crawlin' with them God-awful creatures." He sighed and said, more to himself than to anyone else, "Before long I'll be headin' home to rattlesnake country, all right."

"You gotta admit, though, Sam, spring in Texas is something else, with all those bluebonnets blooming and the trees startin' to green up all over creation," said Jake. The loud music stopped suddenly as someone searched through Clint's stack of CDs for another favorite.

"You got something there all right, but I'll tell you what, I'm gonna miss these mountains when the first flakes begin to fall."

Gulping down his fifth glass of Southern Comfort punch, Jake said loudly enough for the others to hear, "You know somethin', Sam? You're damn lucky you're moving back to Texas. I'm tired of freezing my ass off in this icehouse of a town, so don't go crying in your beer to me about missing the snow."

Although Sam knew Jake was having problems adjusting to life in Spruce Haven, he was not prepared for his hostile attitude. He said, "Hey, relax, Jake, and give it a chance."

"Yeah, I can't wait till the mud season when this white crap melts. That'll be great fun—all slush and mush."

"That's called the unlocking time," said Gerald. "We all dread it, but it's a small price to pay for the rest of the seasons we have here."

Turning to face him, Jake said, "In Texas we don't need to unlock a goddamn thing. Spring happens overnight."

Easing the tension of an awkward moment, Clint said, "Speaking of Sam's return to his homeland, I don't think it's too early to make a toast to his future health and happiness."

The others joined the toast, and soon the music and conversation continued. Sarah managed to take Kathy aside and apologize for Jake's behavior, saying that she needed to take him home before he drank any more.

Sarah caught the angry look on Clint's face and knew if she didn't hurry and get Jake out of there, Clint would throw him out. She looked at Clint and mouthed the words "I'm sorry." She was mortified.

Sam saw Sarah making her way toward him through the

crowded living room to the kitchen, where he and Clint were making popcorn.

"We're leaving now, Sam. I'm sorry about Jake's outburst. He misses Texas and doesn't realize what he's saying when he's had this much to drink."

"Don't give it a second thought. I'm glad the two of you could come to my party."

"And that goes for me too," said Clint, removing a bag of popcorn from the microwave. He walked to the bar where she was standing. "Sarah was a big help to me in getting everything together for your party." He looked at her. "I wish you didn't have to leave."

She looked down at the counter and back at Sam. "We really need to go." She kissed Sam on the cheek, surprising him, and said, "Many more happy birthdays, Sam."

Sam, unaccustomed to displays of affection, shifted slightly on his barstool and said, "Thank you, Sarah, and thanks again for that picture you gave me. It'll remind me of the time I've spent here."

Sam waved good-bye to Jake, who was standing by the door, holding the coats that Kathy had retrieved for him. By the time Sarah reached him, Jake's impatience was obvious. He helped her with her coat, a little roughly, and then they were gone. Sam watched them leave.

Reaching across to help himself to some popcorn, he said, "I feel kinda sorry for Sarah. She didn't seem too happy tonight, even before Jake's performance."

Sam had seen the way Clint looked at Sarah, and he wanted to see Clint's reaction when he made his comment. Sam knew Clint Turner better than anyone else, maybe even better than Clint knew himself, in Sam's view.

"I feel sorry for her too. She deserves better than Jake."

"Someone like you?" asked Sam, stroking his beard.

"Yeah, someone like me." Clint picked up the bowl of popcorn and took it into the living room.

Sam stood up to join the others. He was worried about his friend now that he knew how much Clint cared for Sarah.

*W*hen Sarah and Jake left the party, she insisted on driving. Jake's argumentative mood had escalated by the time they got home. He went straight to the liquor cabinet and grabbed a bottle of scotch. She took the bottle from his hand and said, "Jake, you've had enough."

"You can sure as hell say that again. Enough of this entire goddamn resort."

"Jake, you're drunk. Go to bed."

He staggered toward the living room and lay down on the sofa. Later when Sarah tried to rouse him, she realized it was no use. He had passed out. She removed his boots with difficulty and spread a blanket over him. Leaving the kitchen light on, she went upstairs to their bedroom and sat on the edge of the bed in the dark.

*W*hat's happening to me? I'm losing control of my life. I mustn't think of Clint, yet how can I ever forget the way we made love? Can I ever forgive myself, or will Jake ever forgive me? No, Jake must never know. Our marriage is in too much jeopardy as it is.

Drastic measures needed to be taken to change the course of their marriage. Jake was miserable with his life, and the two of them had drifted apart again. After being with Clint, Sarah wondered if she wanted to try and save her marriage any more.

Having put on her nightgown and robe, Sarah went downstairs to check on Jake and see if she could get him to bed. Unable to wake him, she went upstairs, thinking that she no longer knew what to do to make things right again between them. Sarah realized she had a new complication. Clint had made her feel more alive than she had felt in a long time.

*T*he morning after Sam's birthday party, Clint called Sarah from his office. "I've been worried about you. Did you manage to get Jake settled down last night?"

"Yes, and I'm sorry about the way he acted at the party."

"Meet me at Mid-Glade this afternoon at two thirty. I want to talk to you."

"No, Clint, I can't do that. I have to give my marriage one last chance. I owe that much to Jake."

After a few seconds of silence, he said, "What you're telling me is you're going to just forget about what happened yesterday and go on with your life. Is that it?"

"Please don't make this more difficult for me than it is."

"Sarah, give us a chance. Don't be afraid of your feelings for me."

"Clint, things have moved so fast that I can't think straight. Please don't call me again. It would only make me unhappy."

When she hung up, she felt more despondent than ever. She asked herself if she was in love with him, but she couldn't honestly answer that question. Too much had happened too fast. Besides, she reasoned, even if she did love him, didn't she love Jake more? Surely she did. And surely a marriage of twenty-four years was worth making every possible sacrifice to salvage, compared to a relationship of a few months.

eighteen

On March 28, an expected snowstorm blew in, dumping eighteen inches of snow on an already-weak snowpack and creating a challenge for patrollers who would be conducting their avalanche control work. At six o'clock the following morning, Clint and Sam were on their way to headquarters to plan their strategy, three hours ahead of eager skiers on the way up for their first run.

Sam had learned to love the adrenaline pumping feeling of early morning avalanche work. He especially enjoyed chairlift rides after a fresh snowfall, when he could see the smooth runs below in their natural state. He watched a gray jay take off from a tree limb that sagged under the weight of heavy snow. *I don't see how these critters survive the winter,* he thought. He started to say something about Sarah to Clint as they ascended, but then he decided against it. Since the party, his friend wasn't himself. Sam wished that Clint could forget about Sarah. He had never seen Clint become as emotionally involved with a woman as he was with her.

In gathering routine weather information, Sam found the new snow to be heavy and wet, unusual for southern Colorado, where the snow was typically light powder. The wind was out of the west-southwest at fifteen miles per hour, and the temperature was twenty-nine degrees. The day before, these strong southwesterly winds had created a new load of moisture-heavy snow. He was worried about how these new weather conditions could increase the risk of avalanches.

After Sam had carefully studied all the data, he said, "I think I'd better help the control team above *Ponderosa Bowl* this morning."

"That's a good idea. This new load concerns me. Do you need my help?"

"No, I have you down to help Jim on the avalauncher. With last night's heavy storm and these weather conditions, we need to use it. After you get some action up top, we can start our work on the slide path above Ponderosa." Sam poured a second cup of coffee and took a stale doughnut from his backpack. "Clint, it looks like we'll be busy this morning. You know we've had unusually high temps since the end of January. Now we have all this new wet snow. I don't like the combination." He picked up his assignment sheet for the day's control work. "Let's set aside some time to talk about the hazardous slopes."

"Yeah, that's a good idea. Do you have all the routes and leaders assigned?"

"All except one. I was wondering where to assign Brock, our rookie of the season."

"Why don't you take him on your route? Let him observe a pro in action."

"I think I'll do that. The kid is growing on me. If he'll stay with us, he might make a good avalanche man."

Clint glanced at the clock on the wall. "The crew should be here any minute."

He sat down opposite Sam. "Changing the subject, I've noticed how all your free time has been pretty well taken up with Lois. Is this relationship getting serious?"

Rubbing his beard in a manner that indicated he was thinking before he replied, Sam said, "I'll tell you something that's confidential." He looked away for a moment at the gray sky and the tops of the snow-laden trees. He turned back to face Clint and said, "About a week ago, I asked Lois to marry me."

"Why, Sam, that's great—if she said yes."

Smiling broadly, Sam said, "As a matter of fact, she did. We don't have a date set yet, and we're keeping it a secret for now. You know how the guys will ride me when they find out."

"Congratulations. I hope everything works out for you two."

"Thanks, Clint." He paused a moment. "And if things are meant to ever work out with you and Sarah, they will. I guess you have to admire a woman like that who hangs on to her marriage."

"If the marriage is worth holding onto, I'd agree, but in Sarah's case, I have my doubts." He got up and walked to the window to watch his patrollers skiing to headquarters. Turning away from the window, he walked toward the room where they would assemble the charges for the morning's work.

Sam stood up and followed him. "Clint, give her the space she needs." He patted Clint on the shoulder.

Before taking off for their various routes, the patrollers checked their equipment and turned on their radios. Sam and his team, made up of Gerald, Scott, Gary, and Brock, skied in the direction of *Ponderosa Bowl*, while Clint and Jim hiked about fifty yards up the hill to the small wooden building that housed the avalauncher, which was similar in appearance to an artillery gun. It was used only when a heavy storm moved through and certain conditions prevailed. This powerful avalauncher was capable of firing explosives into steep terrain that the patrollers could not access with hand charges. "Hey, Clint, it's been a month or longer since we fired up this baby," said Jim.

"Let's see if we can make some serious noise," responded Clint, who was glad Sam had asked him to help with the big gun. He radioed Sam that they were ready to fire the first explosive.

The blast from the avalauncher triggered a small slide that was barely visible on the high ridge to the west of headquarters. Sam radioed Clint and said, "You guys can do better than that. Try again."

This time the explosive resounded with a thunderous blast that echoed across the mountains and rumbled in the distant canyons and valleys. High above them, Sam and the others could see massive white clouds of snow that grew in intensity as they shot upward against the gray sky.

Satisfied with the results from the second blast, Sam sent a message to Clint to close down his operation. Sam and the other four patrollers skied along a narrow road, which led from headquarters past the off-ramp for lift 5 to the edge of *Ponderosa Bowl*. Preparing to ascend the steep slope toward the ridge above them, they attached climbing skins to the bottoms of their skis.They began the tiring maneuver of sidestepping to the top of of the avalanche zone. Reaching the higher elevation required tremendous physical skill. The wind had picked up, and a light snow was falling. Carrying the heavy backpacks of explosives added to their hard work. The patrollers were quiet as they made their way up to their destination point.

Once they were high above *Ponderosa Bowl*, they opened their backpacks and removed the explosives. Sam had them to throw simultaneous charges down into the top portion of the bowl. Pressing their palms against their ears, they waited those agonizing few minutes until the explosives went off with a loud belch from the belly of the mountain. But the explosives did not trigger an avalanche.

The patrollers skied down to the next point of testing. Once the five of them had assembled again on the flank of the slide path, Gary lobbed a charge about seventy feet down the slope. The rumble of the explosion echoed around them, but it, too, failed to trigger a release. The snowpack appeared stable.

"To be on the safe side, let's throw some more charges before we ski cut this baby," said Sam. Turning to Brock, he said, "You got a good arm for throwin'. Remember one thing: Once that fuse is on fire, you want to throw the charge the same way every time until you react without havin' to think about it."

"Okay, Sam. I got it." Brock loved the dangerous element of handling the charges and waiting for the earsplitting boom of the explosives. He was proud that Sam had taken notice of his work.

Brock watched Sam as he reached into his backpack to retrieve a two-pound charge, light the fuse with his igniter, and make a mighty heave as he threw the charge. This time they found a few trees to duck behind as they waited for the resounding detonation. Once again, there was no release.

"This hill should have slid by now," said Sam, "with all the snow we've had since the last avalanche. We're going to have to ski cut it."

"Yeah, Sam, I agree," said Gerald."The longer the snow builds on this damn path, the greater the danger."

"Everybody remember," warned Sam, "keep up your speed and let the momentum carry you safely to the other side if you trigger a slide." Sam made the statement for the benefit of Brock, who didn't have the experience of the others.

Gerald set out first, dropping down about forty feet above the point where he had thrown the last bomb. With a kick turn, he skied to the other side.

Brock started to take a turn, but Sam said, "You take the next one."

Sam skied several feet below Gerald's tracks. He was almost to the center of the bowl when he heard the menacing crackle of the snow cover fracturing above him. When the slab broke up underneath him, he knew he couldn't make it to the other side.

He released his skis, dropped his poles, and removed his backpack in rapid movements. Within seconds he found himself turning cartwheels like a cat that had been thrown into a clothes dryer. He tried to use a swimming motion to stay on the surface, but the force of the snow was too great. He felt as if his arms were being pulled from his body by a ferocious animal. He struggled to cover his mouth, but the effort was useless. *Don't panic*, he told himself.

He felt the motion around him stop. His lungs screamed out for air.

Blocks of cement all around.

Unbearable pressure.

Darkness.

Alone.

At headquarters Clint heard the sharp report on the radio: "Sam's caught! Sam's caught! About a hundred yards above Ponderosa!"

Clint felt helpless. He noted the time. Grabbing his backpack, he jammed his boots into his skis and shoved off on the road that led to the upper bowl. He knew his well-trained patrollers were locating the beacon from Sam's transceiver. When he heard the roar of a snowmobile behind him, he turned around to see one of his patrollers slowing down to give him a ride. When they arrived near the scene, Clint looked up to see the patrollers wielding their shovels, piercing the cement-like surface. He dumped his backpack and grabbed a shovel. He and the other patroller hiked up the broken slide path, straining to go as fast as they could.

Brock yelled out to them, "We have a strike!" Clint pushed upward, willing his body to find more strength and speed.

Finding Sam's gloved hand, the three patrollers worked frantically, pushing snow from Sam's face and body. He was unconscious, his eyes open and staring. After cleaning vomit and snow from Sam's mouth and nose, Gerald quickly ventilated the lungs, using mouth-to-mouth resuscitation two times. Finding no pulse, he and Scott immediately initiated cardiopulmonary resuscitation. Scott compressed Sam's chest five times and then Gerald held Sam's nose and breathed into his mouth once.

When Clint arrived, the others shook their heads, but not one of them dared to give up on Sam. Clint relieved Gerald and they continued CPR.

A few minutes later, five more patrollers arrived with oxygen and blankets. Two of them administered the oxygen as Brock and Gerald spread blankets over Sam's body and tucked them underneath him. His face had already turned blue; his dark eyebrows and heavy beard were encrusted with snow and ice.

As Clint watched, he refused to give up hope, praying that any second Sam would show some sign of life. When the doctor from the clinic arrived, he knelt down in the snow and placed his fingers on Sam's throat to feel for the carotid artery. He shook his head and said, "Boys, you've been working on him for over an hour; it's time to give it up." He closed Sam's eyes and pulled the blanket up to cover his face. Putting a hand on Clint's shoulder, he said, "I'm sorry. Your people did all they could do."

Clint got up from the snow and wiped his eyes. He radioed the dispatcher to send in the county coroner. Two patrollers volunteered to stay and take Sam's body down to the clinic in a toboggan.

Clint couldn't bear to stay a moment longer. He walked unevenly across the avalanche debris to the side of the slope. His shoulders heaved in uncontrollable sobs as he wept for his beloved friend.

S arah turned on the small TV in the kitchen to catch the local news while she fixed lunch. Reaching for her sandwich, she stopped when she heard the newscaster say, "There was an avalanche tragedy at Spruce Haven, Colorado, today. Ski patroller Sam Bishop was killed early this morning on routine avalanche control work. Fellow patrollers found his body in four feet of debris, where he had been buried for eleven minutes. Sam Bishop was the snow safety director for Spruce Haven Ski Resort."

After clicking off the set, she backed up to the edge of the counter and struggled to comprehend what she had just heard. Sarah couldn't breathe; there wasn't enough oxygen in the room. Nature had betrayed Sam, sneaking up on him, trapping him, then swallowing him up in her white jaws of death. Sam had seemed indestructible, one of those men who could defy anyone or anything with his sheer brute strength.

And now Sam was gone.

Clint must be devastated. She went into the kitchen and dialed Kathy's number at the ski shop to see if they had heard the sad news.

"Oh, Sarah, Neal found out a few hours ago. I've been too stunned to call anyone. It's just too awful."

"I know Clint must be devastated."

"Yes, I'm sure he's taking it pretty hard. Neal went up to headquarters to be with him."

"Let me know if you hear anything, anything at all," said Sarah, her voice breaking with emotion.

"He did say Sam's body will be flown to Texas as soon as it can be arranged." She took a deep breath before she continued. "We also know a memorial service will be held here tomorrow evening at the small chapel. His friends from Crested Butte will be coming. I'll give you a call when I get all the details."

"Thanks, Kathy. I appreciate it."

Sarah called Jake and let him know about Sam. Putting her head in her hands, she collapsed on the sofa and began to sob for the way Sam's life had ended. Her heart ached for Clint and all the other patrollers.

arly that evening Sarah went upstairs to call Clint. She had considered telling Jake that she was going to call him and offer her condolences, but she changed her mind when he said he wouldn't be attending the memorial service with her. He was watching TV and didn't want to discuss Sam's accident any further, adding that it was unfortunate, but accidents happened. With his back to her, he had waved his hand in the air, telling her to go to the service if it would make her feel better, that nothing could be done for Sam now.

Kathy had called earlier to say the service would be held in the chapel at six o'clock the next evening.

When Clint answered the phone, Sarah tried to find her voice, which sounded weak and far away to her. "Clint, this is Sarah. I just wanted to call and tell you how sorry I am about Sam. You've been on my mind all afternoon."

"Sarah." His voice cracked, and there was silence for a moment. "It's been a terrible shock for the group."

"I won't keep you. I can imagine what an exhausting day it has been for you." She could feel the tears sliding down her face, and she couldn't speak. The silence on the other end of the line told her that Clint had choked up just as she had. "I'll see you tomorrow at the chapel."

"Sarah, I know this is asking a lot, but could I see you tomorrow before the service?"

"I don't know—"

"I've volunteered to give the eulogy, and it would help if I could see you a few minutes. I'll meet you on the deck at Sprucetop around two o'clock."

"I'll be there."

She hung up the phone and went into the bathroom to splash her face with cold water. When she lay down on the bed and closed her eyes, she imagined what it must have been like for Sam: the great masses of snow tumbling down the mountain, roaring like Niagara Falls, burying him in a dark tomb of ice and snow. How could she have refused to meet Clint, she asked herself. The despair in his voice made it impossible to say no.

The following afternoon on her way to the mountaintop restaurant, Sarah skied to the edge of *Ponderosa Bowl* and stopped a moment to think of Sam. As she looked high above the bowl where the avalanche control work had taken place, she found it difficult to imagine that only the day before the scene had been one of tragedy. The sun shone with a blinding brightness, and she could hear the laughter of skiers behind her.

As she made her way up the steps of Sprucetop, she spotted Clint coming toward her. After a brief hug, he led her to a table on the deck. "Thanks for coming."

"It must be difficult for your patrollers to carry on with their work as if nothing happened yesterday."

"Yes . . . it's tough today for everyone. We knew there was danger of an avalanche, but we thought we had taken all the necessary precautions." He paused and looked up at the mountain. "Today I found myself expecting to see him when I went up to headquarters, like always."

"Sam was always so kind to me." Her eyes welled up with tears.

Clint took her hand. "He liked you a lot, Sarah. He was always looking out for your welfare."

She looked off into the distance and was silent. Finding her composure, she said, "Kathy told me you're planning to fly to Texas in the morning in order to attend the services in Sweetwater the next day."

"Right. I fly to DFW in the morning and catch a plane to Abilene and drive to Sweetwater. It's going to be a tight schedule, but I feel I should be there to represent the patrol."

"I know his folks will appreciate it," Sarah said, withdrawing her hand from his.

"Are you still planning to be at the chapel this evening?" asked Clint, studying her face intently

"Of course I'll be there." She stood up. There was really nothing else to say.

"I think I can get through it easier if I know that." Clint stood up and they embraced quickly. "I need to get back to headquarters to check on a couple of things. Thanks again, Sarah." Clint hugged her again and whispered in her ear, "I desperately needed to see you."

*A*s Clint surveyed the faces before him in the small chapel, he looked for Sarah, relieved when his eyes met hers. Knowing that Sam would have wanted comments to be brief, he had decided there would be no long speeches. Clint repeated his silent prayer that he would find the strength to control his emotions before a group that included so many patrollers and their families. He saw a number of familiar faces from Crested Butte.

Clint's eyes rested on those of Sam's intended bride. Clint vowed he would keep their secret. How well he knew the grief in her eyes.

"*I* am proud to say Sam was my friend, for he made all of us who call ourselves ski patrollers honored to do our jobs. Sam took a genuine interest in his profession. We all know he was in the habit of going to the clinic to check on an injured skier. He was highly knowledgeable and cautious about his work, always making an extra effort to be the best snow safety expert he could be. Sam's accident was not one that could have been prevented. Sam's death left us with a valuable lesson. We must never let down our guard, for avalanches are not predictable. The mountain made its claim, and in doing so, it took one of the best. All of us are going to miss him. Although Sam took teasing about his home state good-naturedly, he loved these mountains, and so it is fitting that this is where he died. But he would have wanted his final resting place to be in Texas."

With these closing comments, Clint took his seat in the front row. The strains of Willie Nelson's voice singing "No Place But Texas" filled the small chapel. Clint's eyes welled with tears when he heard the second stanza of Sam's favorite song about how the cowboy would want to be buried beside the Pedernales River beneath an oak tree, where he could see the longhorns grazing. When Clint walked out the chapel doors, he looked up at the mountains in the darkness before him. For the rest of his life, those words would ring in his ears: "Sam's caught."

He felt Neal's arm around his shoulders, and he turned to hug his friend, who shared in his grief. Clint caught sight of Sarah standing beside Kathy.

Sarah came toward him and said, "Sam would have liked what you said tonight."

He encircled her in his arms and said softly in her ear, "You mean more to me than you can possibly know. Thank you for coming."

When they parted, she looked up at him and said, "My thoughts will be with you on your way to Texas tomorrow. I hate that you have to go alone."

She left, avoiding the small clusters of people gathered outside the chapel. As she walked to the condo, her heart beat rapidly. The service had been an emotional ordeal. The impact of Clint's parting words made her realize she could no longer deny that she loved this strong, yet sensitive man.

nineteen

The first week in April, when Jake was in the bedroom packing for a business trip to Denver, he told Sarah about Spruceland's critical financial condition, a situation he had known about for at least a month. He told her that one of J.T.'s partners, the Midland oil man, had gone bankrupt because of the oil slump in Texas.

"Right now, the future looks grim for Spruceland Estates unless J.T. can find additional financial backing. The bank in Denver is getting shaky about backing us. We plan to present our proposal to a wealthy Denver man who has shown interest in the development, and, hopefully, the three of us will meet with the bankers."

"Jake, why didn't you tell me about all this financial trouble?" She was furious with him.

He closed the suitcase. "I didn't want to worry you about it." He clicked the fasteners in place as if to emphasize that the subject was closed.

"Jake, this helps me to understand the pressures you've been under. No wonder you've been so on edge. All this time I thought you were unhappy with me. You should have told me sooner."

"You're right. It seems we haven't been doing much talking about anything lately." He picked up his suitcase and started to leave the room.

His matter-of-fact tone implied a hopelessness that filled the air. "Jake, wait. Why don't I call and see if I can get an airline reservation and join you? I'd like to be with you."

"Sarah, there isn't going to be any free time for us to spend together. J.T. will be there when I arrive to go over figures with me.

We have the important meetings tomorrow, and I have an early evening return flight.

"What about tonight? We could have room service bring up an elegant dinner with champagne and the works."

Without turning to face her, he said, "I have a lot on my mind, Sarah. In fact, I have to get some papers together." With this pretense, he left the room and went downstairs. He felt like a monster, knowing that he would be spending the night with Rhonda, whom he hadn't seen since January. He had lied about J.T. being there when he arrived. J.T. wasn't coming in from Dallas until ten o'clock the next morning.

Disappointed that Jake had been so set against her traveling with him, Sarah felt despondent for a moment until she thought of an idea, a way to surprise Jake. She walked to the stair railing on the landing and called to him. "Where will you be staying in case I need to get in touch with you?"

"Where I always stay, at the Sheraton, near the airport."

Although she was not an impulsive person, Sarah phoned to see if she could get a reservation for a flight leaving sometime after Jake's. Pleased to find she could catch a 4:20 PM flight with United, she began packing, confident that Jake wouldn't come upstairs.

When she was almost finished, Jake called up the stairs. "Sarah, I'm leaving now."

"Okay, I'm coming down."

When she gave him a quick kiss good-bye, she had to try hard not to show her excitement. "Good luck. I love you," she called after him as he made his way outside, but she knew he wouldn't turn around to respond.

A gnawing fear inside told her Jake wanted to escape, perhaps forever. She went to the living room window and watched him drive away in the shiny black jeep. Sarah felt the darkness of depression descend upon her as the jeep disappeared. Should she let him go?

Refusing to allow more negative thoughts, Sarah told herself that the surprise visit could spark some romance in their marriage. She wanted to forget about Clint, and it was becoming almost impossible. Sarah knew time was running short to reverse the downward spiral of her marriage.

When her plane arrived at Stapleton Airport, Sarah went outside to look for a Sheraton Hotel shuttle. During the fifteen-minute wait, she began to wonder if Jake would be upset by her surprise visit, but by the time she arrived at the hotel, located near the entrance to the airport, she had regained her confidence.

She located the courtesy phones and had the operator ring Jake's room. She smiled to herself, knowing he would think she was calling from Spruce Haven. *Wait until I tell him I'm downstairs in the lobby.* She decided if he didn't answer his phone, she wouldn't leave a message, she would just have a glass of wine and wait for him in the bar. When he didn't answer his phone, she thought about telling the desk clerk that she was his wife and had a driver's license to prove it. Perhaps someone would at least send her small bag up to the room, or even let her in so that she could really surprise him. The longer she waited, the more foolish she felt. Then she remembered Jake had told her he and J.T. had to go over some reports. Perhaps they were in J.T.'s room.

Again, Sarah went to the courtesy phones, but the operator told her she did not show a J.T. Wright registered at the hotel. She slumped down on the soft cushions of a sofa, wishing she hadn't come to Denver, realizing for the first time, in the cold reality of the present moment, that one surprise visit was not going to be the magical solution to fix her marriage.

Afraid she would miss his arrival, she decided to keep her seat rather than go to the bar. As if in a bad dream, she saw Jake and Rhonda enter the lobby and walk toward the elevators. Sarah blinked in disbelief. The pulsing of her heart drummed in her ears.

Just before the elevator door opened, Jake leaned down and kissed Rhonda on the cheek, pulling her to him. Sarah grabbed her purse and her overnight bag. Fearing they would see her, she hurried out the lobby doors. She couldn't think clearly. Her head pounded with bullet-like thoughts:

All this time.
Rhonda and Jake.

Lies. Lies. Lies. All of it lies.
I'll go back in there.
I'll make him face me.
No, I can't. Not now.
I want to go home to Spruce Haven.
How could he have done this to me?

When she saw an airport shuttle pull up to the curb, she raced to board it, to find an escape. Feeling faint, she collapsed into her seat.

Jake helped Rhonda out of her coat and hung it in the small closet. "Come here and turn around. I'll unzip your dress. I've been wanting to get you out of that number ever since I met you at the airport."

"Not so fast, Jake." She sat on the edge of the bed, crossing her long, slender legs. She smoothed back the blonde hair that had fallen forward onto her face. "Look, I'm getting tired of always having to sneak around to be with you. I thought by now you would have asked Sarah for a divorce so that you and I could start thinking about marriage. It's time you came to Dallas where you belong."

Jake started to pace the floor. "Believe me, I've tried, but there hasn't been a good time. And now all hell has broken loose on the financial end of the project. Until we get that problem resolved with the bank tomorrow, I can't ask J.T. for a job in Dallas." He stopped in front of Rhonda, grabbed both of her wrists, and pulled her up to him. As he began unzipping her black jersey dress, he said, "I didn't think you flew all the way to Denver to talk."

United had a 6:30 PM flight to Gunnison. Once Sarah had her boarding pass, she sat down to wait for her flight. The thought struck her that she hadn't eaten anything since early that morning. She felt a wave of dizziness and nausea, but she didn't have time to get any food before they called her flight.

Damn you, Jake Hansen, she thought. *Damn you for breaking my heart like this, for making me believe your affair with Rhonda was over. When did you start seeing her again? Probably after my surgery because you couldn't stand the sight of me.*

She could feel the tears rolling down her cheeks. She was conscious of others staring at her, but she didn't care. She was barely aware of where she was or even who she was. She almost turned to the stranger sitting next to her to say that she had just seen her husband with his lover. Why shouldn't she be entitled to cry, to scream? The rage in her heart grew when she thought of how Jake had been with Rhonda on other trips to Denver.

All these miserable months of trying to get Jake to open up and talk to me. Why has he deceived me like this—again? We should have ended the whole mess long ago, when I first found out about the two of them.

On the flight to Gunnison, Sarah struggled to avoid the image of Jake and Rhonda in their hotel room. She thought of all the obvious signs of Jake's infidelity for the past several months: drastic mood swings, selling the lot, drinking too much, spending late hours at the club, and avoiding intimacies. Why hadn't she seen it? She was so stupid, so utterly stupid. At this point, she knew Jake was indeed the man Kevin had seen leaving the motel room with Rhonda that November day they left Carsonville. So all this time, the affair had continued.

As the wheels touched the Gunnison Airport runway, Sarah felt the sudden jolt of reality that she was alone. Walking through the small airport to the main entrance, she wiped the tears from her eyes again. She couldn't seem to stop crying.

She left Gunnison and drove out Highway 135. With a firm grip on the steering wheel, she stared straight ahead at the utter blackness of the night, where all her dreams had disintegrated. She had stopped crying, but now she felt heavy, almost drugged. The isolated stretch of highway in front of her intensified her feelings of loneliness and rejection. When the lights of Crested Butte came into view, she strained to see the brightly lit Spruce Haven sign on Evergreen Road. When Spruce Haven came into view, Sarah realized she would somehow have to find the strength to face the pain that lay ahead.

As soon as she closed the front door behind her, she dropped her bags and went to the kitchen to call Jake. First, however, she decided to mix herself a strong drink, something she wasn't in the habit of doing. The first few gulps sent her head reeling, because she still hadn't eaten.

She picked up the phone and tried to focus as she dialed the Sheraton in Denver and asked for Jake's room. When he answered, she said, "I know all about you and Rhonda. I was at the hotel earlier when the two of you came in together."

"What are you talking about? What do you mean you were here earlier?"

The anger inside helped her to keep tears under control as she explained the entire episode. He made no effort to refute any of it. Her second shock of the evening came when he told her he had been trying to get up his courage to ask her for a divorce for some time. He and Rhonda had plans to be married.

"Tell me, Jake. I'm curious. Do you even have meetings scheduled tomorrow, or was that all a pack of lies, too?"

"No, I do have meetings. I won't be home until tomorrow evening. We'll talk then. Don't worry; I'll get my things and go to a hotel. I'll make this as painless for you as I can."

She started crying, unable to talk any more, although she had so much more she had planned to say.

Finally Jake said, "I'm sorry you had to find out this way, Sarah. I never meant to hurt—"

Sarah slammed down the phone on his empty words. On unsteady feet, she made her way to the sofa and sat down heavily, grateful for the enveloping softness of the leather cushions. The picture on the end table of her and Jake standing by the Christmas tree reminded her of the holidays, when he got snowed in at Stapleton and had to stay over for Christmas Eve. *How convenient,* she thought, *for you and Rhonda.*

It all made sense why Jake never wanted her to go along on his trips to Denver. Sarah picked up the framed snapshot and flung it against the fireplace. She fell onto the sofa pillows, and she cried until she finally fell asleep.

twenty

The next morning Sarah woke with a terrible headache and the sharp, renewed pain of the previous evening's experience. She fixed some coffee and toast and looked outside at the melting snow, a sight that increased her depression when she thought of how the earth would soon thaw, bringing an end to the ski season, an end to the adventure that she and Jake had attempted, and an end to her marriage.

Her eye caught the glimmer of broken glass by the fireplace, evidence of her destructive mood the night before. Kneeling down to pick up the shards of glass, she thought how they resembled the broken fragments of her marriage, shattered pieces that could never be mended. A life without Jake was incomprehensible to Sarah after all their years together.

I'll have to find a new identity as a single person, decide how to make a living for myself, decide where to live. One thing is for certain: I'm not leaving these mountains I've grown to love. Then she thought of having to tell Catrina, and the tears started again. *I'll stay here in Spruce Haven for now.*

She admitted to herself that the most compelling reason for staying in Spruce Haven was the possibility of a relationship with Clint, the man whom she had come to care for deeply despite her efforts to ignore her feelings. With a twinge of guilt, she reminded herself that she hadn't been blameless in her actions. She, too, had strayed beyond the boundaries of matrimony. She remembered when they were together and how he had made her feel loved and desirable. That thought helped her to combat the overwhelming feelings of rejection that Jake had caused.

Wanting to file for a divorce as soon as possible, Sarah looked in the phone book for an attorney in Gunnison and made an appointment for Friday morning. While she was there, she planned to apply for an English teaching position in one of the upper grades and look into the possibility of finding an apartment.

Telling her family about the divorce was out of the question for right now, because she wanted to be in charge of her emotions when she called them. Knowing her family as she did, she knew they would want her to come to Texas and either resume her old job or move to Fort Worth to be closer to all of them. She needed to give herself time to absorb all that had taken place. She wanted to give more thought to her plan to stay in Spruce Haven. Even Sarah realized she was still in shock.

Reflecting on their time In Spruce Haven, she could see where it all began to come apart soon after the Christmas holidays. *All the signs were there*, thought Sarah. *I just didn't want to see them.*

Sarah dreaded the thought of seeing Jake that evening, but she had to face him. They had to reach an agreement on the myriad of issues that come about when a long-standing marriage dissolves. She started to cry again. At least this time there would be no more lies.

When Sarah heard Jake's key turn in the lock, she took another sip of wine, trying desperately to settle her ragged nerves and calm her racing heart. Setting his bags by the front door, he headed toward the liquor cabinet and saw Sarah sitting on the sofa.

"I think I'm going to need a stiff drink."

Sarah remained seated on the leather sectional. Having promised herself she would let him start the conversation, she bit her lower lip and took another sip of wine.

Taking his seat at the opposite end of the sofa, Jake took a long sip of his drink and began. "Sarah, let me say first of all that I'm sorry for the way this whole thing has turned out. I know I told you that last night and you hung up on me, but let me try to explain."

"Jake, the time for explanations has run out; we've moved

beyond that. What has happened has happened. Let's not make this more difficult than it has to be for either one of us." She was surprised that she had found a calm, self-assured voice. She began to feel more confident about the ordeal that lay ahead.

"Okay," Jake began again. "I admit I met up with Rhonda before we left town last November, but, Sarah, I swear to God, that was the only time I saw her after you found out about the two of us. You have to believe me on that score. It's important to me."

"Yeah, whatever. I believe you. Now, let's talk about where we go from here."

Finishing his drink, Jake set the glass down and said, "I want you to know that in the beginning after we moved here, I really was excited about building our new home in the mountains. Gradually, I began to see that I couldn't live here, but I could tell you were crazy about the idea. It didn't help that Rhonda started hounding me with phone calls at the office. I ignored her and told her to leave me alone. She knew I was going to be in Denver the evening of the twenty-second, and she just appeared at the hotel. That damn snowstorm had us trapped there until Christmas Day."

"Oh, you poor thing. Blame it on the snowstorm. Really, Jake, I don't want to hear a chronological rundown of each time you two got together, so let's drop the melodrama. The point is, we are way beyond explanations and excuses. Right now I want to talk about the divorce, finances, future plans."

Jake nodded. "You know I'll be generous. You take the money from the sale of the house in Carsonville, the furniture, the Suburban. We'll split the other assets. I'll have my attorney take care of everything."

"That won't be necessary. I've already made an appointment with an attorney in Gunnison for Friday morning."

With a stunned look on his face, Jake said, "You didn't waste any time. Have you told Catrina?" At the mention of his daughter's name, a pained look crossed his face.

"No, I want to talk about how we're going to deal with Catrina. I have no intention of telling her about your long-standing affair. Maybe later she'll put the pieces together. Right now she only needs to deal with one shock at a time. In fact, I don't want to tell her on the phone. I've made reservations to fly to Fort Worth and tell the family in person. It's going to be hard on Catrina. You know that."

Jake put his head in his hands, not speaking for several minutes. "She's going to hate me when she realizes this whole mess was my fault."

"Look, Jake. I'm going to tell her we've had some problems. I'll say that we've grown apart and we decided this was the best route to take. I suppose if you and Rhonda plan on getting married, she'll have to find out eventually, but that's your problem, not mine." She waited for him to respond.

Jake got up to mix another drink. Sarah poked at the dying embers in the fire and put another log in the fireplace. She stood staring out at the black night, wishing this conversation could find a stopping place, wishing he would leave soon. Her knees were trembling and she didn't know how much longer she could pretend to be so calm. She didn't want to cry in front of him because she didn't want his pity. She wanted to settle key issues and keep her pride intact.

When he returned from the kitchen, she resumed her spot on the sofa. Since he hadn't responded to her previous comment about marrying Rhonda, she gathered her courage and asked the question that had been on her mind all day. "So, are you and Rhonda planning to get married?"

"It looks that way, at least right now. That's what Rhonda wants."

The idea of Rhonda taking her place as Mrs. Jake Hansen hit her with the stark realization that she would soon be giving up her role to another woman. For the first time, Sarah found herself starting to feel sorry for her husband. She knew Rhonda was the sort of woman who would not give up until she had her way. Sarah searched for the right words.

"And what do you want, Jake?"

At first he shrugged his broad shoulders and stared into the fire. "I guess I see Rhonda as a ticket to the big city life. It hasn't been an easy decision, Sarah. That's why it's taken me so long to come to a conclusion. I want you to believe that."

Wanting to shift the topic from Rhonda, she changed the subject. "Are you going to quit your job with Spruceland Estates?"

"I'll be out of the picture as soon as J.T. finds a replacement for me. I talked to J.T. after the meeting with the banker. I told him about Rhonda, about us getting a divorce, about how I missed building big homes in Dallas. He offered me a job with his construction firm."

Sarah found comfort in knowing Jake would be leaving Spruce Haven. At the same time she resented the way he seemed to have his future planned, and the way he had kept the truth from her until he was left with no choice.

"Jake, it sounds as though you have it all worked out." She finished her glass of wine and turned toward him. She looked directly into the dark brown eyes that she had once loved.

"You know I'll always be interested in what happens in your life. I hate myself for the way I've hurt you." He started to move closer to her, as if he wanted to reach out to her, maybe touch her hand.

If he touches me, I will fall apart. She got up from the sofa and headed to the stairs. Before going upstairs, she stopped, turned, and said, "You have a room waiting for you at the Elk Horn. I told the front desk that I didn't know how long you'd be there. Now please, take your things and leave. We don't have anything else to say to each other." She took a deep breath, surprised at her strong voice and sense of control. The ball was in her court for a change.

Jake got up and walked toward her, keeping a safe distance. He had half expected her to throw him out as soon as he walked in the front door. "Sarah, remember we signed a six-month lease on this place, so you have another month or so left, and I'll gladly take care of a month-to-month payment until you decide where you want to live. Are you going back to Texas, or will you stay here?"

"Oh, I'll be leaving Spruce Haven; I can't afford the high rent. But I'll stay close to the ski mountains. I may move to Gunnison if I can find a teaching job there. But Jake, don't worry about me. I'm a big girl—I can take care of myself. Now I'm asking you for the second time to leave before I start saying things I'll regret later."

Advancing a few steps in her direction, Jake said, "Sarah, I know you love it here. I know I'm guilty of letting you down, letting us down, but I hope you find the happiness you deserve . . . here where you belong." He wanted to reach out and hold her one last time, but she was already on her way up the stairs with her back to him.

With a heavy heart, he put on his jacket and picked up his suitcase. He opened the door to leave for the hotel in Spruce Haven. A part of him wondered if he had just made the biggest mistake of his life.

Before the door closed, Sarah came to the upstairs landing and called out to him, "Jake, one more thing. I'm going to Crested Butte tomorrow for one last ski outing. I'll be gone all day. When I get here around five o'clock, I don't want to see any of your stuff here. Okay?"

"Sure, I'll take care of it," he said slowly, realizing the impact of what was happening.

When Jake closed the door behind him, Sarah knew he had walked out of her life forever, leaving behind twenty-four years of memories. This time, Sarah didn't cry. Instead she felt a lifeless ache of sadness. Even the sparks of anger had subsided, and only the dull gray ashes of dead emotion remained. She went upstairs to put on her swimsuit and grab her thick robe. She turned on the Jacuzzi and waited for it to warm up. Slipping into the hot, bubbly water, she felt the tension in her whole body fade. She leaned back with a folded towel under her neck and looked up at the stars. A sense of tranquility enveloped her. Thoughts of Clint drifted in and out of her mind. But she reminded herself to stay focused on one thing at a time. Right now, she needed to take care of ending a marriage and starting a new life for herself.

twenty-one

Brilliant sunshine greeted Sarah as she set out for Crested Butte. How appropriate, she mused, to think that the day after she had arrived in Spruce Haven, she had skied to celebrate the beginning of a ski season, and now, at Crested Butte, she would be skiing to celebrate the end of a ski season. Both times she felt the excitement of beginning a new chapter in her life.

Sarah's spirits soared as she drove to the town of Crested Butte and followed Gothic Road three miles to the ski resort. An inner voice told her that she would always feel a special connection to this place of dreams.

Driving past the cemetery, she remembered that in another month or so she'd be coming here to spend an afternoon looking at the tombstones as part of the research for her novel. For weeks she had neglected her writing. What with Sam's accident and all the problems in her marriage, she hadn't been inclined to write. *At last,* she thought, *I'll be able to concentrate on my characters.*

At the base of the mountain, she found there were few people skiing, and there were no lines at the lifts. Someone told her these skiers were mainly locals taking advantage of the tourists being gone. That made her feel good, because she decided she was definitely a local now. Every time she rode the chairlift and looked out at the purity of this snow-covered haven, she felt cleansed of the bitterness of the past months.

Spring was on its way, and she would be blessed to see another of nature's miracles unfold around her. The sudden drone of a snowmobile below her on the lift startled her, snapping her attention to Clint. Sam's memorial service was the last time she had seen him. Thinking of a future with Clint seemed out of the question right now. Besides, she barely knew the man, and for all she knew he had decided to move on, granting her wish to be left alone to concentrate on her marriage. After she left the chairlift, she skied to one side to decide which run to take. Still lost in her thoughts, she considered how she and Jake had gone through the motions of trying to convince themselves the move would solve their marital problems. Thinking about those times, she realized how exhausting those efforts had been for both of them. She knew the anger and the hurt would stab at her heart at unexpected times, and there would be days of sadness and depression.

But she told herself she was a stronger person now, not afraid of the future. She used her poles to push off for her longest run of the day, beginning the long descent of upper *Treasury* and continuing all the way to the East River chairlift. She loved to ski because her mind went blank, and only the run in front of her occupied her complete attention. At the close of the day, when she reached the Suburban in the parking lot, she looked up at the mountain and said her farewell for the season, promising to return for the next one.

When she got home that evening, she was relieved to see that all of Jake's things were gone. She decided the first big step had been taken. Her body was exhausted from all the hard skiing; that night she slept soundly for the first time in many nights. Not once did she wake up, to be hit with that dull ache in her heart of knowing her marriage had come to an end.

A few days later, Sarah drove to Gunnison to see her attorney and leave an application at the school administration office. When she stopped by the grocery store to buy a few needed items, she saw Kathy at the end of the aisle. Sarah quickly turned around and pushed her cart into the check-out line. She was afraid she would confide in Kathy about their upcoming divorce, and she didn't want Clint to hear about it from anyone else but her.

"Sarah, wait up," yelled Kathy. "I haven't seen you since . . . well,

I guess it was Sam's service. You and Jake are keeping a low profile lately."

"Well, you know . . . it's the usual stuff with Spruceland clients, and construction is underway on three homes. How have you and Neal been doing lately?"

"Oh, pretty good. I don't know if Jake told you or not, but we decided not to buy that lot in Spruceland Estates."

"Actually, he didn't mention it, but he's been pretty busy."

"We bought into a time share in Florida, so we'll spend the summers there for a nice change."

"That sounds wonderful, Kathy. The two of you work so hard in the winter; you deserve some time away in a nice warm climate."

"By the way, Sarah, did you see this morning's paper?"

"No, why?"

"Oh, there's a nice article about Clint. He's been appointed mountain manager for Crested Butte Mountain Resort. Isn't that a great promotion?"

"Yes, I'm happy for him."

"I need to finish up here and let you do the same. Call me and we'll get together."

"Yeah, sure. It was good to see you," Sarah called after her friend.

She was so glad for Clint that she wanted to call him right away, but she resisted the urge, wanting more time before she told him about the impending divorce. Besides, the dreaded trip to Fort Worth was fast approaching. She had practiced explaining to Catrina that her parents had grown apart, and it was time for them to go their separate ways. She would let Jake tell her about Rhonda in his own time and his own way. Sarah was willing to do anything to spare her daughter more hurt than necessary. Calling Clint could wait until she returned from Fort Worth.

The next afternoon the weather was warm and bright, and Sarah decided to walk to the post office on Main Street. The mountain had officially closed, like the official end of her marriage, she thought. She hadn't heard from Jake, which was fine with her. They had covered the major issues. She figured that the dull ache of disappointment from a failed marriage would take a long time to fade into the past.

As she was leaving the post office, Clint came in, dressed in jeans and a plaid flannel shirt.

"Hi, Clint. Congratulations on your promotion. I'm so happy for you." She was pleased to see his warm, sensitive face. Without warning, she started blinking back tears.

Taking her by the arm, he led her outside into the bright sunlight. "You don't look too happy. Come with me." Opening the door of the Blazer, he said, "Here, get in and we can talk more privately." He went around to the driver's side and climbed in. "Sarah, tell me what's wrong."

When she started talking, she couldn't stop; the words spilled out of her like some terrible poison that needed to be expelled from her body. All the days of wearing a mask, of pretending she had her emotions under control, of hiding the dull pain even from herself, came to a resounding conclusion, like the finale of a fireworks display. Except for her attorney, Clint was the first person with whom she had shared the heart-wrenching story of finding her husband with his mistress.

Clint said, "I'm sorry that it's been such a devastating experience for you." He took her hand in his.

"Oh, Clint, I feel so stupid not to have seen it coming. The signs were there, but I kept ignoring them, the same way I did nearly a year ago."

"You should have called me from the airport in Gunnison. That must have been a terrible drive in the state you were in. You know I would have come to get you."

"You have this thing about rescuing people, don't you?" said Sarah as she dug in her handbag for more Kleenex. She took a deep breath and let out a big sigh. For the first time since the confrontation with Jake, her heart felt lighter. She even showed a hint of a smile as she wiped the tears from her face.

"Only beautiful women like you."

"I must look dreadful with all this mascara running down my face."

"You look fine to me."

Sarah pulled down the sun visor and was glad to see a mirror. She wiped away more smudges.

"Oh, Clint, I dread having to face Catrina tomorrow and tell her we're getting a divorce. And of course, my parents will be worried about me, and they'll try to convince me to come home."

"I don't want you running off to Texas."

"I'll only be there for a week. You'd be proud of me. I've been a busy girl, looking into moving to Gunnison and finding a teaching job there, since it's so much cheaper than Spruce Haven.

"I'm proud of you for facing all this head-on. You need to concentrate on other things in your life . . . like me. You know, the last advice Sam gave me about you was to give you some space, and that's what I've been trying to do."

Hearing Sam's name, Sarah said softly, "I know you must miss him terribly."

"That I do," he answered. "We all do. I think this change in my job is coming at a good time. You know, patrolling for me will never be the same without Sam. He used to tell me I had ways to stay connected with the mountains. Some people thought he was a little rough around the edges, but Sam had a good understanding about life." Clint glanced at Sarah and said, "Look at me. I'm rambling on and on. I guess that's the most I've said to anyone since the accident."

"I'm glad you can share your feelings with me." She reached for the door handle of the Blazer and said, "Clint, it was good to see you, but I'll let you get on with your day."

"Wait, Sarah . . . I have an idea. I'm going to kidnap you for a few hours."

"Would you mind telling me where you're taking me?" She took her hand off the door handle. Sarah was glad for the diversion, for the chance to keep her mind occupied until she left for Fort Worth the following morning.

"Can't tell you. It's a surprise. First we have to swing by the mountain center so I can let them know I'm taking the afternoon off. Neal took me out for lunch to celebrate my promotion. Lucky for me that I dropped by to check my mailbox and happened to find you." He grinned and looked at her. "You were going to call me, weren't you?"

"Yes, of course. I was thrilled to hear about your new job. I know how much it must mean to you to be going to Crested Butte."

"Yes, I feel like I'm going home," said Clint. "When I got the call from the general manager of Crested Butte Mountain Resort, I couldn't believe how lucky I was to get an opportunity for the interview." Clint winked at her. "You know, at my age a desk job starts to look pretty inviting."

After Clint pulled out of the Mountain Center parking lot, he headed out on Evergreen Road and turned off on a side road before reaching Highway 135.

"Now I want you to close your eyes, and no peeking until I tell you it's okay."

Sarah obeyed, leaning back and closing her eyes. *Here I am*, she thought, *on this beautiful afternoon in April with this man who has come into my life in such an exciting way. But I don't dare hope for a future with Clint. I'm tired of living my life wrapped around dreams. I'm going to take whatever life offers me at any given time.*

Clint said, "Okay, you can open your eyes, but we're not there yet."

She opened her eyes. The road they were on ran alongside a small rushing stream for a couple of miles. An endless valley spread out before them, offering a tranquil setting with a few scattered homes and horses grazing in pastures nearby.

Clint turned on to a rock drive that led to a modest log home with five or six steps leading to a huge covered front porch with large windows on either side of the front door. Off to one side was a cluster of small aspens.

"This is my surprise. It's my new home—well, new to me anyway. It's actually about ten years old. I've been looking for a place near my new job. What do you think?" He turned to look at Sarah.

"Clint, it looks so much like you."

"I don't know if that's a compliment or not."

"I mean it looks strong and rugged."

"That doesn't sound like a bad description." He smiled at her. I won't be moving in for another couple of weeks. Maybe you could help me pick out new furniture; it's going to need a woman's touch."

He squeezed her hand, stepped out of the Blazer, and walked around to open the door for her. "I wanted you to be the first to see it. It's the first home I've ever owned."

He put his arm around her as they walked up the front steps. He stopped and pointed to the far corner of the front porch. "Do those wind chimes look familiar?"

Sarah smiled and saw a broad grin break across his suntanned face. "Yes, of course I do. Those are like the ones you gave your sister."

"I bought two sets that day because I knew that before long I would have my own home."

As Clint unlocked the front door, Sarah knew that this time she wasn't closing a door behind her, as she had done in the past. Before going inside she turned around and gazed at the valley before her, imagining how it would look once the snow melted and the white oxeye daisies raised their tender heads. Taking her by the hand, Clint led her inside. Sarah broke the vow she had made to herself earlier, for dreams filled her heart like the faraway melody of wind chimes playing softly in the cool mountain breeze.

Printed in the United States
93859LV00006BB/191/A